W9-BSH-069

Final Undertaking

Also by Mark de Castrique
Dangerous Undertaking
Grave Undertaking
Foolish Undertaking

Final Undertaking

Mark de Castrique

Poisoned Pen Press

First Edition 2007

10 9 8 7 6 5 4 3 2 1

Library of Congress Catalog Card Number: 2006929249

ISBN: 1-59058-229-2 (978-1-59058-229-9) Hardcover

Poisoned Pen Press
6962 E. First Ave., Ste. 103
Scottsdale, AZ 85251
www.poisonedpenpress.com
info@poisonedpenpress.com

Printed in the United States of America

For my father, Arch

Acknowledgments

Thanks to the usual suspects who have helped Barry Clayton through all four seasons of his adventures: Steve Greene, whose ideas, attention to detail, and police expertise qualify him as an honorary deputy of Gainesboro; Barbara Peters, Robert Rosenwald, and the great staff at Poisoned Pen Press, who gave Barry a literary home; my agent Linda Allen and my proof readers—my wife, Linda, daughters, Lindsay and Melissa, and new son-in-law, Pete—who all try to keep me from looking stupid, a never-ending task.

For this book I'm indebted to Dr. Bill Cloud and Dr. Jim Plonk for unpaid medical advice. Any mistakes are entirely of my own making. Thanks to Roy Spring for information on Delray Beach, and my father, Arch, for insights into the funeral business.

Finally, Barry Clayton cannot succeed as a sleuth without the support of librarians, booksellers, and dedicated readers who keep his mountain town alive. Thank you for the vital role you play in the ongoing story.

Chapter One

"The banjo's bigger than the picker." Susan laughed and set up her folding chair at the edge of the curb. She motioned me to do the same.

About twenty yards away, a portable stage decorated with red, white, and blue bunting stood in the middle of Main Street. A towheaded boy of no more than six climbed up on a wooden stool. An old man in bib overalls handed the youngster a five-string Gibson, and then tucked his fiddle under his whiskered chin.

I settled into the comfort of my canvas camp chair. "That kid's probably been playing banjo since before he could walk. Same goes for great grandpa. The Dickens family's been calling square dances around here for over sixty years."

Susan sneezed. "Well, I'd like to dosado, if I can breathe." She pulled a nasal inhaler from her jeans' pocket and gave a shot up each nostril. "Nothing worse than a summer cold."

"Nothing worse than a doctor who can't cure herself," I said. "I prescribe a couple whirls around the street with me stepping on your feet and you'll forget all about your cold."

The ancient fiddle player, Roscoe Dickens, stepped up to a mike, the fiddle still under his chin, and cleared his throat. "Thank y'all for coming out this evening. It's good to be back in Gainesboro."

Back in Gainesboro? Roscoe made it sound like they'd been on a world tour with The Rolling Stones. The family lived on the outskirts of the county, and my funeral home, Clayton and

Clayton, had been burying them as long as they'd been pickin' and grinnin'. He introduced the rest of the family—granddaughter on mandolin, a son on guitar, grandson on bass, and granddaughter-in-law on flute—she had to be an import from the Brevard Music Center. And finally on banjo, little Roscoe Albert Dickens the Fourth. I sure hoped they called him Al.

"Our first number's Down Yonder and we've set this one aside for the Laurel County Cloggers. So step back, give them room, and we'll commence the square dancing shortly."

From across the street a group wearing yellow plaid shirts and dark blue pants broke into precise lines three deep and six dancers across. The predominant hair color was silver. The men were outnumbered two to one, and the body shapes were as varied as a shelf full of recycled jelly glasses. Roscoe sawed out the first notes, the band kicked in, and thirty-six metal-tapped shoes started pounding out an intricate rhythm pattern. Folks lining the curb and the sawhorses that marked off the dance area clapped along. Every face wore a smile.

The Friday Night Street Stomp, as the Chamber of Commerce billed it, drew tourists and locals downtown from June to Labor Day. Each week a different band treated the crowd to an evening of live music. Over the summer, the styles ranged from big band to beach music to classic rock and roll. Tonight, traditional mountain music launched the season, and the clear June sky and cool, soft breeze enticed a record turnout.

Across the street, I saw Mayor Sammy Whitlock schmoozing the spectators. His rotund body was clad in white pants and a red shirt, making him look like a fishing bob bouncing along the flow of the sidewalk. I had to give His Honor credit for being a vocal supporter of the event and authorizing his well-guarded funds to boost the street lighting. Although it was already seven, the evening's festivities could go on for hours thanks to the improved illumination.

"Mr. Clayton?"

I twisted around. Fletcher Shaw waved to me from behind an elderly man in a wheelchair. At first I thought Fletcher was with him, but the motorized chair moved farther down the sidewalk and Fletcher stepped forward. He had two lawn chairs under his arm and a pretty blonde by his side.

"Any room?" he asked.

"Sure." I slid a few feet to the left and Susan did the same. Fletcher unfolded one of the chairs, placed it by Susan and offered the seat to his companion. As she sat down, I recognized her as Cindy Todd, the daughter of Helen Todd, who owned the Cardinal Café. The local diner had been in the Todd family for years and was where I'd devoured countless meals ever since first eating from a booster seat. I hadn't seen little Cindy since she'd left for college several years ago. Her tight jeans and bare midriff showed she'd blossomed from a gangly teenager into a very attractive young woman.

"Hi." I reached over and shook her hand. "Remember me? Barry Clayton. And this is my friend Susan Miller. Are you home for the summer?"

"Just two weeks. Then I start an internship with Bank of America in Charlotte."

"You're at UNC-Charlotte?" Susan asked.

"I'll be a senior." Cindy shook her head in disbelief. "The first in my family to go to college."

"Congratulations. I'd shake your hand but I'm afraid I'll give you my cold." Susan nodded to Fletcher. "And it's nice to finally meet you."

"I'm sorry," I said. "I thought you'd met."

Fletcher grinned. "I feel like we have. Mr. Clayton talks about you all the time."

I laughed. My opinion of the young man jumped up a notch. "First of all, I want both of you to call me Barry. I'm not that much older than either of you. And second, Fletcher, your internship at Clayton and Clayton might not be as glamorous as Bank of America, but you've already mastered Funeral Director Diplomacy 101. Obviously you sweet-talked Cindy to the dance."

Cindy blushed. "I asked him. My mom introduced us at lunch today."

"During my second piece of apple pie," Fletcher admitted.
"I asked if he planned to dance that off tonight, and here we are." Cindy gave him a wink that made me wonder if my summer intern might bail on me for a Charlotte funeral home.

Clayton and Clayton had never had an intern before, but the growing influx of summer tourists, many of whom were pushing the eighty-plus age range, had increased the number of those senior citizens who wouldn't last till fall. The request from the Cincinnati College of Mortuary Science to employ one of their students over the summer break coincided with our seasonal surge in business. Fletcher Shaw had arrived two weeks ago and was adjusting to life in a small mountain town as well as anyone from a suburb of Detroit could be expected. Better, considering he now sat beside one of the prettiest girls in western North Carolina.

A line of the cloggers pranced near the curb. I tapped the armrest of my chair in time to the music and turned to Cindy. "Well, I hope you'll translate ol' Roscoe's mountain twang for Fletcher. Otherwise, he's likely to misunderstand and grab some burly mountaineer. That could be a promenade to the hospital."

Cindy laughed and looked at Susan. "Then I'm glad we've got a surgeon here. Mom says you're the best, or at least you've had the most practice from patching up Barry."

"I call him my walking resumé." Susan wasn't kidding.

Fletcher and Cindy looked at me for a response, but I wasn't about to get into a litany of the injuries my unofficial detective work had inflicted upon my body. "I just hope I can get through the square dance in one piece."

I turned my attention to the crowd and caught sight of Sheriff Tommy Lee Wadkins across the street. He gave me a wave and pointed to his uniform. He mouthed the words "on duty," but with his wife, Patsy, on his arm, he looked anything but on duty. I expected he'd be out swinging his bride left and right before the evening was over.

The Laurel County Cloggers finished with a flourish and received an enthusiastic round of applause. As they clickety-clacked off the street, Roscoe Dickens invited any and all to join the first square dance.

"Just the basics," he said. "We save the fancy steps for when y'all are sweatin'."

I turned to Susan. "Want to give it a try?"

She sniffled. "I'd better not. If colds are passed through hand contact, I'll wipe out nearly fifty people."

"Why don't you dance with Cindy?" Fletcher asked me. "Then I can see what the calls mean."

I stood up. "You game?"

Cindy bounced to her feet. "Sure. Just don't laugh at me. I fell down the last time."

"Don't worry," Susan said. "If you do, everyone will know it's because Barry tripped you."

I grabbed Cindy's hand and we hurried out to the street. Roscoe needed a manageable number and sometimes he had to subtract dancers to make things work. The old man counted couples off as odd and even, and then explained a few basic moves. Cindy and I listened as if receiving orders for a commando raid. Neither one of us wanted to screw up. After several practice trials without music, Roscoe pronounced us fit to dance, and the band started playing Arkansas Traveler. The first call sent our big circle moving left, some shuffling, some skipping, but all getting into the rhythm of the tune.

My favorite part was when the men and women moved around the circle in opposite directions, weaving in and out, going from left hand to right. I could jump seventy years in a single swing as a laughing ten-year-old followed a rejuvenated octogenarian. Roscoe skillfully maneuvered us through our newly learned steps until reunited partners strutted their stuff in a promenade finale. Cindy and I bowed to each other, and then at Susan and Fletcher sitting on the curb. They clapped their approval.

As we headed toward them, an elderly gentleman stepped off the curb. His grim expression caught my eye, and I could see that more than his hand was buried in his tan windbreaker.

"Get behind me," I whispered to Cindy.

Before she could move, the man pulled a pistol from his pocket. "Lincoln!"

The couple beside us froze.

"You bastard." The man raised his gun. "This is for Lucy."

I saw a blur out of the corner of my eye as the man next to me grabbed his partner and hurled her at the old man. The girl slammed into the gunman and two shots rang out from his pistol. Cindy cried out, and then a chorus of screams erupted from the panicked crowd as people desperately scrambled to safety. Cindy fell against me. I caught her around the waist and felt warm blood between my fingers.

The other girl lay on the pavement with blood flowing from her head and stomach. The man with the gun looked down at her and then at me. The man she'd been dancing with had disappeared.

I held up my hand. "Drop the gun. No need for innocent people to get hurt." I saw Tommy Lee circling behind the man, motioning the few stunned spectators who remained to clear out. If I could keep the man talking long enough, Tommy Lee would get the jump on him.

"He took my Lucy from me," the man repeated.

"Then we'll catch him. We'll bring him to justice."

Tommy Lee was twenty feet away, coming in at an angle with his gun drawn.

"No. No good." The man quickly stepped to his right and spun around facing Tommy Lee.

That move put Cindy and me behind him and in the line of Tommy Lee's fire. Tommy Lee hesitated, and his shot came a fraction of a second after the man pulled his trigger. To my horror, both men collapsed to the pavement.

Cindy whimpered in pain. I stood in utter disbelief, gazing at the scene. In the glare of the mayor's new lighting, pools of bright red blood flowed from three bodies in the street and a fourth clutched in my arms.

Chapter Two

"Susan! Cindy's hit!" I gently lowered Cindy to the pavement, careful to keep her wounded side elevated.

As Susan and Fletcher ran toward us, I searched the crowd and saw the mayor backed against a storefront window. "Whitlock, find a deputy. Have him radio for four ambulances." I didn't know if the county EMS had four ambulances.

The petrified politician shook off his fright and hurried as fast as his stubby legs could carry him toward the next block, where traffic was being diverted.

Susan knelt beside me. "I've got her. Check Tommy Lee."

"Are there any doctors here?" I shouted to the crowd as I ran to Tommy Lee.

One of the Laurel County Cloggers patted the hand of the woman beside him and joined me by the sheriff. "Walter Bond. Retired, but I spent ten years in the ER."

Tommy Lee groaned. His one eye flickered open. The ever-present black patch covered the other. "God damn," he whispered. "Gun-downed on Main Street in my own town."

His wife Patsy knelt beside him. Tears streamed down her face, but her voice was steady. "Quiet," she urged.

He gave a faint nod. "Right chest wound. Check the girl. Secure the scene." Then he lost consciousness.

As Dr. Bond began checking Tommy Lee, I saw Susan run from Cindy to the other wounded girl. She knelt down and put her hand on the girl's carotid artery. I ran over to do whatever I could to help.

"Fletcher's putting direct pressure on Cindy's wound. This one has a faint pulse. Bullet hit her abdomen, and there's a head injury where she hit the pavement." Susan sighed. "It'll be touch and go. Tommy Lee?"

"The guy with him used to work ER. Chest wound. If the bleeding's not too bad, he's got a good chance."

"Check the old guy," Susan said, and focused all her attention on the girl.

I went over to the shooter and knelt down beside him. The man lay on his back. His eyes stared up at the night sky, but he no longer saw anything on this side of infinity. The hole in his jacket showed Tommy Lee's shot went through the heart. As a decorated vet from Vietnam, the sheriff had instinctively fired with deadly accuracy, even as a bullet tore through his chest.

I looked up to see Deputy Reece Hutchins running toward me. Behind him came the mayor, his face as red as his shirt. Maybe the fourth ambulance would be needed after all.

Reece looked at Tommy Lee lying between Patsy and the doctor. "Is he—?" He couldn't bring himself to say any more. His lip quivered and his hands twitched by his side.

Reece and I had had our differences. I found him arrogant and territorial. I'd come to suspect part of that attitude was because he resented the special friendship his boss and I had developed. But there was never any doubt as to his loyalty to Tommy Lee. The pain on his face spoke clearer than any words.

"He's alive, but it's serious. Cindy Todd has a gunshot wound in her right side. The other girl's hanging on by a thread." I nodded at the dead man lying at my feet. "This one's the shooter. He didn't make it."

Reece didn't make a move. He kept looking back at Tommy Lee as if the unconscious man would give him orders.

"Tommy Lee said secure the scene," I finally said. "He'd want you to be in charge."

The breath caught in Reece's chest. He could only nod.

I stood up and leaned close to him. "There's a mystery here, Reece. This guy was gunning for somebody else. A white male, paunchy, about fifty. I didn't get a good look at him, but the shooter called him Lincoln." I pointed to the girl Susan was attending to. "The son of a bitch used that girl as a shield. I have a feeling he's the reason behind all this. The reason Tommy Lee got shot."

The wail of sirens pierced the air.

"Then we'll get him." Reece grabbed my arm. "Will you go to the hospital? Keep me posted?"

"Sure." I looked at the old man's body again. "Let me know if you get an ID. It'll be the first question out of Tommy Lee's mouth."

We both smiled in spite of the dire situation. We knew Tommy Lee too well.

While Reece cleared the street in preparation for the ambulances, I made a quick round of the injured. Fletcher kept his hand pressed against Cindy's side. His face was nearly as pale as hers, and she looked like she was going into shock.

Susan had stripped the unknown girl's blouse away from the stomach wound and used the cloth as a compress. "I think the bullet went through clean. The head injury could be more serious, but I won't know till I get her in OR."

"Is she the priority?"

"They're all a priority."

I saw Fletcher whispering encouragement to Cindy. Patsy was stroking Tommy Lee's forehead, and Dr. Bond was bent close to the sheriff's chest.

"First ambulance here takes you and this girl," I told Susan. I could see Reece flagging an emergency team at the cross street. A second vehicle with flashing lights came from farther down the block. Both cut their sirens and I didn't hear another.

My gut tightened. I knew what Tommy Lee would want. He'd gone back for a dying comrade in the face of enemy fire. His bravery cost him an eye, but he'd have done it again without hesitation.

Susan must have read my mind. "I don't think Cindy's as bad as Tommy Lee."

"Are you sure about that?"

"I can't be one hundred percent sure."

"Then Cindy goes next." I looked around in desperation. Cars had been banned from the street for the dance. I turned to the stage. The Dickens family stood like a Grand Ol' Opry tableau, instruments quiet in their hands. The mandolin player had her arm around the pint-sized banjo picker. His face was buried in her blouse. The lanky grandson leaned against his big bass fiddle, staring out as if watching a movie.

"Hey," I yelled. "How'd you get that bass here?"

"In our van," the young man answered.

"Where is it?"

"Behind the stage."

"Empty it out. We need it."

He looked to his grandpa.

"You heard the man," Roscoe said. "Git crackin'."

The EMTs hit like a SWAT team. Portable gurneys appeared and Susan helped direct the load-in.

I ran alongside her as the unknown girl was transported to an ambulance. "I've got a van, if you want it."

She turned to the EMT behind her. "What do you think? Is a van better than a delay?"

"We've got a small stretcher for bringing people out of ravines. We could put a vehicle in the pocket and be at the hospital in five minutes."

"The pocket?" I asked.

"Between the two ambulances," he explained. "A convoy."

Two patrol cars pulled to the curb. I saw Deputy Steve Wakefield hop out of one, his shirt half unbuttoned. Word on the scanner must have mobilized even the off-duty officers.

"All right," I said. "Get this girl in and give me the stretcher. We'll put Tommy Lee in the van."

Dr. Bond, Reece Hutchins, Wakefield, and an EMT helped me get Tommy Lee strapped on the stretcher. Patsy walked with us as we carried him behind the stage. The jostling must have roused him. He groaned and opened his eye as we approached a rusted Econo-van with the hand-lettered words *DICKENS MOUNTAIN MUSIC: Best Square Dancing Round These Parts*.

"Always wanted to be in a band," Tommy Lee muttered.

"Good," I said. "Your first gig's at the hospital."

"Just don't book me in your damn funeral home."

At the emergency room, I caught Susan as she headed to scrub.

"I'll be with Patsy. If you can, have someone get me an ID on the girl. Who's on call?"

"O'Malley's on his way," Susan yelled over her shoulder as she ran down the hall. "Chandler's already here. We'll share OR staff as best we can."

Double doors closed behind her and I was alone. Three surgeons, three victims. No, there had been four. I wondered who the dead man was, lying in the street. I'd never seen him before, but, as the town undertaker, I was the only one who could help him now.

In the waiting room, I found Helen Todd sitting with Fletcher and Patsy. Helen wore sweatpants and an extra large tee shirt with a bright red cardinal and the word *café* under it. Promotional wardrobe for her diner.

I guessed the tee shirt also served as her pajamas since Helen had probably been in bed. She got up at four in the morning to make sure her patrons would have a hot meal at six.

When Helen saw me, she burst into tears. "Oh, Barry." She got to her feet and I hugged her without saying anything. "Tell me she's going to be all right."

"We think so. They've got her in surgery. She never lost consciousness, Helen. Susan says that's a good sign."

Patsy had also stood up. I could tell she was trying hard not to cry. "Anything on Tommy Lee?"

I shook my head. Her husband had lost consciousness again halfway to the hospital. But Dr. O'Malley, the head of Susan's

clinic, was a thoracic specialist and I knew he'd be the one operating on Tommy Lee. "We probably won't hear for a while. Can
I do anything for you?"

Her eyes moistened. "No. I'd better call the kids. Kenny's
got a car at the house."

Tommy Lee and Patsy had two great children. Kenny was
home for the summer from N.C. State and Samantha was finishing her first year in high school. They'd be a comfort when
they arrived.

Standing behind Patsy, Fletcher asked me, "Is there something
I can do? Anyone I should call?"

I thought how the news would spread like wildfire through
our little community. I expected concerned friends would soon
fill the waiting room. "Yes. You can tell my mother. But not over
the phone." Mom loved Tommy Lee and his family. I wanted
someone to tell her in person.

"Sure," Fletcher said. "I'll sit with her for a while. See if I can
help with your father."

"Thanks." I shook his hand. "Tell her not to wait up for me.
I'll call if there's any update."

Fletcher left, and I was grateful for the young man's sensitivity.
He'd told his advisor he wanted an internship in a small, quiet
town, preferably with a family funeral business. I hoped he hadn't
gotten more than he bargained for. Family meant he would have
to adjust to the ways of my seventy-five-year-old Uncle Wayne
and my Alzheimer's-afflicted father. I'd anticipated that would
be a challenge. I hadn't figured that the small, quiet town would
have a Friday night shootout to rival the OK Corral.

Fletcher had been gone only a few minutes when a nurse
stuck her head in the door. "Mr. Clayton?"

"Yes." I stood up.

"May I speak with you a moment?" The nurse waited for me
to join her in the hall.

Patsy and Helen paled, worried that I would be given bad
news for one of them.

"I'll be right back," I said.

The nurse retreated a few yards to pull me out of earshot of the others. With a gloved hand, she held out a small beige pouch attached to an elastic belt. Blood stained half the material. I recognized the pouch as a passport carrier to be worn close to the body. I'd used one like it when I'd traveled through Europe several years ago.

"You'd better glove before examining this. We cut it off the girl. Dr. Miller said you'd want to see it." The nurse opened a door behind her. "You can use this treatment room. Gloves are on the shelf. I've got to get back to OR."

"How are things going?"

"Everyone's alive." Her face gave no clue as to how alive.

I pulled the latex gloves over my hands and took the pouch. The nurse closed the door, leaving me alone. I laid the blood-soaked belt on the paper protecting the examination table. The girl must have worn it under the low waistline of her jeans, because I hadn't noticed it when Susan treated her at the scene.

At this point, I looked at everything as evidence and was glad all contact with the belt had been through gloved hands. The pouch itself was flat and not much larger than a four-by-six notecard. Whatever she was carrying in it couldn't be very thick. Maybe emergency money or some identification cards. My first thought was to turn the pouch over to Reece without opening it, but I knew it might be hours before he could get to the hospital. If there was a chance the girl's identification was in the pouch, both Reece and the hospital personnel needed to know now.

The snap yielded easily enough. I lifted the flap and slipped two fingers inside. I felt crisp bills and a plastic card. I pulled them clear, trying to avoid the blood. The money was all new twenties and the plastic was a VISA card issued by Wachovia. *Lucy Kowalski* was the name embossed on the face. I searched the pouch a second time, but there was no driver's license or other photo ID that could prove the girl on the operating table was Lucy Kowalski. Lucy. "This is for Lucy," the old man had shouted. Here was the connection in my hand. But what did it mean?

I counted the twenties. The girl had been carrying exactly five hundred dollars. I replaced the bills and the credit card, closed the pouch and wrapped the belt in tissue from a dispenser. Then I tucked it in the front pocket of my pants.

When I stepped back into the waiting room, I told Patsy and Helen we had no update. The nurse's only information concerned the unidentified girl, and her name might be Lucy Kowalski.

"Never heard of her," Patsy said.

"Me neither." Helen frowned. "Why do you say might be?"

"She had one credit card in a money belt. No other identification."

"I don't remember that name coming through the restaurant. I'm pretty good at keeping names and faces together."

Pretty good didn't begin to describe Helen's memory. I'd seen her shock a tourist by remembering his name a year later.

"Tommy Lee will start a trace and then—" I stopped in mid-sentence. Tommy Lee lay on an operating table. "Well, I'll get this to Reece."

Patsy sat down and buried her face in her hands. A few minutes later, her children, Kenny and Samantha, arrived. Samantha was crying. As a young college man, Kenny tried to keep his composure, but I'd conducted enough funerals to recognize the grief churning just beneath the surface.

I stepped out to the main lobby, off the emergency room. The night would be a long one and I wouldn't leave until I had word from Susan. I told the duty nurse I'd be outside, getting some fresh air, and be sure and have someone find me if there was any news.

The entrance offered a few benches along a landscaped walkway where people could smoke free of the health standards imposed by the hospital. Several people were sitting on the benches, indulging their habit, determined to someday become business for both the hospital and me. I took my stroll in another direction where I could be alone with my thoughts.

The shooting played like a video loop in my head. The old man's determined look changing to confusion as he stared at the unidentified fallen girl. Was she his Lucy? Had he killed someone he loved? Then Tommy Lee's expression as the man whirled around. Uncertainty. Was he afraid to pull the trigger because Cindy and I might be hit? Or had he thought the old man wouldn't fire? I prayed to God I'd be able to ask him.

In the meantime, the recycling images stirred one immediate question—who was the man who ran away? Who was Lincoln? Then my police instincts kicked in. I hadn't been thinking clearly. I needed to get Lucy Kowalski's name to Reece. The first few hours after a crime can be critical to its solution. And here I stood with money and Lucy Kowalski's credit card in my pocket and my cell phone locked in my jeep a block off Main Street.

I ran back to the hospital. The woman at the main information desk directed me to a bank of phones around the corner. At this time of night, I had my pick. The dispatcher for the Sheriff's Department routed me straight to Reece.

Without so much as a hello, he blurted out the question foremost on his mind. "Any word on Tommy Lee?"

"No. He's still in surgery. No update on the others either."

"Damn. That's not good."

"It means they're still alive."

Reece exhaled into the receiver. "Yeah. You're right."

"Listen, I've got some information on the girl who was shot. Ready to write?"

"Shoot."

"She was carrying five hundred dollars and a credit card in the name of Lucy Kowalski. That's K O W—"

"A L S K I," he finished. "We identified the dead man from his driver's license. Mitch Kowalski of Delray Beach, Florida."

"Reece, just before he shot, Kowalski said, 'He took my Lucy from me.' Maybe the girl was a runaway and Kowalski's the grandfather."

"Maybe, but you know what Tommy Lee thinks about coincidences."

I did. He hated them. He only accepted them as a last resort for explaining events in an investigation. "What's the coincidence?"

"I just got off the phone with a Lieutenant Roy Spring in the Delray Police Department. He knew Mitch Kowalski. And he knew Lucy Kowalski. She's not the girl you've got at the hospital. Lucy Kowalski was Mitch Kowalski's wife. She was in her eighties, and he buried her two weeks ago."

Chapter Three

"He took my Lucy from me." Mitch Kowalski's words rang in my head again, but this time I heard the utter despair. Was he grieving for a dead wife and not the wounded girl in front of him?

My mind jumped to the obvious question. "How'd she die?"

"Drug overdose. OxyContin."

"Foul play?"

"Spring didn't think so. He said the lady was old and her pain kept getting worse. She might have chewed her pills and that destroyed the time-release coating."

That didn't explain Mitch Kowalski's deadly appearance in Gainesboro. "Does this police lieutenant have any clue as to why her husband would try to kill a man named Lincoln?"

"No. But Spring's going to look into it."

I had another idea. "Ask him if there's a granddaughter. Maybe named Lucy. The girl could still be the link."

"Brilliant. Why didn't I think of that?" Reece's sarcasm dripped through the receiver.

Maybe it was the pressure of the situation or maybe Reece just couldn't deal with me giving him advice. Either way I wasn't going to let him bait me. I let silence be my response.

Finally Reece sighed. "Something, ain't it?"

"What?"

"Tommy Lee gets shot on Main Street because some blue-haired lady down in Florida overdosed."

"Reece, the sins of the world can't be stopped at the county line."

"No, they can't. But Tommy Lee sure as hell tried."

Reece was right. Tommy Lee was the kind of sheriff a town like Gainesboro couldn't buy. He had to be home grown, and Tommy Lee was one of a kind, a war hero whose bravery and courage now protected the community he loved. If he didn't pull through, there was no one who could even come close to replacing him.

I promised Reece I'd get back to him in an hour unless I heard something sooner.

A few minutes after eleven, both Susan and O'Malley came to the waiting room. By now more than twenty people, including off-duty deputies and friends and neighbors of Patsy or Helen, had gathered for prayers and support. The room fell silent as the doctors entered.

Dr. O'Malley wore his mask draped around his neck, and exhaustion deepened the wrinkles in his gray-stubbled cheeks. "Mrs. Wadkins," he said softly. His trace of a smile sparked hope in Patsy's eyes.

Kenny grabbed his mother's arm and they walked to the door. Samantha followed a few steps behind, hesitant to come too close to what could be bad news.

When O'Malley had taken them into the hall, Susan gave me a barely perceptible nod. I felt the tension flow out of my body. Tommy Lee would be all right. I then looked at Helen Todd leaning forward on the edge of her chair.

Susan went to her. "Cindy's in recovery, and out of danger. Would you like to come with me?"

The question needed no answer. Helen wiped tears from her eyes, clutched the hands of well-wishers around her, and hurried to see her daughter.

Susan turned to me. "Meet you for a cup of coffee when I'm done."

The hospital cafeteria was nearly deserted when I got there. A few bleary-eyed residents snacked on junk food from vending machines. Hot breakfast would be available at six, but since it wasn't yet midnight, I hoped to be gone long before then. Twenty minutes later I was finishing my second coffee refill when Susan sat down across from me. She'd changed into her street clothes and snagged a honey bun pastry to go with her own black coffee.

"What about your girlish figure?" I asked.

"If you ever hope to see it again, you'll let me eat this guilt-free."

"Can I warm it in the microwave?"

She smiled. "No, thanks. I'd probably be asleep before you got back. What a night." She sipped her coffee while I waited. She was the one with the news. "Tommy Lee was lucky. He lost a lot of blood, but the only vital organ damaged by the bullet was his right lung. The lung will heal but scar tissue will probably limit its efficiency."

"How bad?"

"Well, if he planned to run a marathon someday, he'd better go to Plan B. But with proper recuperation and physical therapy, O'Malley says he should be back to normal activities in six to eight weeks."

"And Cindy?"

Susan took a bite of the honey bun, and then licked her fingers. "I operated on her. Bullet mangled her spleen. Given the area, she did okay. You can live without a spleen. I'm afraid she won't be starting her internship in two weeks."

"How's Helen taking it?"

"No mother likes to see her child hooked up to monitors and IVs, but the words 'she's going to make it' were all Helen wanted to hear."

"And our Jane Doe?"

Susan looked over the rim of her cup in surprise. "You didn't get an ID out of that belt?"

"Not enough to be sure." I shared Reece's information on Lucy and Mitch Kowalski.

"Can Reece put out her description? We need to find next of kin."

Susan's question sounded ominous. "You don't think she'll come around long enough to give her name?"

"The abdomen wound's treatable, but the fall fractured her skull. We put her in an induced coma to keep her motionless. Her cranial pressure is building. If we don't get that under control, the girl may never wake up."

I didn't know what options we had. Take a picture of her in a hospital bed? In her bandages, she'd probably look like a mummy.

Susan stared behind me. "Here comes the big boss and her mouthpiece." She washed down the rest of her pastry with coffee and wiped her hands on her jeans. "O'Malley must not have given them the right quote for a press release."

I turned and saw Pamela Whittier, the chief hospital administrator, crossing the room accompanied by Howard Jefferson, the head of PR. Behind them lagged Ray Chandler, Susan's colleague who had operated on the unidentified girl.

Whittier wore a smartly tailored outfit more appropriate for a nine o'clock board meeting than a midnight encounter in the cafeteria. Jefferson wore a blue pinstripe, too heavy for this time of year, but the perfect wardrobe for the media coverage generated by the shooting. Chandler was still in wrinkled blue scrubs.

The three of them came to our table. Whittier forced a smile. "Good work, Susan."

I stood up. "Barry Clayton. We've met before." I nodded to Jefferson and Chandler.

"Yes, of course," Whittier said. "I understand you helped organize the first response at the scene. Thank you."

I suspected Whittier did remember me. I'd attended several hospital functions with Susan, and this woman hadn't gotten to the top of her profession by missing details, including who was dating one of her star surgeons.

Jefferson I knew only by reputation. He had spent a number of years covering the crime beat for a TV station in Spartanburg, South Carolina, before taking the more lucrative and socially connected PR position at the hospital about two years ago. I estimated him to be around ten years older than Susan and I. He had a reputation of being both feared and respected. Feared because he was quick to run over anyone who got in the way of his career path and respected because he had won a number of prestigious awards for his crime reporting. He was said to have been directly responsible for putting a number of criminals behind bars, thanks to leads and witnesses he'd uncovered.

Whittier looked at Susan, who had remained seated. "I see there's still no name for the girl with the head trauma."

"No, but Barry's working on it."

"Really?" Jefferson said. His brown eyes sharpened as if trying to peer inside my skull.

Whittier pointed to my chair. "Why don't we all sit down and get brought up to date." She motioned for Jefferson and Chandler to take chairs and then she sat close to me. "We need to learn something soon to get proper authorization for the girl's treatment and to give Howard some idea of how to handle the media."

"Are you expecting her to remain on life-support?" I asked.

Whittier looked to Susan, knowing physicians didn't want administrators making medical assessments.

Susan dabbed a tissue at her nose. Now that the pressure in OR was over, her cold symptoms had returned. "That's a question for Ray. He was the girl's primary surgeon."

Ray Chandler was the youngest member of O'Malley's clinic, having just completed his residency at the hospital. He was smart, good looking, and a guy who appreciated Susan for more than just her surgical skills. In other words, I watched him like a hawk.

Chandler gave Whittier a sideways glance. He didn't seem anxious to express an opinion.

"I think we've heard enough from Dr. Chandler," Jefferson said with an edge in his voice. "I've got reporters hounding me about morning deadlines and all he says is the girl could be a minor whose care decisions need to be approved by her parents. Or she could be married. She could be seventeen or she could be twenty." Jefferson puffed himself up. "I can't go out in front of the cameras with vague information like that. I'll look like a fool."

Chandler bristled. "Never stopped you before. I've told you what I know about the girl."

"And it's precious little," Jefferson snapped back.

Whittier raised her hand to bring the quarrel to a halt. "We understand your need for information, Howard, and I'll get it for you." She turned to Susan. "Dr. O'Malley talked to me about airlifting the girl to Charlotte's trauma unit, but he also said the helicopter flight itself wasn't without risk to her condition. And we could be separating her from a family who may not want her moved out of the area. I'm asking you what you think."

Susan's knuckles went white as she gripped her coffee cup in both hands. While neither Whittier nor Jefferson had any direct authority over Susan, Whittier did approve all aspects of how the medical complex was run, including accepting the credentials of its practicing physicians. A surgeon without privileges at the local hospital would find it hard to get patients.

Jefferson, on the other hand, not only controlled the public relations machine in the area but also was known to hold Pamela Whittier's ear. He wasn't above putting in a disparaging word just for spite. Neither Jefferson nor Whittier were people Susan needed to have as enemies.

"And I said you need to ask Ray," Susan answered.

That's my girl, I thought. She'd swordfight Zorro if he made her mad. No wonder I loved her.

Whittier colored at Susan's rebuke. Then she brought herself under control. "I see." She looked past Jefferson to Chandler. "Do you agree with Dr. O'Malley that the girl shouldn't be moved?"

"Yes. We've got her stable here. That's all Charlotte would do at this point. We have to monitor her cranial pressure. We've done what surgery we can at this time."

Whittier spread her ringless fingers on the Formica tabletop and stared at them. "We've all had a long might. I don't mean to be the wicked witch of western North Carolina. I care what all my doctors think, and we'll do whatever you decide is best.

It's just that I care about this hospital and I don't want anything to go wrong."

The words were barely out of Whittier's mouth before Jefferson chimed in. "I agree. I just want to be sure that we're all speaking with one voice when I talk to the media." He gave us his best broadcaster smile. "I'll stall the reporters until we're able to get some more information."

Whittier laid her hand on my forearm. "Barry, now you see why learning the girl's identity will help us all. Is there anything Howard or I can do to assist you?"

Whittier's offer caught Jefferson's attention. "Right, maybe a little publicity would be helpful. Maybe there's already a missing person report on the girl or somebody might recognize her description if I get it on the air."

"I'll mention your offer to Deputy Hutchins. He's in charge of the investigation until we can get Tommy Lee involved." I thought how Tommy Lee would be hell to keep uninvolved. He'd be chomping at the bit to get out of the hospital.

Then an idea struck me as to how Tommy Lee could keep involved in the case and still get some rest and recuperation at the hospital. "Maybe there is something you can do. Would it be possible to have a computer in Tommy Lee's room where he could get emails and updates on the case from the Sheriff's Department?"

Whittier gave my arm a squeeze. "Sure. I'll see to it that the sheriff is put in a room where his deputy can consult with him at all times. Direct phone, internet, and email."

"Let me handle the phone and computer hookup," Jefferson said to Whittier. "I deal with those guys down in Information Technology a lot more than you. They're kind of an odd bunch. I'll call Bumgardner and have him take care of it personally. He's the best."

"Thanks," Whittier said and looked at Susan. "As long as we're not violating doctor's orders."

Susan smiled. "Since when has any doctor told Tommy Lee what to do? His head's as hard as Barry's."

Her diagnosis was right on the money.

I dropped Susan at her condo at one-thirty in the morning. Then I wasn't sure what to do. I didn't want to call the funeral home and wake Mom since she should have been in bed, but I didn't want to leave her hanging if she'd waited up for news. Although I'd telephoned her and Fletcher from the hospital as soon as Cindy and Tommy Lee were out of danger, I'd also promised to give them a progress report before I left. I hadn't. The night had gotten away from me. I decided I'd better drive by before heading to my cabin.

My parents had always lived above our funeral home. Other than the kitchen, the rest of the family living quarters—a den, Mom's sewing room, and two bedrooms—were upstairs. Like me, my father had grown up here. His grandfather had built the house back in 1929 and our business opened in 1930. Clayton and Clayton Funeral Directors was as much a Gainesboro institution as the hospital.

No light shone from the windows on the second level. I figured Mom had gone to bed. But as I turned onto the side street, I noticed a glow coming from the window of the downstairs parlor. Then I saw Fletcher Shaw's silver Honda convertible parked in the driveway. Evidently he and Mom were waiting up for me.

The back door to the kitchen was unlocked. I knew the layout well enough to navigate in the dark, and I went down the hall to the section of the house where we conducted our business. The slumber room, as my Uncle Wayne insisted upon calling it, lay on the right and served for family viewings and visitations. On the opposite side of the foyer was a small parlor for counseling families or receiving visitors in a more intimate setting.

In that room, a single lamp burned with the three-way bulb on its lowest wattage. In the dim light, I could make out Fletcher stretched on the sofa in a position more suitable for the inside of a casket. For a second, I watched to make sure he was breathing.

"Fletcher."

He jumped like I'd discharged a cannon by his head. "Barry. I didn't hear you."

He swung his feet off the sofa and started brushing the cushions as if I might inspect them. He stood up, looking unsure what to do next.

I realized that in his eyes I was the boss. "That's okay. Did my mother go to bed?"

"Yes. We figured you'd have called if there was a change one way or the other."

I motioned for him to sit down and I eased into an armchair by the stone fireplace. A summer mountain fern occupied the hearth in front of the dormant gas logs.

"Everybody's stable," I said, "but the unidentified girl's condition is the most precarious. Cindy and Tommy Lee should have a complete recovery."

"That's good." Fletcher's expression contradicted his words.

"What?"

He looked away from me. "I've been thinking that if I hadn't asked Cindy to dance with you—"

"Then you might have danced with her and she could have stopped in a different place where the bullet could have gone through her head, not her spleen. Fletcher, if you stay in this business, you're going to learn that death is even more unfair than life. You can only help people cope with it, not explain it. Cindy's alive. That's the main thing."

"You sound like my father. Mr. Practical."

"Oh, I have my flights of fancy," I assured him. "But, at some point, we all have to play the cards we're dealt and not stay hung up on the fairness of the dealer."

The young man smiled. "While we were in the waiting room, Cindy's mom told me how you've played your hand. I'd just like to say it's an honor to work for you."

His compliment caught me off guard. Maybe it was the late hour and the ordeal at the hospital. My throat tightened and I felt tears in my eyes. Now I was the one who looked away. I managed to whisper, "Thank you."

Life had dealt some tough cards. Not so much to me, but to Mom and Dad. Alzheimer's had struck my father when he was only in his fifties. For several years he, my mother, and Uncle Wayne struggled to keep the business going while Dad's condition deteriorated. They also looked for a potential buyer, but, at the time, their small-town funeral home wasn't attractive to the big chains.

I'd moved to Charlotte, married, and started my career in law enforcement with the Charlotte Police Department. My flight of fancy was to someday work for the FBI with a posting to a larger city, one where my wife, Rachel, could be happier.

Although my parents never asked me, I saw what needed to be done. So, I returned to Gainesboro at the cost of my career and eventually my marriage. But I'd played those cards into a life I valued. I had Susan and I had a community that depended upon me. Yet, moments like this told me I was still not at peace, and that a part of me regretted what I'd given up.

I didn't know how much Helen had told Fletcher about my past. I certainly didn't want to get into it now. "You were kind to stay," I told him. "You'd better get back to your apartment and grab a few hours' sleep. Tomorrow could be crazy."

"Do you think we'll be involved with the dead man?"

"I don't know. Deputy Hutchins got an ID. Mitch Kowalski of Delray Beach, Florida. Next of kin will need to be notified. I assume we might assist a funeral home down there with prep and shipment of the body." I stepped closer to him. "We'll find out tomorrow. Now get some rest."

He nodded. "Okay. But I didn't stay here just to talk. You had a phone call and I wanted to make sure you got the message."

"Who was it?"

"A nurse in the recovery room. Emily something. It was about the sheriff."

My heart raced. "She called after I left the hospital?"

"I don't think so. Earlier. I told her I thought you were still there. She said the sheriff had asked for you. She told him he couldn't have any visitors other than immediate family until he was in a room."

"So why'd she call?"

"She said the sheriff insisted. He had a message and he wanted it delivered word for word. The nurse apologized and said normally she wouldn't have bothered you, but even though he was still flying from the anesthesia, he was the sheriff. And she said these were his words, not hers."

"Oh, boy," I muttered.

"Yeah. The message is 'as soon as I get my room, have Deputy Barry Clayton get his ass in here.'" Fletcher grinned. "I didn't know you were a deputy."

Chapter Four

Deputy Reece Hutchins leaned against the wall of the hospital corridor. His crisp tan uniform and spit-shined black shoes conveyed authority. The stiff blue folder in his hand proclaimed a purpose, but his pale, thin face projected a fear that was impossible to hide beneath his veneer of officiousness. Reece looked like he was next in line for a colon examination.

"Have you seen him?" I asked. The door to Tommy Lee's room behind Reece was shut.

"No. The nurse at the desk said they're checking the wound's drainage and changing the dressing. The docs will let us know if he can have visitors."

That sounded reasonable. Nearly fifteen hours had passed since the shooting. I'd been able to sleep for three of them. "There's a lounge down the hall. I can wait there till you're finished."

Reece shrugged. "Why? Patsy said he wanted to see us together."

I couldn't hide my surprise. Fletcher hadn't mentioned that detail last night.

"You didn't know?" Only a hint of sarcasm laced Reece's question. Normally he loved having inside information, but today he seemed to be doing his best just to hold himself together.

The door to Tommy Lee's room opened and Susan emerged. "Gentlemen." She winked at me.

"What's the word?" I asked.

Susan nodded her head toward the room. "O'Malley has the last word."

Although I couldn't see the older surgeon, I heard his voice boom loud and clear. "You're not going to do anyone any good if you come out of this hospital one minute earlier than I tell you. So, get over it."

There was a mumbled growl in response.

A few seconds later, Dr. O'Malley stepped into the hall. The scowl on his face didn't soften at the sight of Reece and me. "So, what are you here for? Pin his badge on his bandage?"

"He wanted to see us," Reece stammered.

O'Malley sighed in exasperation. "Sure, why not. He'd probably get out of bed and track you down otherwise. But you can do your buddy a favor by keeping your visit short. He's lost a lot of blood, and he's got a lot of tissue that needs time to heal."

I smiled. "Did you tell him that?"

"Yeah. I might as well have been talking to the damn bedpan." He gave each of us a concerned stare. "Try not to let him get agitated. The calmer he stays, the faster he mends." He turned to Susan. "Let's go check on Cindy Todd."

"How's the other girl?" I asked.

"Hanging by a thread," O'Malley said, and then briskly walked away with Susan hurrying to catch him.

Reece motioned for me to enter first. The room was indirectly lit by a fluorescent bulb mounted to the wall behind the hospital bed. Its soft white light cast an ethereal glow over the sheets and medical equipment. A computer monitor hanging from the ceiling displayed heart rate, blood pressure, oxygenation levels, and several other functions unknown to me. An IV tree held multiple bags of fluids dripping into Tommy Lee's arm. A single bag at the foot of the bed collected urine. From somewhere among the paraphernalia, a barely audible beep sounded with the rhythm of a slow dance tune.

The upper section of the bed was inclined at a thirty-degree angle, and Tommy Lee's head was propped up on two pillows. Never before had I seen him without his eye patch. Scar tissue covered the left socket, leaving a pale void that drew my gaze with hypnotic power. The remnants of mangled flesh seemed to spawn the familiar long, thin scar that crossed his cheek and disappeared into the corner of his mouth. Seeing the whole wound exposed made me wonder how he'd ever made it out of Vietnam alive.

His right eye opened, and then his mouth. The words came out in a guttural whisper. "Well, y'all going to gawk at me or tell me who shot me?"

Reece held up his blue folder like he expected Tommy Lee to read through the cover. "Florida man. Mitch Kowalski. I've spoken to the local police in Delray Beach."

Tommy Lee swallowed with difficulty, and then looked at me. "Hurts to talk, but I can listen. Pull up some chairs."

I noticed the room was at least fifty percent bigger than the regular ones. Howard Jefferson had come through with special accommodations. Not only was there a sofa that pulled out for someone to spend the night, but space allowed for a desk and two extra chairs with enough room to maneuver them bedside. Reece sat to Tommy Lee's left and I took the right.

Reece summarized what he knew about Kowalski and the death of his wife. He had new information that there was no one else in the family named Lucy. Kowalski's only daughter, named Rose, didn't know her father had left Delray Beach, and the police in Florida were going to see if Kowalski had told anyone he was heading for North Carolina.

Reece had also told the Delray police about the credit card in the girl's possession and Kowalski's accusation to the man called Lincoln. He concluded his progress report saying he'd release the body to the daughter when the autopsy was completed and had sent out a description of the unidentified girl to the surrounding counties.

Then Reece pulled several sheets of paper from the folder. "I went in early this morning and got the duty roster. I brought it for you to review."

Tommy Lee stared at him for a few seconds. "Duty roster?"

"Yeah. I figured you'd want to reorganize the rotation while you're laid up. How do you want to cover the office?"

Tommy Lee shot me a quick glance. The duty roster was the last thing on his mind. I looked up at the vital statistics monitor expecting to see his blood pressure shoot off the screen.

"Reece." Tommy Lee's voice strained to remain a whisper. "Listen carefully. I don't give a damn about the duty roster."

Reece flushed. He tucked the papers back in the folder like they were dirty pictures.

Tommy Lee took a slow breath and grimaced. "I don't give a damn because I know I can count on you to take care of it. I'm putting you in charge of all administration. Unless something extraordinary happens, I want you to run things like I was dead."

Reece's head bounced like a bobble-head doll. "Yes, sir. Yes, sir. I won't let you down."

"But I'm not dead. And I'll be coming back. So, take my advice and remember empathy and humility. You'll do fine."

"Empathy and humility," Reece repeated.

I hoped Reece would look the words up in the dictionary since they were a foreign language to him.

"One thing you won't be in charge of is the investigation of this shooting." Tommy Lee whispered the statement like he was doing Reece a big favor.

Reece wasn't buying it. "Why not? It's a major crime."

Tommy Lee swallowed again. The tube used to administer anesthesia during surgery had probably rubbed his throat raw.

"Would you like a little ice?" I asked. The Styrofoam pitcher on the rolling table beside me contained slivers of ice that had not yet melted.

Tommy Lee nodded. I held a cupful close to his chin and let him take a bite. Reece and I sat quietly while he enjoyed the soothing effect of the ice.

After several moments, Tommy Lee pressed on. "Reece, I shot and killed a man. An old man I probably startled into firing. We'll need a thorough investigation, and I'll want the final report sent to the District Attorney's Office for their review. That way we'll minimize any question of a cover-up by some good ol' boys Sheriff's club."

"But he shot you first," Reece said.

"And I expect that to be duly noted in the report. But there's also the man who pushed that girl into the line of fire and got her shot. As far as I'm concerned, he's as culpable as Kowalski for the shooting. Maybe more. I want him found and prosecuted."

Reece looked confused. "But we don't even know who the man is."

Tommy Lee smiled. "No, we don't. And you don't have the time or personnel to find out. That's why I'm going to assign a special deputy reporting directly to me."

I got a numb feeling in the pit of my stomach as cold as the ice in the cup. Deputy Barry Clayton hadn't been a joke.

Reece's jaw dropped. He stared at me. "Him?"

"I haven't asked Barry yet. I wanted you to be part of the discussion."

Reece was still having trouble getting his mouth to close. "But he's only a funeral director."

"Barry's also worked for a big-city police force, he's nearly completed his degree in criminal justice, and he's not confined by a duty roster."

People didn't die according to a duty roster, either. How could I conduct an investigation and run Clayton and Clayton at the same time? But I wasn't about to supply fuel for Reece. This was between Tommy Lee and me.

But Reece wasn't about to give up. Like a terrier with a bone, he just couldn't drop it. "I think the idea stinks. And not because Barry's your friend, but because he doesn't have the experience for something this big."

Tommy Lee sank deeper in his pillows and rubbed his throat. "Reece, I'm too tired and too sore to argue. I was hoping you'd understand, but let me put it this way. I was elected by the people. I serve at their pleasure, and the people I hire serve at my pleasure."

His words had the desired impact. Reece forced a smile. "Get me your sizes, Barry, and I'll order your uniform."

Perfect. I could be the escort for my own funeral processions.

"Just a badge and an ID will be enough," Tommy Lee said. "He won't be with us long."

That prospect brightened Reece's face. "Barry, I'll help you any way I can."

I nodded, and then just stared at Tommy Lee. He looked so vulnerable chained to all that equipment. My heart wanted me to help him; my head wanted me to get the hell out of there. "I'll have to talk to Mom and Uncle Wayne."

"Of course," he whispered. "But I need to know quick."

"I'll let you know one way or the other by noon."

"Fine." He turned to Reece. "Will you write the memo announcing Barry's appointment? If he gives you the okay, sign it for both of us. From you and me."

I could tell Reece savored the sight of his name on an interoffice proclamation. "Right away." He rocked back and forth in his chair, anxious to run with the news.

"Go ahead then," Tommy Lee said. "I've got a few minor things for Barry. Tell everyone I'm as ornery as ever."

Reece stood up. "They'll be glad to hear it." Then he actually saluted.

Tommy Lee lifted one arm a few inches off the sheet and waved his fingers "bye-bye." Reece gave me an earnest man-to-man nod and left.

Tommy Lee tried to restrain a laugh, but the suppressed breath came out in a muffled cough. He winced at the sharp pain.

I didn't find the situation nearly as humorous. "Reece has a point, you know."

"Umm," he grunted. "Tell me if he gets in your way."

"Listen—"

Tommy Lee raised his hand again and cut me off. "I need your help, but like I said I'm too whipped to argue. If you can't do it, fine. Right now, though, think with me. What would you do next?"

I gave him some more ice while I thought over his question. "The credit card. It's physical evidence. We need to track the history of its use. Did Mitch Kowalski get a billing statement that led him here? His wife's tied to the card, the card to the girl in the hospital, the girl to a man named Lincoln, and Lincoln to Kowalski by the fact that he called Lincoln by name." I stopped and thought for a moment. "If it was simple credit card theft, how would Kowalski know Lincoln? Someone either here or in Florida might be able to tie them together."

Tommy Lee closed his eye and smiled. "Go on."

"There's the girl. Who is she? Where's she from? We should get a picture to Kowalski's daughter. The Delray police need to work that end. Maybe some of the Florida summer people up here are from Delray. We need to question them. I'll talk to Susan about the girl's appearance. Is there anything that suggests where she's from? Florida tan? Wardrobe labels?

"Then I'll check reports of items left at the street dance. Maybe they brought folding chairs that never got picked up. If Lincoln came from Delray, he might have been staying at an area motel. I'll see if Reece can have someone work the phones for those inquiries."

I stopped. Tommy Lee's head had sagged to one side with a trace of a smile still clinging to his pale lips. His breath came in regular shallow gasps and the monitor beeped steadily. O'Malley's words came to mind. "The calmer he stays, the faster he mends." I realized my own words to Tommy Lee about the planned investigation had taken a distinct shift. What had started as "we" ended as "I."

Before my father's Alzheimer's, my goal with the Charlotte Police Department had been to make detective and perhaps someday work for the FBI. As I stood there watching Tommy Lee sleep, I heard the voice of my dad before his illness. He often gave me that age-old advice, "Be careful what you wish for. You just might get it."

My time in Charlotte had been spent as a patrolman. I'd been around enough homicide scenes to watch and learn from the detectives. I'd made friends with several of them, but I'd never been in charge of a homicide investigation.

In a large police force like Charlotte, detectives usually worked a homicide in teams of two. One would be the primary detective in charge of the investigation and the other would be assigned to assist with interviews, provide backup for going into dangerous situations, and, perhaps most importantly, be a sounding board for ideas, no matter how crazy. But there was never any doubt that the case was the responsibility of the primary detective. His name appeared on the case file. He got the credit when the case was solved and blame when it wasn't.

One of the veteran detectives in Charlotte took a liking to me, as the mountaineers would say. Old Eddie White schooled me on the way things really worked. He laughed about how when he was the assisting detective, he always knew everything and never made a mistake. But when he was the primary detective he always felt lost as hell and was clueless on what to do next.

I'd always thought Eddie was joking, but now I knew what he was talking about. There was a huge difference between helping Tommy Lee on a case and being the guy ultimately responsible for its solution.

Reece was right. I was a funeral director. A damn good one, and I had obligations to Mom, Dad, and Uncle Wayne. There was much to consider and not much time to decide.

But Tommy Lee had confidence in me. How could I tell him no?

I knew one thing for sure. If I took the job and made a mistake, somebody would literally get away with murder.

Chapter Five

"I need to discuss something with all of you." I continued standing while everyone found a seat in the parlor.

Mom led Dad to the sofa. They'd been out in the backyard where he could get some fresh air. She was carrying his customary noon glass of lemonade. My uncle Wayne put his long bony frame in an armchair and cocked his head to give me his good ear. I'd summoned him from the backroom where he'd been inventorying embalming supplies. Fletcher had come into the funeral home that Saturday to help Uncle Wayne since he figured I'd be tied up at the hospital. Fletcher took the matching armchair opposite Wayne.

I pulled the wooden comb-back Windsor from the back corner of the parlor and sat where everyone could see me. Mom, Uncle Wayne, and Fletcher looked at me expectantly. Dad's limited attention focused on the straw in his drink, his doctor's way of making the act of swallowing more deliberate.

"You all know Tommy Lee's out of danger, but it'll be a while before he's out of the hospital."

"Fine man, fine family," Wayne said.

"Yes. Well, he's asked me to help him with the case."

"I thought he killed the man?" Fletcher said.

"But we don't know why the man was there or who he was really trying to kill. And there's the unidentified girl."

"And poor little Cindy," Mom added, probably remembering her as six years old and coloring at a table in Helen's diner.

"You've got to help him," Wayne said. "No two ways about it. He'd take the case if it were you."

Fletcher looked at my uncle, trying to make sense of his statement. Wayne's logic sometimes defied explanation. Of course Tommy Lee would take the case, that was his job. The question was would Tommy Lee conduct a funeral if I were laid up in the hospital? He would damn sure try.

"Right," I agreed, and winked at Fletcher. "But Tommy Lee doesn't also work in a funeral home."

"It's your brain he wants," Wayne said. "You can use that here."

"He's asked me to become a deputy and head up the investigation."

"A deputy?" Mom glanced at her brother. "Full time?"

"He knows I can't be full time, but as much time as I can spare. The department is small and with Tommy Lee out he's put Reece Hutchins in charge of all administrative duties."

Uncle Wayne shook his head. "Reece Hutchins couldn't find his own nose if it were right there on his face."

"Don't be ugly." Mom smiled apologetically at Fletcher.

Wayne didn't look at all apologetic. "I'll talk to Freddy about giving us more help."

Mom shook her head. "Freddy was complaining yesterday that he's over promised the Florida people."

Freddy Mott had worked part time for us for years. He was invaluable whenever we had funerals close together or a larger than normal service. But Freddy also worked as a carpenter and handyman, and the summer people always had projects for him. He made a lot more money hammering nails than lifting caskets.

"Florida people." Wayne waved his hand dismissively. "Tommy Lee's one of our own, Connie."

As brother and sister, the only physical trait they shared was curly white hair. My uncle was older, taller, and set in his ways. Mom stood a little over five feet and would make the perfect kindly plump grandmother if I ever remarried and contributed to the gene pool. Still they were as close as a brother and sister could be. If anybody picked on one, he'd have to deal with the wrath of the other. But they could punch each other's buttons and raise a simple disagreement into an intractable debate.

Fletcher put his hands on his knees and leaned forward. "I can help as much as you need me."

"But Barry's supposed to be teaching you," Wayne said.

Fletcher turned to my uncle. "Mr. Thompson, I know I can learn so much from you."

Wayne blushed and cleared his throat. "Well, there's that."

I smiled. The kid would do all right. "And Tommy Lee promised to fire me as soon as we wrap things up."

"Won't it be dangerous?" Mom asked. "The man had a gun."

"We're just trying to find out who he was. His wife died a few weeks ago in Florida and he may have simply snapped." I didn't tell her I'd witnessed the target of his attack throw a girl into the line of fire. Or the credit card. "I'll be fine, Mom."

She turned to Fletcher. "He has a scar for every time he's said that."

Dad stood up holding his empty glass. He looked around the room in alarm until he saw my mother right next to him. "Home."

"I'll take him upstairs." Mom took the glass from Dad's hand and walked him slowly from the room.

"He's doing that more and more," Wayne said. "Just breaks your heart."

Fletcher stared at the floor. What could he say?

"Thank you for coming in," I told him. "Looks like you're going to have a busy summer."

"That's what I wanted, but I hate it's under these circumstances."

"You make your plans, and then life happens." Uncle Wayne the philosopher leaned back in the armchair. "Make sure Barry gives you my number in case you need to reach me."

"Good. I'll put it in my cell."

"Your cell?" Uncle Wayne looked at me. "You've got him staying in Tommy Lee's jail?"

"His cell phone, Uncle Wayne. Not everybody still uses a rotary dial."

"Nothing wrong with my phone. I'm either home or here." He thought for a second. "If he's going to be on twenty-four-hour call, he ought to stay with me."

A flash of panic crossed Fletcher's face. Round the clock with Uncle Wayne would have frightened me as well.

"He's got an apartment out at Daleview Manor," I said. "That's much closer and he can hop on the interstate to get to Asheville where there's some nightlife."

Uncle Wayne grunted. "Nightlife. I got possums and rac-coons. An owl or two." Then he laughed. "Yeah, I wasn't born yesterday. Young fellow like you'd be more interested in foxes. I know. I watch TV."

Uncle Wayne wasn't born yesterday by a long stretch, but if the lifelong bachelor had ever been on a date, the girl probably had worn a hoop skirt.

As soon as the family meeting was over, I phoned Reece and told him he could write the memo announcing my appointment as a deputy sheriff. I realized I'd actually made up my mind in Tommy Lee's hospital room, but wouldn't admit it to myself until seeing Mom and Uncle Wayne. Now that I had their blessing I was eager to jump on the case.

I asked Reece to begin the search for a man named Lincoln and to give me the number for the Delray Police Department. I planned on calling them personally. I could tell Reece still wasn't happy about my role in the department, but I knew he would do his job.

The first thing I needed to do was get back to the hospital and catch Susan as she made afternoon rounds. The comatose girl could be the key to everything, and if she regained consciousness and could speak, I wanted to be there.

When I got to Tommy Lee's floor, I noticed the nurse on duty was Judi Perez. In fact, Judi was hard not to notice. As she stood outside Tommy Lee's door, her loose-fitting hospital uniform did little to hide the figure that should have been on the cover of *Sports Illustrated*'s swimsuit issue.

Judi was a transplant to the mountains of North Carolina. Susan had told me Judi had been a nurse at Cook County Hospital in Chicago until a messy divorce made her seek a change of scenery. She'd come to Gainesboro just to get away from the hassle of the big city for a while, but she'd found that she liked the pace and had never left. Susan thought highly of her, and I was sure the male employees thought constantly of her.

"How are our patients doing?" I asked her.

Judi gave me a broad smile of perfect teeth. "Tommy Lee and Cindy are progressing as expected and our mystery girl is showing some slight improvement. Her cranial pressure has stabilized."

"Any idea when she might regain consciousness?"

"Dr. Chandler called in a consulting neurosurgeon from Asheville to review the readouts but nobody can say for sure when we'll be able to bring her out of her drug-induced coma."

I thought I saw a mist of tears in her eyes.

She took a deep breath. "Crazy isn't it? This is the kind of thing I'd expect to happen in Chicago, but not here. That's why I came to Gainesboro. Things were supposed to be slower and easier."

I touched her shoulder, surprised at the emotion she was expressing. Her muscles tightened as my concern made her realize she'd momentarily lost her professional persona.

"Oh, well. The best laid plans and all that." Judi tossed her head and her soft brown curls settled perfectly around her angelic face. "I'd better get back to work."

I found Patsy sitting bedside with Tommy Lee. Both were asleep, but she woke before I could retreat from the room.

"Stay," she said. "You won't bother me and I think he's finally fallen into a less fitful sleep." Patsy's bleary eyes showed me she could use more than a few hours' rest herself. "He told me you're a deputy."

I should have figured Reece would have let Tommy Lee know as soon as we hung up. "We hope not for long."

"Thank you for doing that." She started to cry and then laughed at her uncontrollable tears. "You live knowing something like this is a possibility. Part of the job. The world's a dangerous place and law enforcement puts Tommy Lee right on the borderline of that danger. But an old man at a square dance." She threw up her hands at the absurdity.

"Something pushed that old man over the border." I stepped closer and gently touched her shoulder. "I want to find out who and why."

"God knows I want you to, otherwise he'll never really rest." She looked at her battle-scarred husband. Tenderly, she adjusted the black patch over his eye. "The mayor came by. He said the merchants association made a thousand-dollar contribution to aid the investigation. Extra overtime if necessary."

"Good." I didn't doubt the sincerity of our community's concern. I also knew everyone wanted the case closed with an explanation that would make the tourists feel safe.

"And Howard Jefferson came by while Mayor Whitlock was here. He said the computer and phone are ready. The hospital's covering all long distance charges."

There was a knock at the door. A metal cart bearing a computer, monitor, and keyboard rolled into the room. The young man behind it looked like anything but a hospital employee. He wore black cargo pants, a tight black tee shirt, and multiple silver rings perforating the rims of his ears. The ID badge dangling from his neck looked as out of place as a third eye on the Mona Lisa.

"Is this the room to be linked to the network?" he asked.

"I guess so," I said. "I requested a computer for the sheriff."

"Then you got it. One of the new dual processor hyper-thread super RAM babies. Sweet."

Patsy eyed him cautiously as if he'd started babbling in tongues.

The man picked up the CPU and his biceps swelled. For a computer geek, he knew his way around a weight room.

"Actually, it's for me," I assured Patsy. "If I'm not in the way, I can work here. Tommy Lee can participate as much or as little as he wants."

Patsy relaxed. "Okay. Howard also asked me if I wanted to restrict visitors."

"Not a bad idea. Have you had inquiries from the press?"

"Some calls at home. Kenny's handling those. I spoke to Melissa Bigham. She's on vacation in Colorado and heard about the shooting. She was concerned about us, not just the news story."

Melissa Bigham was the top reporter for our daily paper, the *Gainesboro Vista*. Although she was a good friend, I was glad she was out of town. When she learned I was a deputy, she'd be hounding me for the inside scoop. At least I had a week's reprieve.

"Howard's running all media inquiries through his office," Patsy said.

"Sounds like they're on top of things."

Patsy laughed.

"What's so funny?"

"Howard's no fool. When I agreed to an authorized visitor's list, he said he'd put the mayor at the top. Whitlock strutted out like he had the keys to the Oval Office."

The computer installer dropped to his knees and unraveled a thick cable to the wall. He popped loose a faceplate in the baseboard, yanked free a multi-pinned connector, and tied the computer's cable into it. He pulled a small screw driver from a Velcro pocket on his thigh and started tightening the plugs together.

I told Patsy I'd stay for a while if she wanted to take a break. She left for lunch and a change of clothes. A few minutes later, the dark wizard scrambled to his feet. He switched on the computer and turned to me. "Take her for a test drive."

I sat down at the desk. When I scrolled the mouse across the pad, the monitor screen turned to blue wallpaper consisting of *Laurel County Memorial* written multiple times, with the hospital's laurel blossom logo framing each corner.

"You're on the system," he said.

I hit enter and a prompt for a password appeared.

"What do I type here?"

"Not my department. You'll have to get a password from administration. They're on the wing directly under us."

"Can I get it over the phone?"

"Probably not. Someone should see you in person. But if you have other questions, call for Nate."

"Nate?"

He twisted his badge around where I could read *Nate Bumgardner*. "See. Here I am. Fast, huh?" He pulled the empty cart out of the room, laughing at his own joke.

Administration occupied one wing off the main lobby. I decided to go straight to Pamela Whittier's office and have her direct me to the proper department. Her administrative assistant sat behind an impressive oak desk, files neatly stacked on one corner, a computer monitor and keyboard occupying a return along the wall.

The furnishings were fitting for the head of a hospital. Tasteful, traditional, and expensive. The only surprise revealed more about my stereotypes. Whittier's assistant was a man.

"May I help you?" he asked in a pleasant, educated voice. The well-groomed gatekeeper wore a conservative red tie and starched white shirt. He looked to be in his early thirties and spoke with the confidence of someone older.

"I'm Barry Clayton. Nate sent me for a password."

"Joel Greene." He stood to greet me with a handshake. "Ms. Whittier thought you might be by. She had a board luncheon that's running long, but she left this."

He retrieved a business envelope from the center drawer of his desk. "This contains the access code for long distance and a temporary password for our computer network. Change the password as soon as you log on and remember it." Greene handed me the envelope as if it might explode. "You're the only one who can get to your files. We take computer security very seriously. Forget the password, and those files are irretrievable."

"Even to Nate?"

Greene smiled. "Nate's a piece of work, isn't he? Fortunately, he stays hidden in central computer operations where he can't scare the patients."

"How'd the hospital find a guy like that?"

"Referral. From Dr. Chandler. Nate had done some freelance computer work for the clinic and Chandler said he was a genius. The former head of Information Technology retired the end of last year. Nate's run circles around him, but with Nate, what you see is what you get."

When I returned to Tommy Lee's room, Susan was making a few notations on his chart. He appeared to be sleeping.

"How's your patient doing?"

"How are you doing?" Tommy Lee croaked, and half-opened his eye. "Solved the case yet?"

I looked at Susan. "I liked him better when he was unconscious."

Tommy Lee grunted and closed his eye.

"He'll be drifting in and out." Susan sounded stuffy and wore a mask as well as latex gloves. "For the next few days his bark will be worse than his bite."

"How's your cold?"

"Going from runny to clogged. My head feels like it's packed with concrete. Doug Larson's got samples of some new over-the-counter medication he suggests I try."

"Want me to pick them up for you? I'm going by the Sheriff's Department later this afternoon." Doug Larson owned Larson's Discount Drugs on Main Street and would be on the way.

"If it's no trouble." Susan walked to the door and returned the chart to the holder.

"Anything on the girl? I heard she might come out of her coma soon."

"Maybe this evening."

"Can I leave word for someone to call me?"

Susan frowned. "She certainly won't be up for a police grilling."

"No, but she might mutter a few words on her own. You know how the mind works."

"All right. I'll speak to the duty nurse." Susan turned to go.

I caught her arm. "One more thing. Do you know where her clothes are stored?"

"Probably in a personal articles bag in her room's closet." Susan pointed to a cabinet by the bathroom. "Why?"

"I'm trying to see if she's local or from Florida. Does she have a tan?"

"Nothing more than normal exposure to the sun. She hasn't been lying out on the beach or in some salon."

"Do you think I could take a few pictures of her? Then I could have an artist's sketch made that would get rid of the bandages."

Susan shrugged. "If it helps find out who she is. You'd better run it by Howard Jefferson, but under the circumstances I think he'd take his chances with HIPAA privacy regulations." She thought for a second longer. "There is one thing about the girl. She has a few tattoos."

"I don't want to hear it." Earlier in the spring Tommy Lee and I had solved a crime based on tattoos I'd found on a body. That adventure nearly cost me my life.

"Nothing so dramatic," Susan said. "A rose on her ankle, a butterfly on her left shoulder. You should list them in the descriptive markings you circulate with any picture. She also has body piercings—multiple ear, one nose, and a tongue. But there was no jewelry or studs in any of them. Some were starting to close over."

"Sounds like she was running with a new crowd."

"Yeah. If she recovers, she might want to think about going back to the old one."

Susan continued with her rounds and I sat down at the computer. I opened the envelope and found the temporary password GAINESBORO CSI. Someone in administration had a sense of humor. I logged on and changed the password to KOWALSKI, figuring that would be a word I wouldn't forget.

I called the Delray Beach Police Department and was told Lieutenant Spring would be in at four. I asked for an email address so I could send him a description of the girl and he could give me an update on any information unearthed about Mitch Kowalski's movements since his wife's death. I concluded the email with my cell phone number and a request he call me.

Patsy returned around three-fifteen with her daughter Samantha. I didn't want to horn in on family time so I said I'd be back after supper. That would give me time to check in with Reece, run up to my cabin, and swing by the funeral home.

To Reece's credit, he had all the paperwork ready to officially put me on the force. He had a deputy shoot a digital photo for my ID card and then included it with a badge in a new leather flip case. Over five years had passed since I'd left the Charlotte police force, and I must admit I felt a thrill at slipping the badge into my pocket.

No one named Lincoln turned up in the first round of canvassing the major motels. Without an accurate description, finding him registered under an assumed name would be difficult. I suggested they include the girl; maybe they'd traveled as father and daughter because of the age difference. An artist's sketch of the girl would help, and Fletcher and Susan had seen Lincoln head on. I'd get them to provide whatever details they could for the composite sketch.

Nothing had been found left on the street. No folding chairs, no abandoned car, no one who had seen where Lincoln had gone. In the aftermath of the shooting, he had disappeared.

I drove up to my cabin to let my yellow lab, Democrat, out for a run and restock lettuce and water for George, the guinea pig. Those two roommates were accustomed to my comings and goings, but Democrat always gave me a pitiful brown-eyed stare that made me feel guilty. His tail accelerated into double time when I whistled him into the jeep. Tonight he'd stay with Mom and enjoy a little pampering.

Tonight I was a sworn officer of the law, and I remembered I needed to carry more than an ID and a badge. I left Democrat in the jeep and returned to the cabin. From the back corner of my sock drawer I retrieved my holstered .38 Special. The nickel-plated Smith & Wesson didn't have the firepower of the Glock that I'd carried as a patrolman, but the five-shot revolver never jammed and was intimidating enough if you were on the wrong side of the barrel.

I had taken an oath to uphold the law and protect the citizens of Laurel County. I had to be prepared to kill in order to honor that oath, and I knew even the most routine investigation could suddenly turn deadly if you crossed paths with the wrong people.

I looped my belt through the holster, positioned the gun just above my right hip, and headed for the funeral home.

When I got there, I found Uncle Wayne and Fletcher sitting at the kitchen table divvying up homemade chocolate chip cookies while Mom stirred something on the stove. Democrat went straight to his cushion in the corner, but kept an alert watch on Mom's every move. If she dropped so much as a crumb, he usually snagged it in midair.

"Can you stay for supper?" Mom asked. "Fletcher's being introduced to grilled pimiento cheese."

I gave Mom a quick wink. "Looks like he's well acquainted with dessert."

"Just a little something to tide them over. I'm also fixing fresh asparagus."

"Hurt me." I grabbed a cookie off the plate. "But I can't stay. I've got to pick something up for Susan."

"Hey, that's stealing," Uncle Wayne said.

"Then I'll put myself under arrest and take another for evidence."

"Has the girl regained consciousness?" Fletcher asked.

"No. Maybe this evening. I plan to be there. I'm also—" I bit off my words in frustration. "What an idiot. I walked off and left my camera."

"Your what?" Uncle Wayne asked in between bites.

"My digital camera. I was going to take a photograph of the girl so an artist can make a sketch."

"A sketch?" Wayne looked puzzled. "Why not just use the picture?"

"Because of the bandages. We need her to look like she did before the shooting."

Fletcher finished his cookie and picked up another. "Photoshop her."

"That's way beyond my computer skills."

"I've got the program and some facial feature plug-ins on my laptop. We use it in coursework for reconstructive cosmetics. I could take the photos and see what I come up with."

"What are y'all talking about?" Uncle Wayne asked.

"Using the computer instead of an artist," Fletcher said. "I saw the girl at the street dance so I've got a good idea about hair length and color. If it doesn't work, you're no worse off. You still have the photos."

"Can you give me anything for the man she was with?" I asked.

He shook his head. "That might take a police artist. I can't draw freehand, but I'll see if I can assemble something close."

Uncle Wayne turned to Fletcher. "Kinda like Mr. Potato Head? Different eyes, different noses? Barry'd play with his for hours."

Fletcher stared blankly at Wayne, trying to connect his twenty-first century computer program to me and a spud.

After a few seconds, I let Fletcher off the hook and answered my uncle. "A real sophisticated Mr. Potato Head. But I still need to go back for my camera."

Fletcher regained his bearings. "I've got a Canon Rebel. I'll use it. Doing the composite might take me a while. Maybe I'd better go now."

I looked at Mom still working at the stove. "I'm not coming between you and your first taste of Mom's grilled pimiento cheese sandwiches. Have supper first. I'll call the hospital and clear your access."

"Be ready in fifteen minutes," Mom said.

Uncle Wayne bit off half a cookie and mumbled, "Mr. Potato Head. Now there was a toy."

Like most of Gainesboro's downtown businesses, Larson's Discount Drugs closed at six on Saturdays. Doug Larson had inherited the business from his father, and it was the last of the Main Street stores going back to the 1950s. Everyone knew the age of Wal-Mart and the super drug chains killed small retailers like Doug. If not for foot traffic and loyalty from longtime customers, Larson's Discount Drugs would never have made it into the twenty-first century.

I entered the store a few minutes before six, which earned me a scowl from the teenage girl behind the register.

"Is Mr. Larson here?"

"In the back. Are you buying something?"

"No. You can close out the register."

She flashed me a smile of braces. Saturday night was definitely date night.

A waist-high counter at the back of the store separated the customers from the shelves of pharmaceuticals on the other side. I didn't see Doug so I rang the bell beside the "drop prescription" slot.

"Just a second," he called.

I stepped farther along the counter and saw him kneeling in front of a large safe. He closed the door, yanked up the handle, and spun the combination dial a few times.

"The family jewels?" I asked.

"Oh, hi, Barry." Doug got to his feet. "The junkies would walk over the family jewels to get what's in here."

The pharmacist wore a white lab coat and blue name badge. His round, pale face and thick glasses made him look like a snow owl.

"Any of it OxyContin?"

His eyes blinked twice. "Yes. I have to keep it under lock and key even when we're open. Guess you don't have to worry about your customers stealing any drugs."

"No. They're certified pain free. I hear that stuff's dangerous."

"Can be. The manufacturer's being sued. People say it works so well they get hooked. They claim the company should have put out more warnings."

"But it's prescription."

"And when the doctor stops prescribing, the only prescription form needed on the street is a couple of Andrew Jacksons—forty dollars a pill rather than four. That's why I keep my safe locked."

"How easy is it to overdose?"

Doug grabbed a bottle of Tylenol from a counter display. "Take too many, you can O.D. on these. Same with OxyContin. But I don't know anyone who crushes, snorts, chews, or injects Tylenol. That's how people die from OxyContin."

Like Lucy Kowalski, I thought.

Doug gave me an inquisitive look. "Why the interest? Are they prescribing OxyContin for Tommy Lee?"

"No. Maybe." I decided the background information on Mitch Kowalski wasn't confidential. "The wife of the man who shot Tommy Lee died two weeks ago in Florida. Police think it was an accidental overdose of OxyContin. She probably chewed the pills."

"There you go. That could do it. I always make customers sign a sheet that they've read the warning for time-released opioids."

"Her name was Lucy Kowalski. Ever fill a prescription for her?"

He stared at the ceiling, thinking. "No. I don't believe so. I can check the records." He looked at his watch. "But I'm supposed to be at the hospital at six-thirty."

"Someone I know?"

He shook his head. "I work an evening shift in their pharmacy. A little extra to help make ends meet."

"I didn't mean to keep you. I actually dropped by to pick up some cold medicine for Susan Miller. She said you had some samples."

Doug walked back to a side shelf. "Yes. Got them in first of the week. 'Cold-B-Gone.' It's like Cold-Eeze, but formulated for a combination viral and allergenic attack. The common summer cold. Everything's a specialty these days." He slid a box of the lozenges over the counter. "Tell her to let me know how they work. I won't recommend them if they're just marketing hype."

"Thanks, Doug. But how much medicine's not marketing hype these days?"

He laughed. "You got that right. Now days customers tell me what brand prescription they want. One elderly lady asked for that Viagra with the side-effect of a four-hour erection for her husband."

"Sounds like a combustible couple."

"Nah. She just wanted to keep him from rolling out of bed."

Susan had gotten back to her condo a few minutes before I arrived. She popped two of Doug's samples in her mouth, and then mumbled would I like dinner.

"Do you want to go out? No sense cooking if you don't feel well."

She plopped on the sofa. "I really just want to get off my feet. I'll fix something simple."

"How 'bout take-out? I could go for Chinese."

An hour later, I was clearing the remnants of tangerine chicken and beef with broccoli from Susan's dining room table. Susan was back on the sofa, but she'd changed into a blue and white jogging suit and she was nursing a cup of green tea. So far Doug Larson's miracle cold remedy had had little effect.

"I'll load the dishwasher," I said. "Why don't you get into bed?"

"I hate that I'm sick. I've never slept with a deputy before."

"Wait till Reece gives me my handcuffs."

As I carried the dishes into her kitchen, my cell phone vibrated on my belt. I was setting my load in the sink when I heard a chirping noise and saw Susan heading for her bedroom.

"Damn. My pager's beeping."

With an uneasy premonition, I flipped open my phone. The incoming number belonged to Fletcher.

"Barry?" His voice was a brittle rasp. "She's dead. Oh, God, she died while I was taking her picture. The girl is dead."

Chapter Six

No one spoke above a whisper even though the person at the center of our attention could no longer hear us.

Susan, Ray Chandler, and Judi Perez stood conferring about the monitor readouts. To a casual glance, the young woman lying in the hospital bed beside them appeared to be sleeping. I didn't need to see the blank video screens or touch the girl's body to recognize the sleep of the dead.

The room in the intensive care unit was smaller than Tommy Lee's so Fletcher and I crammed ourselves into a corner near a storage cabinet. Fletcher rocked back and forth on the balls of his feet, an expensive Canon bouncing against his chest. He hadn't said two words since Susan and I arrived.

Susan had immediately become involved with Chandler and Perez, and I hesitated to speak lest I interrupt their conversation. After five minutes, Chandler and Perez left, but not before giving Fletcher piercing stares as they passed him.

"I didn't touch her," Fletcher muttered.

Susan laid her hand on the girl's shoulder in a final gesture of compassion.

"What happened?" I asked her.

"Cardiac arrest is the preliminary diagnosis."

"A heart attack? Is that something associated with head trauma?"

Susan walked toward us, and then stopped at the foot of the bed. She looked back at the girl. "Not at her age. But she'd suffered abdominal as well as brain injuries, and had received four units of blood. Her pulse had been through more ups and downs than an elevator." She turned to me. "Short of an autopsy, we can only speculate, but we've enough potential causes and complications that holding an autopsy would probably be a waste of time and money."

"And no family to give consent," I added.

Susan spoke to me but glanced at Fletcher. "You can seek an autopsy if you think there's malpractice or foul play involved."

"I don't care what that nurse said, I didn't touch her." Fletcher held up his camera. "I took a few pictures like I told Barry I would."

Susan's glance at Fletcher turned to a hard glare. "Judi said you were bending right over the girl's face when the heart monitor went ballistic."

Fletcher looked at me as if seeking some support. "I'd only been in the room about thirty seconds. I thought I'd get a close-up of her hair."

Susan pressed on. "Really? Her head was pretty well shaved from surgery."

"I didn't know that. I wanted a color sample to build my computer rendering. Then she said something."

"She spoke?" In my excitement, the question came out as a shout.

"Only a few words. More like muttering in her sleep."

"Could you make them out?"

"Billy. I'm pretty sure one of the words was Billy. She repeated it a few times."

Maybe Billy was Lincoln's first name. I wanted to write it down and realized a smart investigator would be carrying a pen and pad. "What else?"

"I think they were letters. R and D. She only said them once and took a short breath in between each. Then the monitor started beeping and the nurse ran in."

"What do you think?" I asked Susan. "Would she come out of a coma if she were dying?"

"Your guess is as good as mine. We expected her to regain consciousness and her erratic pulse rate could have accelerated it."

I looked down at the motionless girl. "And killed her in the process."

"The brain's the most complex organ in the body, so injuries to it create the most complex consequences. I don't know anything else we could have done." Susan's assessment was neither flippant nor callused. Every patient was precious to her, and the girl without a name had been a life entrusted to her care.

"We'll do everything we can to find her family." I turned to Fletcher. "I still want that composite and anything you can create on the man with her." I touched the latch on the cabinet. "Her personal things in here?" I opened the door and saw a plastic bag.

Susan grabbed a box of latex gloves from a nearby trauma cart. "Better glove up."

The girl's clothes had been cut off her. Blood soaked through parts of the wadded fabric. "Where can I examine these?"

"There's a scrub room available for visitors right outside the ICU. I'll need to clear you through." Susan looked from me to Fletcher. "We should leave so the orderlies can do their work."

"Can you have something for me in the morning?" I asked Fletcher.

"When do you want to meet?"

Sunday morning would find most law enforcement operations on skeletal shifts, but the slow time could be good for getting a duty officer's attention. "How about eight o'clock? Then we can send the renderings to the surrounding counties."

"At the funeral home?"

"Yeah. I'll have coffee waiting."

"What have you got for me?" Tommy Lee's weak whisper still carried the urgency of his request.

"Not much," I said. "The worst thing is the girl died."

He closed his eyes and swallowed.

Patsy stood up from the chair beside his bed and motioned me to sit. "Come on, Samantha. Let's get a Coke in the cafeteria."

Samantha had paled at the news of the girl's death, a girl who was only a few years older than she. When they'd gone, I closed the door and pulled the chair closer to Tommy Lee.

"No ID?" he asked.

"Don't try to talk. Save your questions till I finish." I walked him through what had happened since we spoke last. I repeated what Fletcher said he heard the girl say, and then told Tommy Lee I'd found nothing in her clothing that aided her identification. The jeans and blouse were from The Gap and the shoes were Nikes available in every country on the planet. She wore no rings or jewelry, but the signs of body piercings and the two tattoos might be a help in developing leads. I ended with my plan to have Fletcher create the composites by morning so I could distribute them as soon as possible.

"And Florida?"

"That Lieutenant Spring never called me back." I flipped open my phone and saw the dead screen. "Damn, this afternoon I turned my cell off around all the medical equipment and forgot to turn it back on." I checked my watch. Nearly eight-thirty.

"Call him again."

"Let me see if he left a message." I headed for the door. "I'll step out in the hall. Wouldn't want to screw up your monitors."

When the phone powered up, the screen flashed there were two voice mails, both from Lieutenant Spring. In the second one, he left his cell phone number and instructions to call anytime. I decided I'd try him from the hospital phone so Tommy Lee could hear my end of the conversation.

"This is Spring." His voice was deep and all business. Jazz piano played in the background.

"Barry Clayton here. Have I caught you at a bad time?"

"No. This is a good time. I'm sipping a margarita on the terrace of Busch's Restaurant and watching some big ass yacht try to squeeze through the intracoastal waterway. Since all the retirees are up in your mountains, I didn't even have to wait at the bar. What's up?"

"The girl died. We still don't know who she is."

"You think she's from down here?"

"Maybe. I can fax you a photo in the morning."

"Any leads on the guy with her?"

"Someone in the ICU room heard the girl say Billy and the initials R. D. right before she died. Mean anything to you?"

"No. But I'll add them to Kowalski's Lincoln and Lucy."

"I might have a decent composite of Lincoln tomorrow. I'll fax that as well."

For a few seconds, all I heard was piano. "You there?"

"Sorry. I was thinking." He chuckled. "Didn't you hear the rusty gears? That deputy I spoke with earlier, Hutchins?"

"Yes, Reece Hutchins."

"He said you're a funeral director."

I wondered if Reece had tried to undercut my role in the investigation. "I'm also a former police officer."

"Right. Anyway, Kowalski's daughter's flying in tomorrow and she's going to let me into her father's house."

"His daughter doesn't live in Delray?"

"No. Some little town outside Pittsburgh. I thought since you're a funeral director, you could help make arrangements for getting her father's body wherever she's planning interment."

Not a bad suggestion. There was a chance we'd be contacted by the home town funeral director anyway, but this way I could establish a relationship in case the investigation required more of the daughter's cooperation down the road. "Fine. Give her my cell number. She can have her funeral director call me. What time's she arriving?"

"The flight lands at twelve-thirty."

"Good. I should have the girl's picture to you before then."

The bed sheets rustled behind me. I turned and saw Tommy Lee shaking his head.

"Go," he said.

"You want me to leave the room?"

"To Florida."

"Go to Florida? Tomorrow?"

He nodded, and then lay back on his pillow.

Lieutenant Spring had heard only my side of the conversation. "Are you talking to me?"

"No. Sheriff Wadkins."

"I thought he was shot."

"I'm in his hospital room. He wants me to come down there."

"Ordered you," Tommy Lee said without opening his eye.

"He ordered me."

"He's working on the case?" Lieutenant Spring sounded skeptical.

"No, he's working me on the case." For Tommy Lee's benefit I added, "Can you believe it? The man takes a bullet in the chest and then becomes a pain in everybody else's ass."

Spring laughed. "Just like my captain. Let me know your flight schedule. I'll pick you up."

I thanked him and promised to call in the morning.

"Any other orders?" I asked Tommy Lee, not knowing whether he was still awake.

He opened his eye and looked around the room. "Ice."

The pitcher held half ice and half water. I poured the slush into a cup and added a straw. He took a sip and let the cold liquid coat his throat.

"Why do you want me to go to Florida?" I asked. "There's a lot I need to do up here."

"Because whatever brought Kowalski up here to kill a man probably started in Florida, so that's where you need to start."

Tommy Lee was right. Something had turned Kowalski's life upside down and that life had been lived in Florida. "I'll catch the earliest plane even if I have to go in a dog crate."

Tommy Lee took another sip from the straw and licked his cracked lips. "So you think I'm a pain in the ass now? You ain't seen nothing yet."

Chapter Seven

The 737 dropped out of the thick gray clouds only a few miles from Palm Beach International. Streaks of rain flashed by, but the speed of the jet kept my window dry. Beneath me, neighborhoods of stucco condos, both single-story and high-rise, were interspersed among shopping centers and palm-lined boulevards. The few cars traveling on Sunday morning burned their headlights in an effort to see through the gloomy mess. So much for sunny Florida.

My day had started before dawn. I'd canceled my meeting with Fletcher because I had to get to the Asheville airport at five in the morning for my five-fifty flight. Then I suffered a two hour layover in Charlotte before boarding for West Palm Beach. I could have driven to Charlotte in that time, but the unfathomable pricing of the airline industry meant I'd have paid four hundred dollars more for booking the same plane out of Charlotte without the Asheville origination. And people wonder why the carriers are in bankruptcy.

With no baggage other than a legal pad and my digital camera, I moved quickly through the reuniting families and friends to the taxi queue beneath the protective overhang. Twenty yards beyond the pickup point, a dark blue Crown Vic waited by the curb. Leaning against the car's trunk, a balding man in a peach golf shirt casually surveyed the sidewalk traffic. His gaze fixed on me and I nodded that he'd found his quarry.

"Roy Spring." He extended a broad hand and even broader smile. "Welcome to the hurricane capital of the world."

Spring had me by six inches and thirty pounds. His tan face and boyish grin made it hard to judge his age, but I guessed about twenty years separated us.

"Thanks for meeting me. And for giving up your Sunday morning."

"No problem. God lets me skip mass to help a fellow police officer." He winked. "Too bad it's raining. I could have helped you play nine holes." He motioned to the passenger side. "Ready to ride?"

"Yeah. What you see is what I brought. My return flight's at six-thirty."

He glanced at his watch. "Twenty till eleven. Less than two hours till Rose Vandiver arrives."

"So she's married?"

"Divorced. And that town in Pennsylvania is Aliquippa. Two weeks ago she buried her mother up there, and now she goes through it all over again."

I opened the car door and saw a manila envelope on the seat.

Spring slid behind the steering wheel and then realized I still waited outside. "Pick it up. That's for you."

I buckled my seat belt as he pulled away from the curb, and examined the envelope. The flap wasn't glued but the metal clasp kept it sealed. "What's in here?"

"The photos of the girl and her companion." He blasted the horn as an enormous Cadillac changed lanes without looking. "Damn. The bigger the car, the worse the driver."

I pulled out several sheets of photographic paper. The eight-by-ten headshot of the girl surprised me. Fletcher's computer program and his skill had created an incredible likeness that lacked only open eyes to be portrait quality. Brown hair replaced the bandages, and although its length seemed slightly shorter than I remembered, I had no doubt anyone who knew the girl would easily recognize her. The second sheet was a black and white version. A third had taken the photograph and converted it into a line drawing.

Spring glanced over at the pictures. "Your guy's good. Wish we had him down here. How's your department afford someone like him?"

"He doesn't work for the department. He's my summer intern at the funeral home and he did this on his own. His mortuary science courses use computers for facial reconstruction."

"Damn. Guess I'll have to start schmoozing our area undertakers. Jimmy Patton in our department's a whiz on computers but can't draw a decent stick figure to save his life."

I continued thumbing through the sheets. Fletcher had created a similar series for the mystery man, but these varied—a narrower nose in one, a higher forehead in another. I hadn't gotten a head on look at him during the square dance, but Fletcher would have had a clear view when Kowalski challenged the man. This combination of computer-generated images included black and white composites and line drawings. Fletcher hadn't attempted a color version of Lincoln. "I guess he gave us enough variations."

"Like I said, I'm impressed. He emailed these about an hour ago. He said he made the line drawings in case we thought a little vaguer picture might be useful."

"His logic makes sense. Give too detailed an image and if something's wrong, the viewer won't see beyond it. A line drawing lets the witness fill in the details. Pretty smart. I didn't tell him that."

"We'll see what Kowalski's daughter has to say. Maybe start with the line drawings first." Spring swung the unmarked police car onto the ramp for I-95 South. "I told Rose Vandiver we'd meet her at her father's condo at one-thirty. She's picking up a rental car at the airport. In the winter this route is clogged, but this time of year we'll be there in less than thirty minutes."

Delray Beach—fifteen miles. The green interstate sign whipped by as Spring accelerated. He kicked the wipers into high speed as the rain intensified.

"What do we do in the meantime?" I looked back down at the pictures. "Can we cross-reference these with your mug book?"

"Already got a man working back at the station. I thought maybe you and I could do a little old-fashioned legwork, if you're not afraid of getting wet."

Lieutenant Spring left I-95 at Delray's Atlantic Avenue exit and within a few miles turned into one of the planned communities laced with flower gardens, manmade canals, and a maze of cul-de-sacs. The single-story residences were built three or four to a cluster with attached garages. Wrought-iron gates protected small private courtyards. He pulled the car to the curb in front of a central unit. Lights could be seen in the windows of the condos on either side, but the one next to me was dark.

"Is this where Kowalski lived?"

"Yeah. Grab an umbrella. We'll show these pictures to the neighbors."

I followed Spring through one of the gates, stepped over puddles in the uneven walkway and stood a few yards behind him under the cover of an orange umbrella. He rang the bell of the condo to the right of the Kowalskis' and then held his ID up to the peephole. The rain drowned any noise from inside.

"Maybe no one's home," I said.

Spring kept his ID in front of the door as he turned to me. "The average age in this community is seventy-five. My rule is give them at least a second per year to answer."

A minute later, the door cracked open a few inches. A wrinkled face peered beneath the taut security chain.

"Yes?" The elderly woman squinted at us.

Spring handed her his ID. "Police Department, ma'am."

I doubted the woman was tall enough to see through the peephole. She took the ID and disappeared.

"Ma'am?" Spring yelled through the crack.

"Need my glasses."

Spring shook his head and grinned.

After another minute, the door closed and I heard the security chain slide free.

The woman opened the door wide and stared at us over her reading glasses. She wore a pink housecoat and matching knitted slippers. She handed Spring his identification. "If you need a contribution, I can give you a small check. A little more after the first of July when my social security's deposited."

"No, ma'am, we're here on official business."

Her eyes widened and she nodded toward the Kowalskis next door. "Them?"

"Yes, ma'am. Just a few questions. We'll be meeting the Kowalskis' daughter in a little while. We'd prefer not to burden her by asking too many questions if you're able to help us."

The woman removed her glasses and stuck them in an oversized pocket. "Of course," she said solemnly. "Please come in."

Spring and I left our umbrellas by a ceramic duck sitting next to the door, wiped our wet feet on the welcome mat, and crossed the threshold into doily land. The lace designs were everywhere: on the back of the sofa, the armrests of all the chairs, the end tables, under the photographs on the coffee table, and even beneath the Hummel figurines behind the glass in a mahogany breakfront. The air smelled like my grandmother's bedroom used to. A heavy dose of potpourri.

"I'm Mattie Spiegel. Can I get you gentlemen some coffee?"

"None for me," Spring said.

I followed the lieutenant's lead. "Me neither, thank you."

Mattie motioned for us to sit, but Spring continued talking. "I'm Lieutenant Spring as you know, and this is Deputy Barry Clayton." He stepped back so she could have a clear look at me. "He's with the Sheriff's Department in Gainesboro, North Carolina."

I shook the woman's small, dry hand.

"Gainesboro. That's where—" She left the sentence incomplete.

"Yes. Mrs. Kowalski's daughter didn't realize he'd left Florida, and we're trying to determine why he would come to Gainesboro." I stopped, not wanting to take the course of the conversation away from Lieutenant Spring.

"Shuffleboard," Mattie said.

"Shuffleboard?" Spring repeated the word as a question and looked at me for an answer.

"News to me." I turned to Mattie. "What makes you think so, Ms. Spiegel?"

"Mrs. My Mort's been gone ten years but I'll always be Mrs. Spiegel."

"Sorry," I said.

Spring sat on the sofa and patted the cushion next to him. "Please."

The elderly woman sat down beside him and I took a chair on the other side of the coffee table.

"Did Mr. Kowalski play shuffleboard?" Spring asked.

"Oh, my heavens, yes. Lucy too before her pain got too bad." She flexed her fingers. "I have a touch of arthritis in my hands, and in weather like today my shoulder flares up, but that could be bursitis." She looked from Spring to me. "What's the difference between bursitis and arthritis? I used to know."

Spring cleared his throat. He sensed we'd be categorizing bunions in a few moments if he didn't keep Mattie on track. "So Mrs. Kowalski had to give up playing? When?"

"Must have been last fall. They were disappointed they couldn't compete in mixed doubles at the Delray tournament." Mattie lowered her voice like a crowd might be eavesdropping from the kitchen. "I don't know for sure, but I think it could have been some kind of C A N C E R." She spelled the word as if saying it could cause one of us to get it.

"But you don't know that she was under any kind of treatment?" Spring asked.

"Well, she confided that her medicine was very expensive." Mattie nodded at me as if that made the case.

Spring turned his attention to me. "What about Gainesboro and shuffleboard? Is there a connection?"

"The game's popular with the Florida people. Our town has a number of courts. Hendersonville's about thirty minutes away and has hosted national and even world tournaments."

"Lucy mentioned Hendersonville," Mattie said. "And Gainesboro too. They used to spend a month or two in North Carolina every summer."

"But not this summer?" Spring asked.

"No. They couldn't go this year." And then under her breath, she whispered, "Cancer."

I took up the questioning. "Mrs. Spiegel, did Mrs. Kowalski have any in-home healthcare?"

"You mean like hospice?"

"Hospice or an RN or some other medical professional who visited her?"

"No. Mitch always took her to the doctor."

"Did he stay with her round the clock?"

"He would go out during the day, but never overnight. I guess after Lucy passed away, he decided to go to the mountains like they always did." She sighed. "Life goes on, Deputy Clayton."

Spring shifted on the sofa so he could look directly at Mattie. "I don't know how much you know about what happened in Gainesboro, Mrs. Spiegel, but Mr. Kowalski evidently thought someone had harmed Lucy, so much so that he tried to kill him."

"That's what Rebecca Owensby said. They live in the condo on the other side. I can't believe it. Mitch was always so quiet."

"He didn't have a temper?" Spring asked.

"No more than most men. Now my Mort, he could give you an earful."

"We have some pictures we'd like to show you, Mrs. Spiegel. Tell us if you recognize anyone." Spring signaled for me to pass him the envelope.

Mattie paled. "These aren't pictures of the shooting, are they?"

"No, ma'am. Just some people you might have seen with the Kowalskis."

She retrieved her glasses from her housecoat pocket and waited as the lieutenant arranged the images in the order he wanted and set them in two piles facedown on the coffee table.

He handed her the line drawing of the girl. "Does she look familiar?"

Mattie studied the face carefully, moving it back and forth for the best focus. "No. Too young and slim to be their daughter."

Spring exchanged that rendering for the black and white photo composite. "This might be a little clearer."

Again Mattie scrutinized the girl. "Maybe Jennifer."

"Jennifer who?" Spring prompted.

"Jennifer the waitress at the Cracker Barrel in Boynton Beach. Sometimes I'll ride up there with the Owensbys for lunch."

"Did the Kowalskis know her?"

"Maybe. But they preferred Wendy's. Seniors get a free drink, you know."

Spring passed her the color image of the girl. "Is this Jennifer?"

The wrinkles in Mattie's brow deepened. She looked from the black and white to the color picture. "Doesn't look as much like her. Jennifer's hair is browner. But I suppose she could have lightened it since she left."

"She's no longer at the Cracker Barrel?"

"Oh, my, no. She got in the family way. Can't be taking people's orders if your tummy's halfway over the table." Mattie paused. "I think her baby's due about now. Maybe she'll be back by fall."

Disappointment showed on Spring's face as he restacked the sheets. "How about this man?" He gave her the top picture from his second pile.

Mattie examined the line composite of Lincoln. At first, she showed no particular interest. Then her lips puckered and she nodded. "It could be," she said more to herself than to us.

Spring leaned closer. "Could be who?"

"Could be that man who brings her medicine."

He handed her the more detailed rendering.

"Yes. I'm pretty sure he's the one."

I glanced at Spring. He gave me a wink which I took for a green light. "Mrs. Spiegel, did this man work for a pharmacy?"

"I don't think so. I've never seen him at CVS. I asked Lucy about him once. He came by one morning when I was in the courtyard. She said he was a friend who occasionally picked up her refills for her."

My next question came without thinking. "Did he always come when Mr. Kowalski was away?"

Mattie blushed. "Do you think there was some," she hesitated, searching for a palatable phrase, "inappropriate relationship?"

"No, ma'am. I just thought the simple explanation would be he picked up the refills when Mr. Kowalski couldn't."

"That must be it." She relaxed, grateful that she'd avoided a potential episode of Desperate Senior Housewives. "Now that I think of it, I never saw his car when Mitch was home."

I looked at Spring for the follow-up.

"Did she happen to mention his name?" he asked.

"Art."

"Only Art?" Spring held back Lincoln, wanting her to supply the last name on her own.

"Artie. She just called him Artie."

A tingle flashed down the back of my neck. Mattie had said "Artie," but I had heard "R.D." The dying girl hadn't spoken initials. Artie and what Fletcher heard as "R.D." had to be one and the same.

For the next hour, Lieutenant Spring and I checked eight other condos on the street. Only five residents were home, and nothing new came from our inquiries. The other next-door neighbor, Mrs. Owensby, confirmed that she had seen a man resembling Fletcher's composite coming to Lucy Kowalski's condo once or twice, but she didn't know his name. The other neighbors knew even less. No one recognized the girl, and since that was the more accurate of the renderings, I concluded she'd never been seen by anyone we interviewed.

Spring and I grabbed a bite to eat at Wendy's, and he assured me he wasn't old enough to qualify for the free drink. We returned to the Kowalskis' condo around one-thirty and found a white Taurus with an Enterprise rental sticker parked in front of the garage.

"She's here," Spring said. "I'll lead, but don't hesitate to chime in. You did fine with Mrs. Spiegel. Who knows, if people stop dying, you might have a career as a real detective."

I didn't hear any sarcasm in his voice. My own doubts made me want to ask what he meant by that remark, but I kept quiet.

The rain had calmed to a drizzle and we made a quick dash without umbrellas through the courtyard to the front door. Rose Vandiver must have been watching because she met us on the stoop.

I estimated Rose's age to be close to sixty. She carried a few extra pounds, but nothing more than a woman whose years have turned her from maiden to matron. Her straight brown hair showed gray at the roots and her formal black dress was all the more formal given the multiple necklaces, bracelets, and rings she wore. As Susan had once remarked about a woman at a cocktail party, "She has nice jewelry. Too bad she wears it all at once."

Lieutenant Spring introduced himself, then me, and expressed condolences.

"Come on in. I haven't had a chance to go through everything, but you're welcome to look around." She started back into the condo. "I'm at a loss as to why my father went to North Carolina with a gun."

We followed behind her. Where doilies had been the motif at Mattie Spiegel's, foxes were the Kowalskis' obsession. Foxhunt prints adorned the walls. Fox figurines populated the bookshelves, fox caricatures graced the coasters, and fox placemats indicated a setting for four at the dining room table. The only variations in the décor were plaques for shuffleboard championships hanging along the wall behind the sofa and a row of trophies on the top bookshelf.

"Did your parents belong to a hunt club?" I asked.

Rose laughed. "Mom and Dad? The only horses they could ride are outside Wal-Mart and need a quarter a gallop. They went on the fox craze after spending time in Tryon, North Carolina. Threw out all the seascape paintings and driftwood sculptures and tried to bring the mountains down here."

Tryon was an affluent community about forty miles and a thousand feet below Gainesboro. The thermal climate belt generated by the protection of the Appalachian mountains behind the town meant Tryon enjoyed moderate temperatures and a favorable environment for the horse farms that bred some of the finest steeplechase stock in the country. Even I had attended several of the world-renowned Block House races.

"Did they summer in Tryon?" I asked.

"They did before shuffleboard. About six years ago, they started playing down here. Some of their friends compete in tournaments in North Carolina during the summer so Mom and Dad started renting cottages in Gainesboro or Hendersonville to be closer to the action. That was before Mom got too sick."

"What was the nature of your mother's illness?" Spring asked.

"The aftermath of an illness. She had PHN."

Spring looked at me. "Don't know that one."

I was as clueless as he was.

"Post-herpetic neuralgia. About eighteen months ago Mother developed shingles. She just thought she had a rash and delayed five days before going to the doctor. She missed the window for the most effective treatment. The shingles cleared up after a month, but PHN is the residual pain of the nerve damage. Actually worse than the pain of the disease. Debilitating. Her outbreak was around her torso and down her right leg. She said it was like being on fire."

"Was that why she was on OxyContin?" I asked.

"Yes, though I didn't know how much. She also took antidepressants. Time is the only cure, and when you're in your eighties, you don't have a lot of that."

There was no easy way to ask the next question. "OxyContin's an opioid. Do you think your mother became addicted?"

Rose sighed. "I don't know. We talked on the phone several times a week. None of the medicine was helping as much as she wanted. I'd ask Dad the questions I hesitated to put to Mom." Tears filled her eyes. "It's hard when you're a thousand miles away. Maybe if I'd been here."

"Why don't you sit down?" Lieutenant Spring motioned to the sofa. "I know talking about this can be difficult."

"No. I want to show you something." Rose led us through the dining room to the kitchen. She opened a cabinet and exposed a cluster of pill bottles. "Because most of her medicine had to be taken with food, Dad moved them out here."

A small mortar and pestle sat between the pills and plastic containers of individual servings of applesauce like a kid would take in his lunchbox.

"May I?" I reached in before Rose could answer and retrieved the mortar bowl. Residue of white and yellow powder lay on the bottom. "Why did she grind her pills?"

"Size. About a month ago, Mom's doctor put her on potassium for her heart." Rose selected a bottle, uncapped the top and handed the bottle to me. The pale yellow pills inside looked large enough to choke a horse. "My father started grinding them up and mixing them with the applesauce."

"Just the potassium?" I asked.

"I don't know. Maybe he found it easier to give her all the medicine that way."

Spring gnawed on his lower lip and said nothing. He and I realized what must have happened. Mitch Kowalski had ground up his wife's OxyContin and destroyed the time-release coatings. By his own hand, he had given her the overdose.

"But that wasn't what I wanted to show you." Rose grabbed another bottle from the shelf. "I found this right before you got here. It was hidden behind some glasses in the other corner."

She handed the bottle to me and I looked at the label. The bottle was for an OxyContin prescription. The refill authorization had expired six months ago, but there were plenty of pills left.

"Had she stopped taking OxyContin for a while?" I asked.

"Not that I know of. I was checking these right before you arrived."

I opened the top and tapped a few pills into my palm. Then I studied the label again. The prescription called for thirty pills of twenty milligrams each. The ones in my hand were stamped eighty. I showed them to Spring. He had to draw the same conclusion. Mitch Kowalski might have ground up the pills, but Artie Lincoln provided the lethal dose.

"They don't match the prescription," Rose said. "I think the pharmacy screwed up."

I put the pills back in the bottle. "I'm afraid not. Your father tracked down and tried to shoot a man who delivered medicine to your mother. I think that man was supplementing her with more pills than her doctor would prescribe. She kept them in this old bottle."

"My mother was buying drugs illegally?"

"She was in a lot of pain." Spring pulled the computer image of Artie Lincoln from the envelope. "Do you recognize this man?"

Rose looked at the picture for several seconds. "No. Who is he?"

"Mrs. Spiegel told us he brought your mother medicine." Spring pointed at the bottle in my hand. "I think this is the medicine because it's a much higher dosage."

"And then my father found out?"

Spring nodded. "We're not sure how. Maybe Mrs. Spiegel mentioned it to him after your mother died."

"And my father tracked him down."

Neither Spring nor I said anything.

"How would he have known this man was in Gainesboro?"

"Did your mother or your father pay the bills?" I asked.

"My mother. She'd worked as a part-time bookkeeper back in Aliquippa."

"Do you happen to know where she kept the credit card statements?"

Rose looked puzzled. "I guess the writing desk in their bedroom."

She left the kitchen and we followed her down a short hall to the master bedroom. A small desk was tucked in the far corner of the room. Papers and envelopes were neatly stacked on its surface.

I saw several envelopes that looked like they contained bills. "I'm looking for the statement from their Wachovia card."

Rose picked up a few of the envelopes encircled by a rubber band. "The last few months are together." She pulled the top envelope free and handed it to me.

The Wachovia statement covered the billing period ending last week. Seven charges were listed for two cards. Evidently the Kowalskis each carried one. One purchase at the CVS and two Exxon gas charges were on one card; three ATM withdrawals of two hundred dollars and one for five hundred dollars were on the other. The final withdrawal had been in Gainesboro on May 29th, twelve days before the shooting. Mitch Kowalski had gotten the bill and known right where to go.

"Did your mother use an ATM?" I asked.

"Not that I know of. She rarely went out these last few months."

"Can I see some of the other statements?"

Rose handed me all of them. Each had three or four ATM withdrawals on one of the cards. I could see how Lucy Kowalski had paid for her extra OxyContin. Mitch Kowalski must have also understood what his wife had been doing. And he'd found someone whom he could hold responsible for his wife's death. Someone to relieve his guilt. Someone he had to bring to justice himself because he couldn't admit to anyone that he'd pulverized the more potent OxyContin and killed his own wife.

"Did anyone investigate Lucy Kowalski's death?" I asked the question as innocently as I could, not wanting to sound accusatory. I still wasn't sure how Lieutenant Spring felt about my dual roles as novice detective and undertaker.

Spring stirred the ice in his scotch with his forefinger. I nursed a club soda with Rose's Lime. We'd stopped at a forgettable bar about a mile from the airport to kill twenty minutes before I checked in for my flight. A back booth gave us needless privacy because other than the bartender, we were the only people in the place.

Spring licked his finger. "Investigate? Yes, if you mean talked to her attending physician and a few people who knew her. Mitch

Kowalski was genuinely distraught, and we could find no motive that suggested why after fifty-five years of marriage he'd want to do her in." He sipped his drink and then stared into the glass. "You'd be surprised at the number of Lucy Kowalskis who die down here. They're on some prescription for pain and get their meds confused, or just don't want to fight life anymore."

"How many are buying extra pills?"

"That's a problem. A dirty little secret no one wants to pry into. Who's going to throw Grandma in the slammer?" Spring grabbed a fistful of peanuts from the bowl between us and popped them into his mouth.

"So a guy like Artie Lincoln can deal OxyContin with little chance of being busted?"

Spring nodded as he chewed, and then washed the peanuts down with a healthy swallow of scotch. "Lincoln's clients aren't the kind to cause him trouble. If he's not greedy, he can have a steady income as long as he can get enough product to deliver. Look at Lucy. She probably let him carry her debit card."

"Maybe he didn't know she'd died."

"Or he tried to squeeze in a few extra withdrawals. Five hundred's usually the daily max."

My trip to Florida was generating more questions than answers. "But I'm no closer to identifying the girl in the hospital than before I came here. How do she and Lincoln tie together?"

"Hillbilly heroin," Spring muttered.

"What?"

His face glowed red. "Sorry. Didn't mean nothing by it. I've got a friend in the DEA. That's what he calls OxyContin."

"Hillbilly heroin." I shook my head. "Haven't heard that insult before."

Spring squirmed. "He said it's because the first known reports of OxyContin abuse came from Appalachia. Isolated places with high unemployment and a large elderly population. But it's spread all over now."

I laughed and let him off the hook. "Relax. I'm one of those mountaineers who sell only moonshine."

Spring changed the subject. "My DEA friend might know this Artie Lincoln. Sometimes they'll watch the little fish for a while to track the supplier."

I didn't want to lose Spring's initial thought. "But why'd you say hillbilly heroin when I mentioned the girl?"

He shrugged. "She might have been a local up there. Sex ranks right behind money when it comes to getting drugs. Lincoln could have picked her up."

"Then why'd she have the debit card and the five hundred dollars?"

Spring drained his drink and thought a moment. "Maybe she stole it from him."

"She'd have to know the pin number."

"Any of the ATMs up there on video surveillance?"

I saw where he was headed. "Damn. I didn't ask. If Lincoln knew Lucy had died and her husband would now see the statements, he might not have risked being photographed. Use the girl to get the money."

"And if they'd been together a couple of days, she might have made an extra withdrawal he didn't know about."

Spring looked at his watch and then signaled the bartender for another round. "I'm definitely off-duty."

I was still nursing my soda. "I'll check the cash withdrawal times against the bank videos. Do you think that's why Lincoln went to North Carolina? To use the card where nobody knew him?"

Again, Spring swirled the scotch with his finger. "The Serengeti."

"Africa?"

"More like Florida and North Carolina." He stopped talking.

I could tell he enjoyed watching me try to figure out the connection. "Do I have to buy you another drink for the answer?"

Spring laughed. "Nah. Two's my limit. I'm thinking about this documentary I saw once. How the animals of the Serengeti migrate. Thousands of them. Gazelles, wildebeest, like the whole frigging jungle. I can't remember if it was because of food or, like salmon, they were going to mate, but what I found fascinating were the predators that migrated with them. They were forced to follow their prey."

"The snowbirds."

"Exactly. Our seniors migrate winter and summer, from my neck of the jungle to yours. Artie Lincoln might simply have been following his prey." He took a gulp of scotch. "You need to find the watering hole up there."

I laid a twenty on the table to pay for Spring's drinks. "Shuffleboard."

"Bright boy. That's where I'd put my money." Spring raised his glass. "Of course, I'm only a detective, not an undertaker."

Chapter Eight

The red light was blinking on my answering machine in the kitchen. My return flight hadn't arrived in Asheville until after ten-thirty, and by the time I got to the cabin, it was nearly midnight.

On my way home from the airport, I'd checked for messages and had only one from earlier in the afternoon, Uncle Wayne calling to say Mildred Cosgrove had passed away and the family would be at the funeral home the next morning at nine-thirty. This new message had to have been left within the past hour.

I hit the play button. "Barry, it's Fletcher. I thought you'd be home by now. I was talking to Cindy about the dead girl and wondered if I could take tomorrow off. Call if it's a problem."

Fletcher's request posed more of an inconvenience than a problem. I'd have met with the Cosgroves anyway since they were longtime friends of our family, but I'd hoped the rest of the process could be taken care of by Fletcher and my uncle. Freddy Mott might be available to help, but it was too late to call him tonight.

My curiosity got the better of me and I dialed Fletcher's cell phone.

He answered after the first ring. "Sorry I called you so late. Guess tomorrow's not a good day to be away."

"Did you know we had a death?" I doubted if Uncle Wayne had tried to reach him.

"No." Fletcher's voice rose in surprise. "Then I'll be there first thing in the morning."

"Hold on. What's this about the girl?" I took the cordless phone into the living room and sat down on the sofa.

"Actually it was Cindy's idea. I dropped by the hospital tonight to visit."

I jumped in with what should have been my first question. "How is she?"

"A little better. Weak. In pain. But anxious to know what happened."

Aren't we all, I thought. "That's good. Did you see Tommy Lee?"

"No. I tried, but I wasn't on some approved visitors list. And I'm not exactly a favorite of the hospital staff after the incident with the girl."

That was predictable. Both Ray Chandler and Judi Perez had looked like they wanted to kill Fletcher in the ICU. I felt sorry for him. "I'm partly responsible for that list. I'll see that your name is added. We're trying to keep the media away."

"I understand. Anyway, I was telling Cindy what we knew about the girl. The tattoos, the body piercings. I told her I didn't know where you were going to show the pictures. She thought we ought to concentrate on Asheville. She said there's a significant counter-culture group there, almost a street community, and some of them might know her."

Since Gainesboro was a small town and no one had recognized her yet, our likelihood of discovering the girl's identity here was slim. I'd planned to let the law enforcement departments we contacted in other counties handle the distribution of the girl's rendering, but I knew that could be inadequate. We were dependent upon the priority each would give, and for some that may be nothing more than posting the picture on a departmental bulletin board.

"Cindy makes a good point. I'll emphasize that to the Buncombe County Sheriff's Department."

"Okay." Fletcher's disappointment came through loud and clear.

"What were you thinking?"

"That I should do it myself. I'm the right age. I can dress down and not smell like a cop." He paused. He must have remembered I'd been and now was once again a law enforcement officer. "I mean the kids might open up to me if I've got the right cover story."

I stood up and paced in front of the fireplace. His idea showed promise. "And you want to do that tomorrow?"

"It can wait. See if the Asheville police turn up anything first. But I want to help."

I thought for a moment. Fletcher had seen the girl die right in front of him. And some of the hospital staff held the opinion he'd been too zealous with his photography. Fletcher was looking for a way to do something to even the score. And for my investigation, identifying the girl was critical.

I reached my decision. "Listen. Wayne and I can cover tomorrow. But I want to see you before you go to Asheville. There are some things I learned in Florida that might be useful, and I doubt your target group will be out early in the morning."

"Sure thing." He sounded ready to come over to my cabin right then.

I looked at my watch. Five after twelve. "Let's meet at the hospital cafeteria. Seven-thirty. Print some more copies of the pictures you faxed Lieutenant Spring, and we'll show them to Tommy Lee."

"No problem. I'll need them for Asheville anyway."

No problem. Easy to say. I had the feeling our problems were just beginning.

On Monday morning, the hospital cafeteria served a steady stream of coffee to the caffeine junkies desperate to jump-start their week. I scanned the crowded room, checking to make sure Fletcher hadn't beaten me there.

"Hey, buddy. Spare some change?"

I turned around and discovered Fletcher sitting at a table just inside the cafeteria's main door. I'd walked right past him.

The preppy attire he normally wore had been replaced by a wardrobe that would have been rejected by Goodwill—an inside-out black tee shirt that had more wrinkles than a year-old prune. A jagged tear ran along the shoulder of one sleeve, exposing part of a dark blue chain inked around his upper arm. The crude tattoo looked real. He'd jelled his razor-cut hair into a hayfield of short brown spikes tipped with yellow, and the stubble on his chin completed the illusion of a young man angry at the world.

The only thing out of place was his big grin.

"Change? I hope you can change back." I envisioned the faces of Mildred Cosgrove's relatives when I introduced the latest addition to Clayton and Clayton.

"A little mousse, a little Streaks 'N Tips. With one shower, my disguise flows down the drain." Fletcher stood up and pointed to the holes in his threadbare jeans. "Good thing I brought my favorite pair with me."

I noticed we were getting curious looks from the tables nearby. "Let's see what Tommy Lee has to say. They've probably prodded him awake by now."

The duty nurse scowled when I said Fletcher would accompany me, and she insisted on leading us to Tommy Lee's room. We found him picking at the remains of a fruit cup on his breakfast tray.

"Are you okay to receive visitors?" the nurse asked.

Tommy Lee studied Fletcher for a few seconds. "What'd he do to you, son? Assign you the no-frills funerals?"

Fletcher laughed. "You should see the discount casket. I didn't know Tupperware came so big."

The nurse relaxed. "I'll take that as a yes, Mr. President." She left, closing the door behind her.

"Mr. President," I said. "Why not go for king?"

Tommy Lee pushed his food tray away. "Ah, that's something O'Malley started. He tells me I act like President Reagan. Just because Reagan joked to Nancy, 'Honey, I forgot to duck,' and asked his surgeons if they were all Republicans, didn't mean the wound wasn't serious. O'Malley says I've got a lot of damaged tissue that needs to heal and he wants me in here at least another week."

"You do have a tube draining your chest," I pointed out.

"So, I'll have to poke a hole in my shirt. What'd you learn in Florida?"

I turned to Fletcher. "Show him your pictures."

Fletcher pulled the most detailed composites from a manila envelope and handed them to Tommy Lee.

I nodded toward the pictures. "This is what we sent Lieutenant Spring. Then I went with him to talk to the Kowalskis' daughter and their neighbors."

Tommy Lee pointed to the picture of the girl. "Very good," he told Fletcher. "Maybe you should be in charge of the investigation."

Fletcher blushed.

"We'll get to that," I said. "The point is the girl's likeness is accurate, yet no one in Delray Beach recognized her. We figure she's got to be from around here."

Tommy Lee lifted Lincoln's composite. "And him?"

"Worth the flight." I briefed Tommy Lee and Fletcher on Artie Lincoln's possible link to Lucy Kowalski's OxyContin and the debit card we'd found on the girl.

"What do you think's the best way to pick up Lincoln's trail?" Tommy Lee asked.

"Two ways. First, if Lincoln latched onto Lucy Kowalski through a shuffleboard club, then that crowd might know him up here. Second, we still have to identify the girl, and we know Lincoln's trail crossed hers." I nodded to Fletcher. "You're looking at your newest undercover agent."

Tommy Lee shook his head. "Getting you involved is one thing, Barry. But if this is some kind of organized drug ring, Fletcher's got no business getting anywhere near it."

Fletcher took a step closer to the bed. "I'll only be trying to find out the dead girl's name. Who else can melt into Asheville's underground?"

Tommy Lee looked at me. I knew he was running through his options and coming up empty. Finally he asked, "What's the cover story?"

I glanced at Fletcher. "We haven't talked that through. I wanted to see you first."

"That's one smart thing you've done." Tommy Lee shifted on his pillow and couldn't suppress a groan. "So, any ideas?"

"Maybe Fletcher's an old friend trying to find her," I said. "A friend told him she was in Asheville."

"Then why doesn't he know her name?" Tommy Lee asked. "Why's he carrying a picture?"

Fletcher took the composites from Tommy Lee and briefly stared at the unknown girl. "I wasn't going to show any pictures. I wasn't going to ask directly about the girl. I was going to be looking for Lincoln because he owes me money. I got stiffed by the 'man.' Anybody I ask doesn't need to know why. The right people will assume drugs. I'll say the last lead I had put him with a girl and bring in her description that way."

The story sounded credible. I could see Fletcher getting sympathy for being ripped off by someone like Lincoln.

Tommy Lee rubbed his forefinger across his lips and considered the idea. "If anyone sees the guy you describe, how are they going to reach you?"

Fletcher smiled. "My cell phone. That's the only contact info I'll give them. And I've got a Detroit area code. Resurrect my accent a little and the story should fly."

"But your goal is only the name of the girl," Tommy Lee emphasized. "I don't want you tangling with Lincoln."

"Understood," Fletcher agreed.

I still wasn't comfortable. "I wish we had more information so Fletcher can be more specific. Maybe Lieutenant Spring's pulled up a vehicle registration. Be nice if Fletcher could describe Lincoln's car."

I checked the time. Ten after eight. I doubted Spring would be at his office yet, and I needed to be at the funeral home by nine to meet Uncle Wayne and get ready for the Cosgroves. I sat down at the computer. "Spring gave me his email address. I'll tell him what we're doing and ask him to call me with any new information on Lincoln as soon as possible."

"All right, let's do it." Tommy Lee looked at Fletcher. "God knows I've wasted enough breath telling Barry, but maybe you'll listen to me. Be careful. At the slightest hint of trouble, you get your butt back here."

I found Uncle Wayne in the store room checking our embalming supplies.

"Sorry I'm late," I said. "I stopped by the hospital."

"How was everybody?"

"Tommy Lee wanted to break out and Cindy was sleeping."

"That's good. Sounds like they're both mending." Wayne walked to the work sink and washed his hands. "I haven't seen Fletcher yet."

"I gave him the day off."

"The day off?" My uncle stopped scrubbing and turned to me with water dripping from his fingertips. "But the Cosgroves—"

"Fletcher wanted to come in when he learned we had a funeral, but he'd already mentioned a plan to aid the investigation. I thought he should follow through with it."

"Plan?" Wayne cocked his head. "What plan?"

"To go undercover in Asheville. Mix with the kids that might have known the dead girl."

"He's not a policeman."

"No. But me and everybody else in the Sheriff's Department are too old to fool that crowd."

"Damn hippies." Wayne cut the spigot off. "But, Fletcher doesn't look like one of them sex-crazed addicts."

Arguing with my uncle was an art form unto itself and I'd honed my techniques throughout my life. I wisely sidestepped the fact that "hippies" existed forty years in the past. "And that's why he needed the day off. Looking sex-crazed takes practice for a normal person like Fletcher."

Uncle Wayne mulled that over. "I guess it does. Did this plan come out of your trip to Florida?"

I gave him a condensed version of the previous day's discoveries, including Artie Lincoln and the illegal OxyContin supply.

"So the Kowalskis met this Lincoln fellow playing shuffleboard?"

I shrugged. "Possibly. I'll be checking that part out."

Uncle Wayne stared off into space. "Shuffleboard players. They're even older than I am. One foot in the grave and the other on a banana peel. They're at the age where none of them should be buying a green banana either, that's for sure."

"And they sure shouldn't be buying pain killers from Artie Lincoln. I can understand how Mr. Kowalski blamed Lincoln for his wife's death. And I blame Lincoln for the death of the girl. That's why we've got to find him."

Uncle Wayne wiped his hands on a paper towel and then crushed it into a tiny ball. "Yep. We've got to. No two ways about it."

Before Wayne could enlighten me with his plan of attack, Mom called that the Cosgroves had arrived.

Mildred Cosgrove had been my first grade teacher. She'd seemed ancient at that time and I'd thought of her as my teacher ever since, even years later when she'd been long retired. If I ran into her at the curb market or drug store, the very way she called my name sent me back to my desk, holding a giant pencil and trying to print between the lines. Pleasing Mrs. Cosgrove had been the first aspiration I could remember. That was probably true for nearly everyone in town who had passed through her classroom.

Mildred's son, Julius, and his daughter, Dot Cramer, waited in the parlor. Uncle Wayne and I greeted them with our condolences and shared some memories of what a wonderful woman Mildred had been.

"You were one of her prize students." Julius sat on the sofa in an ill-fitting seersucker suit. He had to be in his sixties and kept looking at his daughter for reassurance. "Many's the time she told me, 'that Barry Clayton could have gone anywhere, but he came back.'" A sob caught in his throat. "Seems fitting you'll be the one to bury her."

Dot dabbed at her eyes with a lace handkerchief. "Gran Marmie knew she could count on you, Barry. We'd talked about it just a week ago when she got to feeling poorly."

Dot had been about five years behind me in school. I didn't know her very well, other than seeing her at Julius' tire store. I heard her husband had run off with the Avon lady. Quite the scandal since he'd been the Fuller Brush man. They'd been making sales calls on each other.

"Wayne and I are here to help any way we can. Did Mrs. Cosgrove leave any special requests for the funeral?"

The grieving son and granddaughter exchanged glances. Julius cleared his throat. "Just one. Momma wanted to be buried with her fluffy."

Being buried with a doll or special keepsake wasn't that unusual. The most touching occasions involved the death of a child. Those scenes were heart wrenching as the parents laid some cherished toy in the small casket. Occasionally, an adult would have the same attachment, maybe for a book or special pillow.

"Is her fluffy a quilt or a comforter?" I asked.

Julius took a deep breath. "No. Fluffy's her cat."

"Her cat!" I looked at Wayne, but he simply closed his eyes, wishing himself to God only knew where. "Mr. Cosgrove, I can't put a dead cat in your mother's casket."

Dot blew her nose and sniffled. "That's the other thing. Fluffy ain't dead. Yet."

Chapter Nine

Uncle Wayne's eyes popped open. "Not dead? You mean you want us to put a live cat in Mildred's casket?"

Dot's face flushed and she looked to her father for support.

Julius stiffened, tugging at the narrow lapels of his oversized suit coat like a tortoise pulling himself deeper inside his seersucker shell. "Of course not. We'd take care of making sure Fluffy was properly prepared. And we'd expect to pay extra."

I shook my head. "It's out of the question. I can't condone your killing a cat because the owner died."

Dot's lower lip trembled. "Gran Marmie said we could count on you. You were a good student. You always did what she told you."

"I was a first grader."

"She made us promise." Dot buried her face in her handkerchief and sobbed.

Uncle Wayne got to his feet and stood beside my chair. His tall, lanky frame towered over the rest of us. He pointed his finger at Julius. "Did your mother force her students to break the law?"

"No. She was god-fearing and law abiding till her dying day."

Wayne nodded. "I know she was. And now that she's in heaven, she probably understands rule 6513."

Julius blinked in confusion, and then stared at me. I sure as hell wasn't in heaven and had no idea what Uncle Wayne was talking about. But I tried to look like rule 6513 would have been the first thing Saint Peter proclaimed at the Pearly Gates.

Wayne brought the palms of his hands together as if preparing to lead us in prayer. "Your mother knew it's not against the law to bury a cat, but there's no reason she'd have known about embalming laws. Barry and I are licensed embalmers. We've taken that hypocritic oath just like doctors." Wayne rotated his hands face up like a faith healer ready to touch somebody. "Our embalming skills are to be used only on people. That's rule 6513. As much as we may want to help you, we're prohibited from embalming Fluffy. And we can't mix the embalmed with the unembalmed. It's just not done. You do want your mother properly prepared, don't you?"

Dot peered over the handkerchief. "We've got to have her ready for the viewing. She wanted Doris to do her hair. Now that Gran Marmie knows the embalming rules, I'm sure it's all right."

I sat stunned at my uncle's preposterous explanation and the fact that Dot actually believed it.

Julius frowned at his daughter. He didn't seem to be buying rule 6513. "Then you're going to take care of that damn cat. I want nothing to do with it."

I got the feeling Julius' real impetus for carrying out Mildred Cosgrove's wish was to get poor Fluffy out of the way. He might have put the burial idea in his mother's head.

"We'll talk about it later, Daddy." Dot laid the handkerchief in her lap. "Let's get the funeral planned first."

Uncle Wayne took a deep breath and returned to his chair. I could tell he was proud of his solution to the problem.

We finished meeting with Julius and Dot around eleven. The funeral was scheduled for Thursday and I enlisted Freddy Mott to assist in transporting Mildred's body from the hospital later that afternoon. I'd help Freddy load and Wayne would meet him at the funeral home. That way I could work on the case from Tommy Lee's hospital room for a couple of hours.

My mother came out on the screened back porch. "Will you stay for lunch?"

I was sitting in a wicker rocker, stealing a few minutes to read Monday morning's *Gainesboro Vista*. "No. I'd better run by the

Sheriff's Department for some things. Then I'm heading back to the hospital."

Mom walked across the gray plank floor and stopped close to the screen wall. She watched two cardinals vying for position on our backyard bird feeder. Their squabble knocked more black sunflower seeds to the ground than either could eat. The victors were the little wrens who enjoyed the spoils of someone else's battle.

"Your father wouldn't get up this morning." She spoke the words as much to the birds as to me.

I set the newspaper aside. "Is he sick?"

Mom turned around. I saw the tears come quickly.

"Sick? Barry, he's been sick. We're losing him."

Of course Dad was sick. Alzheimer's was an insidious disease. Insidious because the family had to accommodate it, hell, even accept it. "That's just Dad," I'd said to myself a thousand times. I tried to get beyond the point where every time I looked at him, I saw what was no longer there. I tried to deal with the person he'd become and not dwell upon the person I was losing.

But Mom was losing so much. She and Dad had been married for over fifty years. And every single day having to watch the erosion of a person she loved was taking a terrible toll.

I got up and hugged her. "I know, Mom. I'll check on him."

I released the baby gate at the top of the stairs and leaned it against the wall. We kept the gate wedged in place so Dad wouldn't wander downstairs without my mother's knowledge.

The door to my parents' room was open and I could see the sheets had been kicked to the foot of the bed. The bathroom door in the hall was closed and before I could knock, I heard the commode flush.

My father didn't like being in a closed room, but the bathroom was an exception. I figured years of automatically closing that door had become so engrained the habit would always stay with him.

I waited in the hall. He coughed a few times, trying to clear phlegm from his throat. I waited a few minutes longer, but he didn't come out. "Dad?" I knocked softly on the door. "You all right?"

No answer.

"Dad?" I turned the knob. It was unlocked. The hinges squeaked as I pushed the door in slowly, not wanting to hit him.

Dad stepped away from the basin as the door nudged him. He held out one hand wrapped tightly around his toothbrush. He looked at me and then down at the brush. He was holding the bristles upside down. He obviously had no idea what they were for.

Patsy Wadkins was sitting beside Tommy Lee's bed. She folded the magazine she'd been reading and laid it across her lap when I entered the room. "He's finally fallen asleep," she whispered.

The color in Tommy Lee's face looked better than when I'd seen him earlier and I understood Patsy's unspoken message not to wake him. "I'll be quiet. I've got a few things to do on the computer."

"Will you be here at least thirty minutes?"

"I don't have to be anywhere until three."

Patsy glanced at the wall clock. Ten after two. "I haven't had lunch and now that he's sleeping—"

"Go on. I'll be here."

She started for the door. "And if Susan or O'Malley makes rounds?"

"I'll grill them for all the information they can give me." I saluted her. "Don't forget I'm a deputy."

Patsy laughed. "Barney Fife better watch his back."

After she left, I logged onto the computer and accessed my personal email. Lieutenant Spring had sent me the vehicle registration data for Artie Lincoln. His full name was Arthur Collier Lincoln and he had a Delray Beach address. His car was a 2005 Lincoln. The man liked his name.

I noticed that Spring had sent the email only five minutes earlier. I forwarded the information to Reece Hutchins so he

could issue a BOLO—short for "be on the lookout"—throughout the department and to the surrounding law enforcement
agencies. Then I telephoned to make sure someone gave the
BOLO top priority.

The dispatcher routed me to Deputy Wakefield, a competent officer who'd been at the street dance when the shooting
occurred. He jotted down Lincoln's license and registration
numbers and promised to print out Spring's email for the file.

"I just got off the phone with the regional ATM manager for
Wachovia," Wakefield said.

I cradled the receiver against my neck and flipped open my
notepad. "What's the word?"

"No one's actually screened the security video yet. They don't
have playback capabilities at the Gainesboro branch."

"But they have the tape?"

"Tape or hard drive. The woman referred to it as the media."

I didn't care what they called it. "When can we see it?"

"They're driving it over to Asheville now. If we want, they
can burn us a DVD by Wednesday. They have to do that at their
corporate headquarters in Charlotte."

"Wednesday? Did you tell her this is a murder investigation?"

"You bet. She said our other option was to screen the video
at their main office in Asheville. Here's the address."

I wrote down the information. "Call her back and tell her I
want to come to the main office."

"I already did. They're expecting you at four."

I flipped my pad closed. "Wakefield, you're a good man."

If Freddy brought the hearse right at three, I could take care
of Mildred Cosgrove and be in Asheville by four. I looked at
Tommy Lee. Keep sleeping, old pal. With Lincoln's car now
on everybody's radar screen, maybe we'll get a break before you
wake up.

Since Lieutenant Spring had sent Lincoln's vehicle registration from his office, there was a good chance he was still there.
I called to thank him for his help.

Spring gave me an update. "We've sent a patrol car by Lincoln's condo down here. No sign he's been home."

"Lincoln's had plenty of time to get there. Maybe he's gone to earth someplace up here." I thought for a second. "What's the chance of getting a warrant to search his place?"

"I made the request to my captain an hour ago."

"Good. Maybe you'll find something that tells us where Lincoln's staying."

Spring dropped his voice to a whisper. "Captain Rathbone ordered me to hold off."

I wadded the phone cord in my fist. "Hold off. But we've got a positive ID from the Kowalskis' neighbor."

"Barry. Something's going down. As soon as I mentioned OxyContin, the captain backpedaled."

I'd been a police officer long enough to recognize the warning signs. My inquiries had crossed over into another investigation. I was the guy from out of state and the captain wasn't going to jeopardize his local case for me. "Is Lincoln an informant?"

"I don't think so. I figure he might be a small fish, but if he gets hooked, the big fish get nervous. And we've got some big fishermen casting in our pond who sure as hell don't want someone hooking a minnow right now."

Spring didn't have to spell it out for me. The feds were involved. I didn't like the new hand I'd been dealt. "Can we help them?"

"Yeah. Stay clear. I've a feeling the net's gonna close real quick." Spring laughed. "Maybe the feds will snare Lincoln and toss him your way."

Fat chance. I realized Spring had done all he could for me. "Thanks for sending the car registration."

"No problem. Glad it came through before my little chat with the captain. I'll be in touch." Spring hung up before I could say anything else.

I checked his email again. No mistake. The address header showed he'd sent the vehicle information after he'd gotten his captain's orders to back off. I owed Spring another drink.

The description of Lincoln's car could help Fletcher in Asheville. He hadn't called since he'd left the hospital over five hours ago, and I weighed whether to wait for him to contact me or to ring his cell phone. I decided Fletcher could refuse to answer if he was in the middle of some role play.

"Talk to me." Fletcher barked the words as an order.

"Lincoln drove a light blue Lincoln, Florida plates."

"Tell Barry I'll talk to him when I'm good and ready. I don't know when I'll be back north." His brusque tone was so out of character Fletcher had to be in character.

"I'm coming to Asheville at four to screen security videos. If you're good and ready then, call me."

"When I get my money." Fletcher shouted the words and hung up.

My summer intern had been performing for someone. I hoped he wasn't casting himself in a play with a bad ending.

I worked the phone and computer for another thirty minutes, checking bed-and-breakfast and mom-and-pop motel registries for Artie Lincoln. Nothing turned up.

Tommy Lee slept soundly. I wanted to ask him for any ideas on how to make the most of what little information we had, but I knew his priority was to get the deep healing sleep his body needed.

"Be careful what you wish for." Dad's words rang in my head again. My name was on this case file. I had the duty to find Lincoln and bring him to justice. As far as I was concerned, he was responsible for not only the death of the unidentified girl but also Lucy and Mitch Kowalski as well.

As a police officer, I'd arrested many druggies devastated by addiction. As a funeral director, I had buried them. Drug dealers like Lincoln made a living off the suffering of others, whether they were teen runaways on the street or elderly ladies at the shuffleboard courts. There was no telling how many lives he'd ruined and how many more he would destroy if he wasn't stopped.

At ten till three, I logged off the computer and went down to shipping and receiving. Most people didn't realize the hospital's loading dock not only brought in medical supplies and equipment but was also the location where hearses picked up the deceased. I was well known in the department. Cooper Ludden had been in charge as long as I could remember, and I found him outside one of the roll-up doors. He had a cigar cocked in one corner of his mouth and held a clipboard and pen in his hands. Several workers were unloading boxes from a truck marked *Remington Medical Supplies*, and Cooper checked each one against an order form.

"Barry. Didn't know you had a passenger." The cigar bobbed with each word. Cooper scanned the concrete lot. "Where's your ride?"

"Freddy Mott's meeting me here. I was up visiting the sheriff."

He snatched out the cigar and jabbed the smoking end at me. "Hell of a thing. The man survives Vietnam and then gets shot in his home town. What's the world coming to?"

"I don't know. But it looks like Tommy Lee's gonna be okay."

Cooper jammed the cigar back in his mouth. "Damn good news. I was afraid you were loading him up."

I shuddered to think how close Tommy Lee had come to being my passenger.

"Hold it." Cooper stopped one of his men from setting a box on the forklift. "This carton's got a split in the side. Move it out of the way and we'll count the contents later. The driver can just cool his heels." Cooper turned to me. "You can't imagine the theft that goes on in a place like this. My job's to at least get the stuff in the door. Then it's Hospital Security's problem." He made a notation beside one of the items on his clipboard. "So, who are we saying goodbye to?"

"Mildred Cosgrove."

Cooper shook his head. "Mrs. Cosgrove. Had her in first grade. Fifty years ago. She gave me my first paddling at school. Second day. I couldn't sit down the rest of the morning. Woman put the fear of God in me. After that I did whatever she told me."

"Me too." Up until she wanted a dead cat in her casket, but I kept that thought to myself.

"Here's Freddy." Cooper jutted his chin toward the main gate in the high chain-link fence. Our hearse pulled in and swung wide to back up next to the truck.

"I'll call the morgue. Should have had the paperwork by now." Cooper took the cigar from his mouth and handed it to me. "Hold this. Can't smoke in the building and they're never as good if you have to crush them out and re-light them."

Cooper disappeared into the large storage room. "Feel free to keep her going," he shouted from the shadows.

I looked at the soggy stogie and felt my stomach churn.

"Your momma know you smoke?" Freddy grinned up at me from beside the rear bumper of the hearse. He wore carpenter's overalls and a John Deere cap. Not exactly the dignified look one expected in funeral transportation. But Freddy had been working part time for us since he was a teenager, since before I was born. He'd obviously come from one of his handyman jobs.

"I'm keeping it for Cooper."

"Oh, I won't tell on you." He dropped the tailgate. "Where's Mrs. Cosgrove?"

"Not down from the morgue. And Cooper didn't have any paperwork."

Freddy spit on the pavement. "Figures. Takes forever to check out when you're alive. Being dead only makes it worse."

I couldn't argue with him. We waited a good twenty minutes and I worried I'd be late for my appointment in Asheville. The burning cigar began to warm my fingers before Cooper returned.

"Here you go." Cooper swapped a manila envelope for the remains of his stogie. "When you've been here as long as I have, you can shortcut the system. I had her include five copies of the death certificate."

"Thanks." I handed the envelope to Freddy. "Give this to Wayne in case the family needs it before I come in."

"Sure." Freddy looked at the name handwritten on the front. "Old Mrs. Cosgrove. She paddled me the first day of school."

Cooper puffed out a cloud of blue smoke. "Damn. I thought I had the record."

"Sorry I'm late." I shook hands with Elaine Vincent, a smartly dressed executive who met me in the lobby of Wachovia's largest office in Asheville.

"No problem, Deputy. We used the extra time to isolate the incidents on the tapes. Follow me, please." She turned and led me to a bank of elevators.

"Incidents?"

Elaine pushed the down button. "The branch manager in Gainesboro said you got your date of the ATM transaction from the Kowalskis' statement. We had an additional transaction clear this morning. Five hundred dollars withdrawn last Friday morning."

The day of the shooting. The money on the girl's body.

The elevator doors opened and Elaine motioned for me to enter. I caught a whiff of her light perfume as I stepped past her. Certainly a vast improvement over Cooper Ludden's cigar.

Elaine punched B and the doors closed. As I expected, the security offices were in the basement.

"I hope I'm not keeping you from your work," I said.

"Not at all. This is my work."

"Are you in public relations?"

"No. Bullshit's not my specialty."

Her frankness surprised me. I studied her more closely. Her short blonde hair created a youthful appearance, but the hint of wrinkles around her eyes and throat told me she was a good ten years older than I first thought. Probably at least mid-forties.

Elaine seemed to read my mind. "I'm retired Navy. Twenty years. Enlisted when I was seven."

"That's how old I thought you were."

She laughed. "You should be in PR."

The elevator stopped with a jolt.

"Rock bottom." She stepped back as the doors opened. "I worked in military security. Joined the bank six months ago and I'm supervising the upgrades for western North Carolina."

"We appreciate your cooperation with our case." I motioned for her to go first.

"Cooperation? Unauthorized use of a customer's card is my case. The bank might want to prosecute as well." She detached her name tag from her blue blazer and swiped it through a keypad to the left of the elevator. The adjacent door opened.

"Both Kowalskis are dead." I followed her into a narrow hallway.

"All the more reason to nail the bastard." Elaine knocked on a door at the end of the hall, and then entered without waiting for a response.

The room was about thirty by thirty. We stepped up on a raised platform made of yard-square tiles. I knew enough about computers to guess wiring ran beneath the floor. Racks of what I took to be servers lined the walls on either side. Directly ahead of me stood a console and a bank of computer monitors. I recognized shots from the exterior of this building on Haywood Street and several angles from the first-floor lobby. Other pictures seemed to be from other banks.

"This is Danny Crane." Elaine introduced a young man seated at the console keyboard.

Danny swiveled around and shook my hand. "Pleasure to meet you, officer." He looked away as he spoke, obviously more comfortable staring at a computer screen than another human being.

"Show Deputy Clayton what you've got," Elaine said.

Danny clicked the mouse and the picture on the central monitor vanished. "The quality's going to be pretty crappy. Gainesboro's on our old VHS system."

I leaned closer to the monitor. "Like a tape from Block-buster?"

"Same physical cassette, but the recording speed's reduced. Twenty-four hours per tape. The branch has a machine that holds seven cassettes and the manager changes them once a week. We pulled video from the last transaction on the Kowalskis' state-ment and the one that occurred last Friday. I digitized them in chronological order." Danny slid the mouse across his pad and double-clicked. "It's running half speed."

The monitor showed a fish-eye view of a parking lot. The video refreshed every second instead of every 30th of a second, giving the sense of watching a series of stills rather than smooth motion. Although the picture was in color, most of the frame was filled with gray asphalt. A readout in the bottom corner of the screen showed date and time—Monday, May 29th, 2:45:15 p.m.

"That was Memorial Day," Elaine said. "The ATMs get heavy use on a holiday weekend."

As the seconds ticked by, an edge of a blue car appeared on the right side of the screen. I recognized the hood ornament of a Lincoln. "That's the car."

A few seconds later, a woman stepped up to the ATM. She kept her head down, and her face was partially obscured by the hood of a light green windbreaker. Enough of her chin and nose were visible for me to recognize the dead girl.

"She your victim?" Elaine asked.

"Yes."

She stared at the girl's clothing. "Seems like we had a record-breaking temperature on Memorial Day. Nearly eighty in Asheville."

I'd spent the day with Susan in Pisgah Forest and remembered how hot it had been. "Yes. The sun's bright and the pavement's dry. She wasn't wearing that windbreaker for some isolated thunderstorm."

Danny froze a frame that revealed most of the girl's features. "I'll print this one for you." He clicked the mouse and somewhere in the room a printer stirred to life. "Now for last Friday."

The date changed to June 9th, the day of the shootings, and the time to 7:16:00 a.m. A garish yellow hue bounced off the pavement.

"The sun hadn't come up enough to trip the photo-sensor for the security light," Elaine said.

The clock started running and the girl again entered the frame from the same angle. If she came by car, it had been parked out of camera range. Her outfit was different from what she'd worn that evening. A red tank top and black shorts made her look like she'd been out for an early morning run. But she didn't appear to be breathing hard. In fact she spent most of the time smiling at the security camera. We watched her reach for the cash and then lift her top enough to reveal the pouch Susan had cut off her bleeding body.

Elaine looked at me. "Tell you anything?"

"A lot. I just wish I knew what it meant. The first clip she goes to extremes to hide her identity and the second has her auditioning for American Idol. Why the change?"

Danny froze a shot of the girl staring straight into the lens. The printer started again. Then he put that frame side-by-side with the first one. He pointed to the hood ornament. "That's interesting."

"You recognize the Lincoln?" I asked.

"No. It's interesting the girl came by car but walked up to the ATM. It's a drive-through."

Elaine nodded. "And after the transaction, the car backed up. No chance to see the driver or the license plate."

I began to understand. "The driver didn't want the girl or him to be recognized, which means the second withdrawal must have been made by the girl alone. She wanted the whole world to know she was there."

Danny zoomed into her face. "Maybe she was being held hostage."

"No," Elaine said. "If so, why not take the money and escape?"

I leaned closer to the monitor, trying to read meaning in the dead girl's eyes. "She wanted to be caught. She handed us the evidence, and then didn't live long enough to use it."

"Why?" Elaine and Danny asked the question together.

"I don't know, but I'm sure she would have told us." I thought about Fletcher's report of the girl's dying words—"R.D." and "Billy." We knew "R.D." was Artie. Maybe Billy was the answer to why.

Chapter Ten

The afternoon sun had dipped below the western ridges by the time I stepped out of the Wachovia offices and onto the shadowed sidewalk of Haywood Street. In addition to my case notes, my leather portfolio held several printouts of a freeze frame of the unidentified girl smiling at the security camera. Although Fletcher's composite had been surprisingly accurate, the video from last Friday morning provided an unmistakable likeness recognizable to anyone who knew our mystery girl.

My cell phone vibrated on my belt, signaling I had a voicemail waiting. The below-ground security facility in the bank must have shielded incoming calls. Fletcher had phoned ten minutes ago.

"I'll stay in Asheville till I hear from you." The swagger was gone from his voice and I knew he was alone.

I found an empty bench on the sidewalk along the small park across from the bank. Down the block, two young wannabe fiddlers scratched out Ol' Joe Clark in a mishmash of notes. Their open violin cases would have encouraged more contributions if a sign had read "Will Stop Playing For Cash." I pressed my cell phone to one ear and stuck my finger in the other.

"Where are you?" Fletcher got right to the point.

"Outside the bank on Haywood Street."

"I'm over at Pack Square near a monument."

"Governor Vance. I can walk there in a few minutes."

Fletcher hesitated. "No. Better not. Too many people have seen me. I'll come to you."

"There's a bookstore nearby. Malaprop's." I gave him directions and told him I'd meet him in the mystery section.

Malaprop's Bookstore and Café is an Asheville landmark. Not for unique architecture or a singular location, but for the convergence of cultures that share an enjoyment of the coffee, conversation, and the store's collection of bestsellers and new literary discoveries.

Three distinct lifestyles intersect within the store. There are the locals who've been born and bred in the mountains, the retirees with their silver hair and pension funds, and the new-agers whose hair could be purple, red, or even green, depending upon the day's vibration of the vortex. Walking between the rows of shelves, I'd overhear patrons discussing everything from the Middle East to Middle Earth.

I bypassed the crowd hovering around the café counter and made my way toward the back where the mysteries were stocked. Titles were arranged alphabetically along an island on the left and I browsed the far-end, picking up *Out Cold*, the latest in William Tapply's Brady Coyne series. Despite the warm June day, "out cold" was an appropriate assessment of my investigation.

Two elderly women at the other end of the shelves were debating which cat mystery to buy. I thought about how close Fluffy had come to being a murder victim.

I was ten pages into Brady's New England adventure when Fletcher arrived.

He stepped beside me and pulled a book at random. "Too bad our mystery can't be solved in three hundred pages."

I glanced up to make sure the feline fans were still engrossed in their conversation and then turned to Fletcher. "I'd be happy just to get to a new chapter." I tucked Tapply's novel under my arm. "The café's crowded. Get a table for two. I'll follow in a few minutes and ask to join you. We don't know each other."

Fletcher replaced his book and returned to the front of the store. I made a pretense of scanning a few more titles as I walked along the aisle. As I neared the two women, they smiled and turned toward me.

"Here's a good one." The lady on the left held up a paperback with only the words "The Cat Who" visible above her fingers.

"Thanks, but I just started *The Cat Who Shared a Casket.*" I slipped past them, and took a quick peek over my shoulder. Both women were frantically digging through the shelves.

I bought my book and crossed from the book section of the store to the café. Fletcher sat at a back table. I waited a few minutes in line, ordered a lemonade and carrot-walnut muffin, and then read the dust jacket of my book while I made sure all the tables were occupied. Fletcher drank coffee and read a free tourist magazine.

I eased beside the chair opposite him. "Do you mind if I share your table?"

He didn't look up. "Suit yourself."

As I sat, Fletcher shifted in his chair, turning away from the other patrons. To my surprise, he freed his cell phone from his belt and put it to his ear. I hadn't heard it ring.

"Damn. I was followed."

I glanced toward the front door. A guy wearing threadbare denim overalls, no shirt, and sandals stood at the café counter. Beside him, a woman in a dirty floral-print shift scanned the room. She looked to be in her late teens or early twenties. The man probably had a few years on her. He certainly had a few feet. I pegged him at six-five. His companion only came up to his chest.

Fletcher shielded himself from their view. I slid my chair back and opened my new book. I hoped we looked like two strangers forced to share a table. Fletcher was obviously talking to someone else on his phone.

I turned a page in the book, freezing my eyes on the top line where I could also view the couple. While they waited for their order, the girl moved deeper into the café. Again, she played her gaze over the room and this time caught sight of Fletcher. She quickly withdrew to the man.

"She spotted you," I said.

The girl pointed at us. Mr. Overalls studied Fletcher for a second and then looked at me. I flipped another page. In my peripheral vision, I saw the man wave his hand at the woman behind the counter, refusing the two drinks he'd ordered.

I closed the book. "They're leaving."

The man grabbed the girl by the upper arm and pulled her through the door.

Fletcher wheeled around. "They know the dead girl. They wanted money for her name. I was supposed to meet them later."

I jumped to my feet. "Then we can't let them get away."

With Fletcher close on my heels, I ran through the tables of stunned booklovers. Outside, the sidewalk bustled with pedestrians enjoying late afternoon window shopping. I looked right and left but the couple had disappeared. Across the street, people strolled without any sign that they'd been jostled by the fleeing pair.

Fletcher threw up his hands in exasperation. "Where'd they go?"

"Did they have a car?"

"I met them at the park at the end of Haywood. When we split, they walked in the opposite direction."

I examined the vehicles parked across the street. Halfway down the block, I noticed a black Hummer big enough to transport a SWAT team. The horn beeped and headlights flashed as someone used a remote to unlock the Hummer's doors. A middle-aged woman who looked like she had as much business driving the monstrosity as climbing into the cockpit of an F-14 fighter jet stepped from the curb and walked toward the driver's door of the Hummer. She clutched a shopping bag in one hand and her keys in the other. As she rounded the left front fender, she turned her head and peered back through the windshield.

"Watch the front of the Hummer." I jogged along the sidewalk to where I could see the rear of the vehicle. The stoplight at the end of the block turned green and the heavy two-way traffic formed a barrier as effective as a swift-moving stream.

I pulled my badge, prepared to identify myself if we flushed the couple. Just as the rear of the Hummer came into view, the two sprang from behind the vehicle and ran darting and weaving through the pedestrians.

"There they go!" I ran parallel to the traffic, holding up my badge and motioning the cars to stop. Tires squealed beside me. I jumped into the middle of the street and ran down the center line. An oncoming delivery van swerved to the right. I zigzagged on its tail, momentarily running away from our quarry. When I reached the other side of the street, the two had disappeared around the corner.

Horns blared behind me and I knew Fletcher must be making his mad dash. I turned up Battery Park Avenue and saw the couple half a block away. The girl lagged, unable to keep up. The man flailed his arms, urging her to hurry.

"Police!" I held the badge above my head.

Any thoughts Mr. Overalls had of protecting the woman vanished. He turned tail and bolted like a scared rabbit. The woman cried "Chip" and lunged forward, but her left foot twisted in her thong sandal and she tumbled to the concrete.

As I stood over the girl, winded from the short sprint, she curled into a fetal ball with her face buried in her forearm and started crying.

"I'm Deputy Barry Clayton. I just have some questions. That's all."

"He'll kill me if I talk to you." The words came out in halting, guttural gasps.

"No he won't. Now look at me."

She lifted her head and braced herself on one arm. Tears ran from her dark hollow eyes and clear mucous streamed from her nose. Now that I could get a close look at her, the girl showed all the classic signs of methamphetamine abuse. Her skin was pale and dry and seemed to hang on her frail body. She was sweating far more than a girl her age should, even after a short run. She already had the beginnings of "meth mouth," the black staining of her teeth. In a few more years, they'd be rotten.

I'd seen her kind countless times while on patrol in Charlotte. I would arrest an innocent-looking eighteen-year-old for a first-time drug offense and think her biggest problem should be getting a date for the prom, not getting her next fix. A year later, I'd arrest her again, only this time she looked a hard thirty and there was no innocence left.

Fletcher came up beside me. "Where can we talk to her?"

"You lied to me." The girl screeched like a tormented cat.

I stooped down closer. "Didn't my friend tell you he was looking for someone?"

"Yes."

"That's the truth. We're not interested in you. Now we can go down to police headquarters where everyone will see you and they'll figure you're telling us all sorts of secrets. Or I can put this badge back in my pocket and we'll have a little chat in the open air. Your choice."

She looked at me and then Fletcher. "You only want to know about the girl?"

I nodded. "That's all, although the way your boyfriend ran out on you, I don't think you owe him anything."

"Chip's on parole." She got both feet under her and tried to stand. "He was afraid he was being set up."

I grabbed her right hand and helped her up. She was light as a dandelion wisp, a body that burned meth rather than food. "Set up for what?"

"Nothing." Her eyes narrowed as she looked at Fletcher. "We were just selling information." She turned to me. "Is it true you're police?"

"Yes."

She thought a second. "Chip said this guy might be trying to frame him. Claim Chip offered him drugs."

I got the sense she was making this up. "Where'd y'all meet?"

She leaned on me as she straightened her twisted sandal. "The park at Haywood and Patton."

That was right around the corner, the park across from the bank. "Let's go back there and start over." I turned to Fletcher.

"Would you get my book and papers from Malaprop's? I'll want to show—" I stopped. "I'm sorry. I don't know your name."

"Dale."

The words clicked. Chip and Dale. "Don't get cute with me."

Her anemic pallor reddened slightly. "No. I swear. That's why Chip says we're made for each other."

Dale and I started walking toward the park as Fletcher jogged back to the bookstore. Chip and Dale. A match made in Disney World. I was glad Tommy Lee wasn't there to see the turn my investigation had taken.

Fletcher caught up with us just as we claimed a bench facing Patton Avenue. A late afternoon breeze cooled the air. Dale sat between Fletcher and me, her hands in her lap, nervously picking her fingernails. Fletcher passed me my portfolio and I pulled out the picture of the girl smiling at the security camera.

"Who is this?" I set the photo on Dale's lap.

Dale brushed her fingers across the girl's face. "She's not going to get in trouble, is she?"

"I'm afraid it's more than trouble. She's dead. I'd like to give her a name. I'd like to notify next of kin."

A breath caught in Dale's throat, stifling her cry into a faint squeak. Her hands started shaking. "No. Not Crystal. Not Crystal."

"She was shot. Was that what she was into? Crystal meth?"

Dale kept staring at the picture. "Crystal was her name. Crystal Hodges. She steered clear of meth."

"How did you know her?"

"We worked together. At the Mellow Mushroom. But that's been a while ago."

I glanced at Fletcher. He shrugged. This was new to him.

I took back the picture. "Was that the information you were planning to sell? Her name?"

Dale nodded. "That was Chip's idea. Score some cash."

"Without this photo, how did you know Crystal was the girl we were looking for?"

Dale turned to Fletcher. "Because of what you said."

Fletcher nodded. "That's right. I was sitting on this bench, zoning out in the sunshine. I'd made some inquiries on the street and was hoping word would get to somebody who knew something. After about ten minutes, Dale asked if she could sit down. She said she'd heard I was looking for a man named Lincoln."

"It was Chip's idea for me to talk to you," Dale said. "He was afraid you were a cop."

"I told her the man I was looking for drove a blue Lincoln and I'd heard he'd picked up with a girl in Asheville who looked something like her. Lincoln owed me money and I was going to collect. I made it sound like a threat."

I studied Dale's face. "He scared you?"

"Yeah. I told him the girl wasn't me, and I left. Chip said it sounded like Lincoln owed his supplier. He'd heard Lincoln was into cotton."

"Cotton?" The girl had lost me.

"Oxycotton."

I understood. OxyContin. Things were beginning to fall into place. "How'd you know Crystal was involved with Lincoln?"

"I'd seen them together last week. I didn't know his name, but Crystal got out of the car he was driving."

"So you told Chip what Fletcher said?"

The sound of a burned-out muffler rose above the street noise. A beat up Nissan Sentra cruised down the far lane. Dale looked at the car and gnawed on her lower lip.

"Chip?" I asked.

"Yeah. I guess he's worried about me."

What a guy. The knight in rusted armor had abandoned her on the sidewalk and now watched from the safety of his car.

"You spoke to Chip?" I asked Fletcher.

"Yeah. After Dale left, I waited. In about fifteen minutes, I heard a voice behind me say, 'You supply, huh? You supply Lincoln?' I hadn't seen him come up so I just ignored him. Then, like a bad actor, he said, 'Hey, I'm talking to you.'

"I stood up, opened my phone, and took his picture." Fletcher couldn't help but grin. "That got his attention. I told him I just wanted my bosses to see who I was dealing with. In case we had a misunderstanding. He backed off big time, mumbling he knew the girl I was looking for and he thought her name might be worth something."

"He was willing to sell the girl out to a perfect stranger?" I asked the question for Dale's benefit to point out what a heel the other half of her chipmunk team was.

"Yeah. We settled on two hundred bucks. I told him I didn't have the money with me, but I'd meet him tonight. I gave him my cell number and let him think about the Detroit area code. Guess I spooked him too much since he followed me."

Dale hung her head. "Chip didn't really think you were a cop. He thought you might be setting him up, you know, to kill him."

"He must have nice friends," I said.

Fletcher frowned. "Meth head paranoia."

Dale flinched and looked up the street. The Nissan turned the corner for a second pass down the block. She jumped to her feet and ran toward the car. Fletcher started after her.

"Let her go."

Fletcher turned around. "Why?"

"What are we going to do with her? I think she's told us what she knows. We've got the name Crystal Hodges, the connection to Lincoln and OxyContin, and the Mellow Mushroom as a place of employment. I'd say we've done pretty well."

We watched Dale hop in the Nissan. Chip flipped us the finger and sped off.

I stood up and slapped Fletcher on the back. "And you've got the phone photo of Chip in case we need to track him down again."

"There's only one problem. I'm afraid I took a picture of my thumb."

Fletcher headed back to Gainesboro to assist Uncle Wayne and Freddie with Mildred Cosgrove. I decided to stay in Asheville for supper. A pizza and beer from the Mellow Mushroom sounded like the perfect combination of business and pleasure.

At five-thirty, the evening crowd hadn't yet hit and I was able to get an outside table under a trellis of vines that covered the patio. A slim blonde waitress in hip-hugger jeans brought me a glass of water and a menu.

She pulled an order pad from a pouch in front of her waist. "I'm Karen. Can I get you something else to drink?"

"Yes." I paused as if deciding. "Is Crystal here? She recommended a great beer last time."

Karen smiled sympathetically. "I'm sorry, sir. Crystal no longer works here. Was the beer dark or light?"

"How about Dale?"

Her smile disappeared. "Dale's not here anymore." The tone of her voice told me Dale wasn't missed.

"Quite the turnover. I sure hope you'll be here next time, Karen."

She blushed. "If not, it means I found something better."

"I'll take a double cheese and pepperoni and a Newcastle Brown." I handed her back the menu. "Is the manager here?"

Her smooth forehead wrinkled. "Is there something wrong?"

"Not at all. I've just got a question about the franchise. See if he can spare me five minutes."

The waitress left, unconvinced that I wasn't about to register some complaint.

A few minutes later, a portly man in his mid-forties came to the table with an empty glass and my bottle of beer. His black hair and moustache were liberally salted with gray and his dark brown eyes cautiously appraised me. "Karen said you wanted to speak to me."

I flipped open my badge. "Just a few questions. I didn't want to alarm anyone."

He gave a quick glance to either side to make sure I wasn't scaring his customers, and sat down at the table. "I'm Joe Patterson. Is there some problem?" He pushed the bottle and glass in front of me like a peace offering.

I slid Crystal's picture to him. "Know this girl?"

He looked down at the photo. "Sure. Crystal Hodges. Is she in some sort of trouble?"

I sidestepped his question. "She doesn't work here anymore?"

"She quit two weeks ago. Said she had an unexpected opportunity."

"A new job?"

"Something in health care. She didn't say much about it. Said she'd get some career training."

I gave Patterson the composite of Artie Lincoln. "Did you ever see her with this man?"

He studied the image carefully. "Maybe. Kind of a common face. I think I've seen him in here. Crystal might have waited on him."

"How about Dale?"

He frowned. "Now there's someone I'd expect you to ask about."

"Were she and Crystal friends?"

"They got along I guess. I don't get involved in my employees' personal lives."

"Unless it affects the job." I slowly poured the brown ale into my glass. "Is that what happened with Dale?"

Patterson shrugged. "Personnel issues are supposed to be confidential."

"And young women like Crystal are supposed to die of old age."

Patterson looked like I'd slapped him. "She's dead?"

"You heard about the shooting in Gainesboro last Friday?"

"Oh, Jesus." He ran his fingers through his hair and looked at the photo again. "Are you sure?"

"Dale identified this picture less than twenty minutes ago. I haven't even had a chance to notify her family."

"God damn Dale. What did that slut get Crystal hooked into?"

I reached over and tapped Lincoln's composite. "We suspect this man of dealing OxyContin, but we don't know why Crystal was with him."

Patterson sighed. "And I don't know why she would have lied to me. Why make up a story about health care?"

"Maybe she valued your opinion of her."

"I'd like to think so." He looked around at his customers enjoying the food and fresh air. At the next table, a pair of red-haired twins no older than six fought over a last slice of pizza. "We run a nice business. A lot of families come here. Every employee knows our company has a zero-tolerance drug policy. About a month ago Dale tested positive and she was gone. But Crystal."

"Does your company do random tests?"

"Yes, and Crystal passed every time." Patterson thought for a second. "Do you think she knew she wouldn't pass the next time?"

"As far as we can tell she was clean. She might have just been in the wrong place at the wrong time." I took back the pictures. "There's no reason for you to think less of her."

He nodded. "How can I help?"

I rubbed my hand across my chin, thinking of what lay ahead. "I need you to check Crystal's records so I can contact her next of kin."

Patterson got up without speaking. There was nothing to say. I took a swallow of beer and tried to resolve the conflicting portrait being drawn of Crystal Hodges. Within a few minutes, Karen came with my small pizza. I'd lost my appetite.

"Tell you what," I told her. "Please give that to the next table with my compliments." I motioned to the family with the twins and their double-sized appetites.

"Mr. Patterson told me it's on the house."

"That's very kind of him, but I insist on paying." I pulled my credit card. "Go ahead and ring it up. Remember the customer's always right."

Karen did as she was told. I received a hearty thanks from the harried parents and another from Karen for my generous tip.

A few minutes later, Patterson returned with a sheet of white typing paper. "Sorry for the delay. I copied off the information rather than bring out the file. Crystal listed her mother, Carol Hodges, as the person to notify in case of an emergency. It's a Weaverville address and I've also got a phone number."

"This is something I have to do in person."

"Good." Patterson handed me the folded sheet. "And I hope you'll come back, Officer."

I realized I hadn't given him my name. "Clayton. Deputy Barry Clayton."

He shook my hand. "Karen said you wouldn't accept dinner on the house. Promise me you'll stop by when you're off-duty and give me the pleasure."

"It's a deal."

"And if there's anything else I can do for Crystal."

"If you think of something, you can reach me through the Laurel County Sheriff's Department." I was about to leave when I remembered a question I'd forgotten to ask Dale. "Mr. Patterson, did Crystal ever mention someone named Billy?"

"Not that I recall. Could that have been her boyfriend?"

A question I should have asked. "Did she have one?"

"Some boy used to pick her up after work when she first started, but I haven't seen him in a while."

"How long had she been here?"

"Almost a year. She got the job right after she turned eighteen. We always check because we have to be very careful with the employment laws for minors."

"And you think the boy's name was Billy?"

"I don't know. Just a suggestion."

I thanked him and turned to leave.

"Deputy Clayton."

"Yes."

"Tell Crystal's mother that her daughter was my best employee. I'm very sorry."

After leaving the Mellow Mushroom, I called into the Sheriff's Department and got directions to Carol Hodges' home.

She lived off Highway 25 between Asheville and Weaverville, a distance of about fifteen miles.

Although the days were rapidly approaching the summer solstice, longer light really meant a longer dusk. The sun would disappear behind the high ridges of the Appalachia Mountains and leave the valleys in purple shadows for hours. I turned on the jeep's headlights as much to be seen as to see.

Even in the deepening twilight, the outside world presented a clearer picture than the inside of my mind. Crystal Hodges was turning into an enigma. The credit card and the five hundred dollars made her look like a common thief, a tramp who picked up a sugar daddy and then picked his pocket. But her behavior at the ATM told a different story. The first withdrawal came with part of Artie Lincoln's car in view, and Crystal went to great lengths to conceal her identity. I had to believe she'd been coached. That made the second withdrawal all the more peculiar. Why the mugging for the camera?

If Crystal was into the drug scene, her friendship with Dale was easily explained. But both Karen and Joe Patterson made clear distinctions between the two women. I wondered where Chip fit into this puzzle. When had he been paroled and for what crime? Had he led to Dale's drug problem and the loss of her job? Chip was the one who knew Lincoln dealt OxyContin. Had he been the connection between Lincoln and Crystal?

Amid all my speculation, one fact loomed ahead of me. Crystal Hodges had been somebody's daughter. I was about to break the news that could break a heart. As a funeral director, my job meant I helped people deal with grief, but that grief was already present when they came to see me. Now, I was the one bringing the heartbreak, and that made a hell of a difference.

Carol Hodges lived on one of the numerous side roads that branched off the main highway like veins in a mountain fern. When pioneers first settled this area, every cove wide enough for a stream and a logging trail sprouted a few homesteads that over the centuries became communities named for their geographic landmark—Reems Creek Falls, Herron Cove, Dark Hollow.

Unlike the real estate boom of the last thirty years which saw the ridgelines undergo the malignant spread of vacation homes perched on every outcropping that provided a spectacular view, the mountaineers had built for a more basic purpose—survival. Cabins nestled within the shelter of windbreaks near enough to water for convenience but not so close that flashfloods could sweep them away.

The Hodges' residence sat on the footprint of one of the early settlements. The small clapboard house stood close to the road, marked only by a dented mailbox with a faded rural route number. To the left of the single-story home, I saw the crumbling remains of an isolated stone chimney, a withering vestige of a cabin that had burned or rotted out years ago. Perhaps the last trace of the Hodges family's first impact on the Appalachian wilderness.

A dirt driveway led to the steps alongside the front porch. Two cars were parked adjacent to one another, a late model Ford Focus and an older Dodge sedan. I stopped where my jeep would be easily visible to anyone inside.

Unkempt patches of lawn lost ground to greener moss and brown sprigs of rabbit tobacco. Lightning bugs danced in the cooling air and, somewhere farther down the road, a coon hound bayed.

I could see several lights burning in the front room, and the interior shadows were disturbed by the flicker of a television screen. I got out of the jeep and slammed the door. My news deserved at least a minimal warning.

As I crossed the yard, the yellow porch light came on. I kept walking, my hands away from my side. The door opened and a women stood behind the closed screen door. Her right side was hidden by the jamb and I suspected a shotgun was within easy reach.

I stopped. "Mrs. Carol Hodges?"

"Yes." Her voice was high-pitched and challenging. "Who are you?"

"Deputy Barry Clayton. From over in Laurel County. I can show you my ID if it's all right to come closer."

"Laurel County?" Her face couldn't hide her confusion. "What do you want with me?"

I stepped up on the porch and held out my badge. "I need to talk to you about your daughter."

As she glanced at my identification, I gave her a quick once over. She wore jeans and a gray sweatshirt. Her brown hair was pulled straight back and streaks of silver appeared as unwanted highlights. She was probably mid-forties, although the harsh glare of the bug-repellent porch bulb tacked five years on her sharp features.

She looked up and searched my face. "Is Crystal in trouble?"

"Do you mind if I come in?"

My question told her enough. Her tight lips trembled and from somewhere in that part of the soul that connects mothers with their children, the pain came. "Oh no. Tell me she's all right."

I moved closer to the door.

She staggered back on wobbly knees. "Then just tell me she's hurt."

"I'm so sorry, Mrs. Hodges." Once in the house, I looked for the nearest chair, knowing she was about to collapse. There was a sofa to my left. Across the room, Vanna White turned letters on "Wheel of Fortune." The category was Before and After. Carol Hodges stumbled toward me into that moment that would always be after.

I steered her to a corner of the frayed sofa and I sat at the opposite end. As gently as I could, I told her of last Friday's shooting and all that had been done to try and save her daughter's life. She interrupted me only once, to ask if I thought Crystal had suffered.

I told her no, since she never regained consciousness. I had so many questions to ask Carol Hodges, but I couldn't bring myself to start interviewing her. All I could ask was if she had someone who could be with her.

She made a vain effort to wipe the tears from her eyes. "My sister's over in Black Mountain. I'll call her." She started to get up but fell back crying again. "I'm sorry. I can't do it right now."

"That's all right. Don't worry. If you give me the number, I'll call for you."

She nodded, and buried her face in her hands. "First Billy. Now Crystal. How could God let this happen to my babies?"

Chapter Eleven

I grabbed a cup of scorched coffee from the hospital cafeteria and took a back elevator up to Tommy Lee's room. The morning bustle was over and I expected Tommy Lee to be sleeping after his usual visit from Susan and O'Malley.

Instead I found him propped up on two pillows with a copy of the *Gainesboro Vista* spread on the rolling table that extended over his lap. He was still wired to the gills with monitors and IVs, but the color in his face clearly showed he was on the mend.

"Nice of you to saunter in before noon."

It was only nine-thirty.

"I can come back when you're unconscious."

Tommy Lee managed a weak laugh. "So, our girl has a name—Hodges."

I glanced at the newspaper. "Her name's in the *Vista*?"

He shook his head. "Reece dropped by this morning. He'd been by the office and learned you'd called in for directions last night—Hodges in Weaverville. The guess about the girl was mine."

I pulled a chair up close to his bed. "Crystal Hodges. Her twin brother Billy died about eighteen months ago. OxyContin overdose."

"Damn. And she didn't have enough sense to stay away from the stuff herself?"

"I think it's more complicated. Crystal Hodges might have been on a mission to get back at the people she held responsible for her brother's death." I gave Tommy Lee the details of Crystal's performance at the ATM and Fletcher's discovery of the link between Crystal and Artie Lincoln that was probably set up through Chip and Dale.

"Only you would get involved in a case with Chip and Dale," Tommy Lee said. "Who's next? Goofy?"

"I figure that's who I'm reporting to."

He waved a hand for me to cut the comedy and continue.

"I spoke with Crystal's aunt last night for a few minutes. The mom had raised the children single-handedly. They'd given her the normal troubles, nothing serious. Crystal was a bit boy-crazy and the wilder of the two, but her brother watched over her."

"Then how'd he get mixed up with OxyContin?"

"He was into football, a pretty good high school player with college prospects. Fall before last, some of the team members got hold of some OxyContin so they could imitate the pros and play through the pain. Pretty soon that became just an excuse to party whether there was pain or not. One night Billy took too much. Dead at eighteen."

I could tell from his expression Tommy Lee had heard the story all too often. "What did Crystal think she could do?"

"Her aunt said Crystal withdrew at first. Barely kept her grades up enough to graduate. She worked as many hours as she could get at the Mellow Mushroom. The only outside interest she showed was the internet. Then about six months ago, she started following a lawsuit."

"Lawsuit. Against who?"

"The people who make OxyContin. Crystal had found a website called oxyabusekills.com."

"Nice PR," Tommy Lee said. "The drug company probably had to triple their ad budget."

"There's a government investigation of claims that the pharmaceutical company pushed the drug on the market without disclosing all the dangers. They're fighting more than public opinion. Doug Larson mentioned it to me the other day." I got up and moved to the computer. "I was going to check it out. Crystal's aunt said the girl became obsessed with making someone pay."

Tommy Lee sat quietly while I logged on.

"Here it is." I scrolled down the site. "Lots of links, a request for stories of personal tragedies, pictures of congressmen and state attorney generals lamenting prescription drug abuse, rallies with parents and teens protesting. I can see how Crystal could get caught up if she thought she could blame someone for Billy's death."

Tommy Lee cleared his throat. "What irony. The twin sister whose brother died of OxyContin abuse is killed by the husband whose wife died from the same thing."

"Even more ironic, I think Mitch Kowalski shot the one person who might have brought Lincoln down. Instead both he and Crystal are dead."

Tommy Lee sighed. "Kowalski's death is thanks to me."

"Don't be so hard on yourself. Kowalski wouldn't have been pointing a loaded gun at you if it hadn't been for Lincoln."

Tommy Lee shook off the temptation of self-blame. "Any leads on where Lincoln could be?"

"No. Crystal had quit her job. She told her boss she was going into health care."

Tommy Lee looked around the room. "Like a hospital?"

"She didn't have any formal nurse's training. Maybe she just said that."

"Remember what Susan said about the girl's body? She had a few tattoos not readily visible and some body piercings."

I saw where Tommy Lee was headed. "Piercings that were starting to heal over. Nose and tongue. She'd stopped wearing the more extreme rings."

Tommy Lee nodded. "Maybe she was going into a new job. She had to look straighter."

"And it's coincidence she hooked up with Lincoln?" My sarcastic tone was unnecessary because in this case I shared Tommy Lee's distrust of coincidences.

"Lincoln was the new job. He recruited her."

"You've lost me. He was paying her to shack up with him?"

Tommy Lee grabbed his cup of water and took a slow sip. I had to be mindful not to press him too much longer. "If you need to rest, you can tell me later."

"All I've been doing is resting. Resting and thinking." He squinted his one eye at me. "What's the difference between meth and OxyContin?"

"One's legal."

"Right. Crystal meth can be made by any nitwit with a high school chemistry set and a month's supply of cough medicine, while OxyContin is made by a legitimate company from a patented formula. Lincoln could get meth from practically anywhere, but he has to have some good sources to get enough OxyContin to be running a business like he is. Sources like distributors, pharmacies, hospitals, and doctor's offices."

"We don't know how many pills Lincoln was moving. He could have been a small-time operator."

"Even a small-time operator needs sources. Maybe he wasn't getting all his pills in Florida."

"He gets Crystal a job where she can get the pills?"

Tommy Lee licked his lips like a wolf savoring a lamb. "One possibility, if we're to believe everything you've been told. At least it gives you a lead."

He didn't have to paint me a picture. "I'll get Crystal's photo to as many area drugstores and hospitals as I can."

"And Lincoln's composite." Tommy Lee closed his eye as the last of his energy left him. "Ask them here," he whispered. "They've probably got a list of every place you need."

I left Tommy Lee's room and found Joel Greene at his desk outside Pamela Whittier's office, engaged with entering data in his computer. He was wearing another dark suit and white shirt, but the red tie had been exchanged for a phosphorescent green one. Even a straight-laced administrative assistant must have a flamboyant side.

He gave me a broad smile. "Deputy Clayton. How are things going?"

"We've made some progress. The girl who died is Crystal Hodges. Thompson's Funeral Home in Buncombe County will be handling the arrangements."

Greene made a note on a steno pad he kept by the phone. "Then there's to be no autopsy."

"Not unless hospital policy requires one given the circumstances."

"No. We just weren't sure what the family would want." He looked relieved at not having to ask them the autopsy question.

"I've got a favor to ask."

Greene spread out his hands, offering the world. "We're at your disposal."

I laid the photograph of Crystal Hodges on his desk. "We have reason to believe Hodges might have recently been hired or applied for work in health care."

"I'll check with human resources."

"Do you also have a list of area pharmacies, nursing homes, and other medical facilities?"

His eyes widened. "That's a pretty broad net."

"That's why I need to get started."

He looked at the photo. "I could fax this for you. I don't know for sure, but we probably have an automatic distribution system. I'll check with Nate Bumgardner in Information Technology. We deal with pharmacies and nursing homes daily, and patients are being transferred between hospitals all the time."

His proposal would save me hours of legwork. "Terrific." I set the composite of Lincoln beside Crystal's photo. "I need this one to go as well."

Greene studied the composite. "Did he apply for work?"

"No, but he might have been in a position to recommend the girl."

I could tell something was troubling Greene. "I'm not sure how to handle the request," he said.

"Don't worry. I can draft the cover letter, or if you prefer, print me a list of the fax numbers and I'll handle all of it from the Sheriff's Department."

"No. We've got everything batched on speed dial. But the cover letter's a good idea." He reached for a steno pad sitting neatly on the corner of his desk. "You can dictate it if you like."

I thought about the way the inquiry should be phrased. "I need to use our official stationery. I'm sure I can have a template sent as an email attachment. I'll write the letter in the sheriff's hospital room and forward it for you to print."

Greene handed me his card. "My email address is on the bottom. I'll scan these pictures and when your letter's ready, you can send it to me and I'll handle the faxes electronically. We'll give the recipients the option of emailing their responses straight to you."

From behind him, the door marked *Private* opened and Pamela Whittier stepped out. She looked annoyed. "Joel. What's taking so long?"

Greene's hands flew across his keyboard punching in data. "I'll have those figures for you in just a minute."

"My fault," I said. "I'm afraid I've kept him from his work."

Pamela forced a smile. "I've made it clear to Joel that assisting the police is his work. Has he been helpful?"

"Extremely."

"Then carry on." Pamela backed into her office and gently closed the door.

Greene relaxed. "Thank you."

"She runs a tight ship."

"She has to." Greene glanced back at the closed door. "I feel lucky to work for her. I've got a master's in hospital administration, but no degree prepares you for the day-to-day pressures of running a place like this."

"Sorry I'm adding to it."

"Actually, you're not. Having law enforcement in the hospital is something I'd like more of." Greene lowered his voice. "Frankly, we could use the expertise. Theft and fraud are rife throughout the health care industry. We try to stay on top of it, but short of frisking everyone, including doctors and administrators, there's no foolproof way to catch it all. If you think you've got the problem under control, then you're kidding yourself. You just haven't discovered the new scam yet."

Greene's fears only reinforced my suspicions of Lincoln's activities. I pointed to the pictures of Crystal and Lincoln. "You're sure this won't be any trouble?"

"No problem." He grinned. "You heard the boss. It's my job."

When I got back to the room, Tommy Lee had fallen asleep. I sat at the computer and composed the cover letter while waiting for the department to email a stationery template. After my request for information about Crystal Hodges and Artie Lincoln was complete, I phoned Joel Greene and told him to check his email inbox and distribute the photos. It was eleven o'clock. With a little luck, we could have a lead before the end of the afternoon.

I called the funeral home to see how things were going with the preparations for Mildred Cosgrove. The family visitation was scheduled for the next evening. The memorial service would be held at Crab Apple Valley Baptist Church at ten on Thursday followed by the graveside interment.

My mother answered the phone. "Wayne's not here. He had Freddy come in to help Fletcher."

"Where's Uncle Wayne?"

"He told Freddy he had something important to do."

Important things for my uncle to do amounted to getting a haircut every two weeks and changing the oil in his car.

"Didn't he have a haircut last week?"

"Yes. So maybe it was his car." Mom knew her brother better than anyone.

"Let me speak to Freddy and make sure he's got enough help."

"He ran out to the hardware store. Something about repairing the lock on the back screen door."

I started to ask for Fletcher, but then remembered what had prompted Freddy's handyman work. "Has Dad been downstairs?" Last week Mom had found him in the backyard in his pajamas after he wandered from the breakfast table.

"No. He was weak on his feet this morning. Not as bad as yesterday, but a little disoriented."

Describing an Alzheimer's patient as a little disoriented was an understatement. Dad was always disoriented, but I knew Mom sensed something was different. "Shouldn't Dr. Milliken see him?"

Mom sighed. "I'll call for an appointment. Maybe they can work us in tomorrow."

"Tell Fletcher I'll be by later this afternoon." I hung up, feeling uneasy that I wasn't at the funeral home to supervise my intern or to help with Dad.

I could have gone straight over there, but with the pictures of Crystal and Lincoln blanketing the health care industry and creating the possibility of new leads, I wanted to stay focused on the case. In Florida, Lieutenant Spring and I had learned the Kowalskis were linked to Gainesboro through shuffleboard. I had yet to tap into that connection.

A beautiful June day meant the parking lot at the Laurel County Senior Center looked like a Buick dealership. The predominant bumper sticker read "Ask Me About My Grandchildren." I found an open space at the far end and maneuvered my jeep between a new LaCrosse and an older Century.

A slight breeze cooled the effects of the noon sun. Double doors to the main building were wide open and I could see rows of card tables set up inside the multi-purpose room. I guessed either a contract bridge or canasta tournament was in progress. From around the side of the building, I heard the sharp smack of colliding shuffleboard disks. The games were being played outside behind the activity center in a space surrounded by a ten-foot-high chain fence.

I entered the shuffleboard area through an open gate and followed a covered walkway that dissected an array of thirty or forty courts. The long concrete boards were clean and the lines and numerals of their scoring pyramids freshly painted. Nearly half the courts were engaged in fierce competitions—most with four players, two at each end, some with two players in singles' matches, and a few with three players in some kind of rotation. Red and black disks slid along the smooth surfaces as competitors tried to place them in the scoring zones or knock their opponent's disks clear or, better yet, into the ten-off penalty space.

As scores were posted on a board at the head of each court, laughter and good-natured teasing rose from the players. The scene reflected the shiniest moments of the golden years and was a far cry from the nursing homes and geriatric wards that awaited so many senior citizens. I could understand why Lucy Kowalski would have tried anything to reclaim her active life.

The walkway ended at a small patio and concession stand. During tournaments, spectators could follow the fortunes of their friends and families while enjoying a sandwich or cold drink. Many of the retirees brought their own lunches, but prominent signs informed them that food not purchased on-site must be consumed at the many picnic tables outside the court area.

I decided to start my questioning with the people on the patio. Several tables hosted lively conversations and I moved toward a particularly animated group of four women and one man. The old gentleman had his back to me, and as the ladies noticed my approach, I got the strange sensation that I'd crossed into the Twilight Zone. The man's curly white hair was as distinctive as a fingerprint. He turned to see what had attracted the attention of his harem, and I don't know who was more surprised—me or Uncle Wayne.

I froze. Wayne's finger shot up to his lips, signaling me to be quiet. The command was unnecessary. I was speechless. The life-long bachelor was wearing Bermuda shorts and a Hawaiian shirt. His bony white legs terminated in scuffed bowling shoes. The green shorts still had a size label stapled to a belt loop, and the shirt must have dated back to when Hawaii was a territory.

A slender, elderly lady on Wayne's left smiled at me. "Are you looking for someone?"

"Bathroom," I managed to mumble.

Wayne cleared his throat as if auditioning for the Royal Shakespeare Company. "I'll show the lad the way."

As he got out of his chair, a plump woman to his right snagged his arm. "We're saving your seat so don't be too long."

The other women nodded in agreement.

"Don't worry. I wouldn't want any of you sending me to the kitchen."

Although I had no idea what my uncle meant, the women giggled like he was Jay Leno.

"Follow me, sir." As he passed, he whispered, "We don't know each other."

The men's room was inside the activity building. We walked in silence until we entered the restroom and checked the double stalls to make sure we were alone. Then I just stared at him.

"What's the matter?" He looked in the mirror over the sinks as if I'd discovered lettuce between his teeth.

"What do you think you're doing?"

"I'm undercover. You sent Fletcher to Asheville because you were too old to fit in with them hippies. Well, you're too young to fit in here."

I threw up my hands. "But I was going to talk to these people straight up. They aren't criminals."

"How do you know that? Old people like money."

There's nothing worse than being halfway into an argument with Uncle Wayne and realizing he's right. "Are you trying to sell pills to them?"

Wayne noticed the tag on his shorts and ripped it free. "Your mom and dad gave me these for Christmas."

"Last Christmas?"

"No. Must have been '74, maybe '75. When I was thinking about going to Myrtle Beach. I still might."

I wasn't going to be sidetracked by a three-decade-delayed vacation. "What are you telling those women?"

"That it was a shame about Mitch Kowalski. That's all I had to say. Then Ethel, she's the stocky one, she said she'd seen Mitch last Friday. He was upset and he was looking for Artie Lincoln. Then Ruth, she's the one with liver spots all over her hands, she said Lincoln had been here the day before. Then she told the other women her arthritis was feeling better."

"Arthritis?"

Wayne nodded. "Yes. Lincoln came by one day and Ruth's arthritis felt better the next. Jumped from one subject to the next without rhyme or reason. These women sure like to talk about their ailments."

I realized Wayne had probably found another one of Lincoln's customers. "Did you ask any questions about Lincoln?"

"I didn't get the chance. You came up."

I looked at his ridiculous outfit and smiled. "Sorry. You should have told me."

"And you would've talked me out of it. What do I do now?"

In a building full of men with prostate conditions, an empty restroom was a rare occurrence. Before someone interrupted us, I needed to think fast and let my uncle make the most of his charade. "Give them your phone number."

"At the funeral home?"

"Your home number. Tell them it's a delicate situation, but Artie Lincoln owes you some money. You'd appreciate them letting you know if they see him so you can have the chance to talk with him. But that he might try to avoid you if he knew you were coming."

Uncle Wayne frowned. "You think they'll believe that?"

"Sure. They like you. They laugh at your jokes. Now let's get out of here before they start wondering why two guys are hanging out in the bathroom so long." As we headed back to Wayne's groupies, I had to ask. "What does being sent to the kitchen mean anyway?"

"The kitchen's the ten-off area on the court." Wayne puffed himself up proudly. "I went to the library and got a book on shuffleboard so I could throw some terms around. I wasn't born yesterday."

"No, you weren't. But I don't think the kitchen is the room in the house those women are interested in."

He stared at me.

I winked. "Be careful or you'll really be undercover."

Wayne's face turned as red as a mountain apple.

Chapter Twelve

With assurances from Uncle Wayne that he wouldn't embellish our plan, I returned to the hospital in hopes that someone in the network of health care providers had recognized Crystal or Lincoln.

Tommy Lee sat in a bedside chair, attached to an IV pole and monitor. He flipped through a pamphlet with one hand and held a can of apple juice in the other.

"Does your nurse know you're out of bed?"

"Your girlfriend told me my vacation's over. Susan says I'm ready to start walking a few steps." He looked up at his IV. "Of course, I have to drag my pal everywhere, including the bathroom. Thank God the catheter's out."

I glanced at the pamphlet. "What are you reading?"

"Information on pulmonary recovery. How to breathe when your lung's turned to hash. If I'm a good boy, I might be out of here a few days early."

"Meaning?"

"This weekend. I guess my body's been shot up enough it knows what to do." He set the pamphlet on the bed. "So how are you doing?"

"We sent the photos to every doctor's office, drugstore, hospital, and nursing home in the area. I hope I've had some emails come in. And I've learned Mitch Kowalski was looking for Lincoln last Friday at the shuffleboard courts. Lincoln had been there the day before and I've got good reason to believe he's supplying up here as well."

"You've been busy."

"I've had unwanted help." I gave Tommy Lee a detailed description of secret agent double-O-seventy-five.

"Stop. I'm not supposed to laugh." Tears streaked his face. He hadn't shed a drop when he'd been shot, but the vision of Wayne and the bevy of beauties was too much for him. "Your uncle doesn't know what he's unleashed. For some of those women he's the perfect catch—a man with a pulse. And you had him give them his home phone number?"

"It seemed like a good idea at the time."

"Maybe this woman Ruth knows how to get a hold of Lincoln. She might talk to Wayne later if she can get him alone."

"I'll tell him she's the gal to court, although he described her as the one with the liver spots. Not the slickest pickup line I've ever heard."

Tommy Lee laughed again, and then coughed with pain. "You're killing me. Shut up and get on the computer."

I logged in and checked my email. Replies had come from two hospitals, five nursing homes, and eight drugstores. "Fifteen negatives. None of them recognized Crystal or Lincoln."

"I'd be shocked if we struck gold with the first responses. How many inquiries did you make?"

"Over sixty."

"Then there's still a good possibility something will turn up." Tommy Lee patted the arm of his chair like a judge tapping a gavel. "Give them a day. Some might want to call rather than send information over the internet."

My cell phone vibrated and I pulled it from my belt.

"See," Tommy Lee said.

I checked the caller ID and recognized a Florida area code. "Must be Roy Spring."

The police lieutenant dispensed with any chitchat. "I've got a web page for you. Ready to write."

I grabbed a pen and flipped my pad to a clean sheet. "Go ahead."

"It's www.dea.gov/pubs and then click on press releases."

"The U.S. Drug Enforcement Agency?"

"Yep. There was a nice little press conference this morning down at our courthouse. My chief got his picture taken with the DEA Special Agent in Charge of Southeast Florida. They busted a ring of public school employees forging prescriptions for OxyContin. A federal grand jury returned a seventy-three count indictment."

"Public schools?"

"Ten bus drivers, seven custodial staff, and a school cashier among others. A little nest a doctor had formed that passed phony prescriptions and filed fraudulent insurance claims for reimbursement. We're talking about a conspiracy that got thousands of tablets from pharmacies. Then the defendants would sell the OxyContin to a co-defendant who moved them on the street for forty bucks a pill."

I winked at Tommy Lee. "Let me guess. That co-defendant was Artie Lincoln."

"No. Artie Lincoln's name never showed up."

My expression must have clued Tommy Lee that I'd jumped the gun. "What's wrong?" he asked. "They couldn't indict him?"

I waved him to be quiet because I had my own questions for Spring. "Then why'd they tell you to stay clear of Lincoln?"

"Because I told my chief Lincoln was involved in OxyContin. He and the feds didn't want me crashing a party just as the band struck up the final number. But now they're real interested, especially since you've got a lead they don't."

I wrote *DEA* on my pad, underlined it and held it up for Tommy Lee to see. "What do they want?" I asked Spring.

"Right now, just an update on developments."

I repeated the request for Tommy Lee's benefit.

He frowned. "Hell, we don't have time to check in with the feds every half hour. Let them build their own damn case."

Spring heard Tommy Lee's growl. "I agree with your sheriff, but if you could give me something to take back to my chief, while his picture's in the news and everybody's buddy buddy, I'd appreciate it. Even an email summary's fine."

While Spring spoke, I jotted *we owe him* on my pad and flashed Tommy Lee the note.

"Whatever," he whispered.

"All right, Roy. Let me give you the long version over the phone so I can keep the written summary short." I told him what we knew about Crystal and the possible connection to a job in the health care industry.

"Sounds like a version of what we busted down here," Spring said.

"Maybe someone's franchising the OxyContin business and Lincoln has the golden arches for western North Carolina."

"I'll keep you posted on the case down here so you can look for similarities. Good luck when the feds come trampling through your investigation." Spring hung up.

I found the DEA website and read Tommy Lee the news release. The information provided a few more details, but Spring had already given us the essentials.

Tommy Lee shifted in his chair, trying to keep the hospital gown intact. "Trouble is we don't know if Lincoln was a little fish in a big Delray Beach pond or a big fish in a little Gainesboro pond."

I opened a blank Word document to begin my case narrative for Lieutenant Spring. "Maybe he's a frog jumping from puddle to puddle."

A knock came from the door behind me.

A raspy voice said, "I don't know about frogs, but it's time my patient hopped back in bed."

I turned and saw Susan crossing to Tommy Lee. "You sound terrible. You're the one who should be in bed."

"Actually I feel a little better. My head's clogged but at least my nose isn't running like a leaky faucet. I prescribed myself an antibiotic and an allergy medication. I suspect there might be a touch of a sinus infection."

"Do you file an insurance claim for a doctor's visit?" Tommy Lee asked.

"Only if I want a command performance before the medical examination board. Technically I should have had O'Malley write my prescription, but Doug Larson knows I don't abuse erythromycin. It's not exactly a party drug."

"Not like OxyContin." I gave Susan a brief update, including our inquiries as to Crystal's new job possibilities.

"I'll make sure the clinic responds to the fax." She took Tommy Lee's arm and helped him back in bed. "You've sat up enough today. Tomorrow we'll break it up—some in the morning and some in the afternoon."

Tommy Lee gave a slight groan as he slid across the sheet. His face paled with the exertion and I knew his workday was over.

"Are you about through?" Susan asked me.

"I've just got to type a short report. You want to grab supper later?"

She shook her head. "I'm going to take your advice and go to bed early. The antibiotics sap my strength. My goal's to shake this cold by the weekend and then your job will be to show me a good time."

"Doctor's orders," Tommy Lee mumbled.

"No argument from me. We're all due a good time."

Susan blew me a kiss as she left. I spent thirty minutes compiling my report to Lieutenant Spring, and for twenty-nine of those minutes, I listened to Tommy Lee snore.

"Did you get Dad a doctor's appointment?" I asked Mom as she set a plate of hot fried chicken and steamed asparagus in front of me. Her invitation to join her for supper meant I wouldn't endure leftovers at my cabin.

"Yes, I'm taking him at ten tomorrow morning."

Democrat whined beside me, enticed by the aroma. I snapped my fingers and pointed to his bed in the corner of the kitchen. He might not be the best trained dog in the world, but I never allowed him to beg at the table. He slunk over and lay down.

Mom sat across from me. "Democrat looks so pitiful."

"He's been fed. He's doing that for your benefit so don't sneak him anything."

Mom laughed. "Don't be critical. I saw the same look on your face when you walked in the kitchen."

"Yeah, but I'm cuter."

"I invited Fletcher to eat with us, but he wanted to drop by the hospital."

"More for me." I took a bite from a leg.

"He likes Cindy, doesn't he?"

"What's not to like? And he feels bad she got shot."

Mom was the only person I knew who didn't eat chicken with her fingers. Instead, she delicately cut the meat away from a thigh. "Fletcher's a nice boy. He worked hard with Freddy this afternoon. And he spent some time on the phone with Mildred Cosgrove's family. Now we've only got a few more things to do before the visitation tomorrow night."

"Did Uncle Wayne come back?"

Mom eyed me suspiciously. "What's he up to? He stopped by to check in with Freddy and told me he was helping you."

"Did he look like he'd walked out of an episode of 'Love Boat' meets 'Gilligan's Island'?"

"Yes. And he had on bowling shoes. He hasn't gone bowling in over thirty years. Should I take him to the doctor as well?"

"No. He's taken up shuffleboard. At least for one afternoon. Mr. Kowalski often played here."

Mom set down her fork. "Your uncle's not in danger, is he?"

In my mind, I saw Wayne at the table with the four elderly women. "Not the kind you think."

She shook her head, knowing it was better not to ask.

After supper I took a cup of coffee back to my office and called my uncle. I wanted to tell him Ruth was the woman deserving his attention. The phone rang a long time and I thought he must have gone to bed early after his exhausting ordeal. At last a whispery voice answered, "Hello."

"Uncle Wayne?"

"Barry." His voice regained its strength.

"Are you all right?"

"I thought you were one of the women. Three of them called tonight."

"About Lincoln?"

"No. About going to Friday's street dance. They want me to be their escort."

"You'd go with all three?"

"They asked me separately, but I ain't going with none of them."

I set my coffee on the desk and leaned back, maliciously enjoying my uncle's dilemma. "You should have held back the charm this morning."

"I was just being friendly. Maybe it was the shirt. They must think I get around."

I bit my knuckles to keep from laughing.

"I should have minded my own business."

I felt sorry for the old guy. "You were just trying to help me, Uncle Wayne. I appreciate it. Was Ruth one of the three who called you?"

"No. I thought sure you were going to be her."

"She's the one most likely to see Lincoln again."

"I don't have to take her to the dance, do I?" He sounded like a little kid whining at his chores.

"No, just be nice to her. Tell her you have to help your nephew Friday night."

I heard him take in a breath and knew the crisis had passed.

"Okay. But I'm never going within ten miles of those shuffle-board courts again."

I took my coffee and Democrat upstairs to spend some time with Dad. At the top of the steps, I held the lab's collar while I undid the safety gate. Otherwise Democrat could bound into the den and startle my father. Dad loved having the dog in the room, but sudden appearances made him anxious.

Dad sat in his easy chair and studied the back of his hands. The TV played an unwatched episode of "Sponge Bob Square Pants." I think my father just liked the sound of the character voices because when I'd turned it off in the past, he became agitated.

Dad's face was flushed and his breathing a little labored. Mom hadn't changed him out of his pajamas from last night and when I walked in, he spoke only one word. "Bed."

I patted one of his hands. "No. It's not time yet. Democrat and I came up to visit."

The dog gently laid his head on my dad's knee.

"Democrat," Dad repeated. He scratched behind the dog's ear and said the name again.

Sometimes this went on for two minutes or twenty minutes. Neither Dad nor Democrat seemed to mind.

Not only was my father's color off, but his face seemed puffy. I reached out slowly and touched his forehead. His skin felt warm although the room was cool. I knew there should be a thermometer in the bathroom and I thought Democrat would provide a distraction so that I could check my dad for a fever without too much resistance.

As I stepped into the hall, my cell phone vibrated.

"Barry. It's Fletcher." His voice was barely above a whisper.

"What is it?"

"I think I've found Lincoln."

My heart raced and I headed down the stairs. "Where?"

"Here. At my apartment complex. When I came in from the hospital, I noticed a blue Lincoln parked a few spaces away."

"Does it have a Florida plate?"

"No. North Carolina. I know that's wrong, but the only inspection sticker on the windshield is from Florida. So is the dealership insignia on the trunk."

"He switched plates so we wouldn't spot his car."

"What should I do?"

I mouthed "I'll be back" to Mom as I passed through the kitchen and out the back door.

"Barry?"

"I'm thinking." I didn't want Fletcher confronting Lincoln and I would need backup from the department. "Can you see his car from where you are?"

"No. There's a van blocking my view. The Lincoln's closer to the exit. That's how I noticed it as I drove in."

"Then try to find a spot where you can watch it. Maybe move your car out on the street. Don't stop him. If he leaves, follow from a safe distance and phone in. I'm on my way."

One nice thing about a small town is that everyone is ten minutes away from everything. I speed-dialed the Sheriff's Department as I started my jeep. "This is an emergency," I told the dispatcher. "Get me Reece."

Reece must have been in the office because he picked up immediately.

"Hutchins here."

"Reece, it's Barry. I think we've found Lincoln."

"Where?"

"Daleview Manor. My intern's staying there and he noticed a car that matches the description. I'm on my way. Can you send two men?"

"Me and Wakefield."

I paused to find the right words. "Reece, I don't want there to be any misunderstanding at the scene. This is my collar and we need to play it my way for the good of the whole investigation."

For a few seconds, I heard only silence. Reece was also choosing his words.

"Then I'll try not to screw it up."

I let his sarcasm roll off me. "Come in quietly and park where you won't spook him. I'll probably be in the manager's office."

Daleview Manor was a glorified single-story mom-and-pop motel. Minor renovations had changed paired rooms into so-called suites with one side converted into a living room and kitchenette. They were clean and popular with the retirees who didn't have the money to rent a summer cottage.

By the time I arrived, the evening darkness had descended enough to trigger the streetlights and I saw Fletcher's convertible parked in the dimmest point between two of them. The parking lot entrance was bordered on either side by a thick boxwood hedge. I positioned my jeep diagonally across the single lane and raised the hood like I had engine trouble.

Fletcher walked up beside me. "Smart move. He'll have to leave on foot."

"I'm going into the office. You pretend to be the jeep's owner." I handed Fletcher a flashlight from the glove compartment and locked the doors. "Anyone wants you to push the jeep aside, tell them the transmission's locked up and a wrecker's on the way."

I left him to play his role and walked up to a unit with the word *Manager* on the door. From inside, I could hear one of the cable news shows with all the guests screaming at once. I knocked loudly.

In less than a minute, the door opened and an older man with thinning gray hair stepped out. Although I didn't know his name, I'd seen him around town. At first I thought he was wearing orange lipstick, but when he raised his hand, I noticed his fingers were the same color. He'd been snacking on Cheetos.

"Sorry. We're full up."

I showed my identification. "You've got a guest we need to speak with."

He licked his orange lips nervously. "We run a good place here."

"What's your name?"

"Sid Mulray."

"I know you run a good place. But the guy I want is not so good. Bring the passkey."

He glanced over his shoulder. "What should I tell my wife?"

"That Fletcher Shaw has a plumbing problem."

His eyes widened. "He's the guy? He seemed so nice."

"He is nice. He's not the one. I'm looking for the man who drives the blue Lincoln."

"Mr. Wilson? He just checked in this afternoon. Called for the last unit."

"Then let's go welcome him." I had an idea. "Bring a registration form."

"But he filled one out when he got his key."

"And you just spilled coffee on it, didn't you?"

Mulray smiled. "I guess I did."

As Mulray went back inside, Reece and Wakefield arrived. I gave them a quick rundown.

"The manager said he just checked in this afternoon. Going by the name of Wilson. I'm having the manager knock on the door. Reece, you and I'll stand out of sight to either side. When the door opens, I'll ease where I can see him. If it's Lincoln, we'll arrest him for credit card theft and sort the other charges out later. Wakefield, when we know the unit, I'll want you behind it in case he gets suspicious and escapes out the back."

Mulray came out, surprised to see the reinforcements. "There won't be any shooting, will there?"

"No. We do this all the time."

"All the time," echoed Reece and Wakefield.

"What's the unit number and how can we get behind it?" I asked.

"Number seven. It's third from the end. There's an alley just beyond the hedge, but there's no back doors. Only a bathroom window."

I nodded to Wakefield. "We'll give you a couple minutes to get in position. My intern's got the parking lot blocked with my jeep."

Wakefield unsnapped his holster and left.

"What do you want me to do?" Mulray's voice had acquired a distinct quiver.

"Knock on the door. Tell him you hate to bother him but you need his signature again."

He nodded. I hoped the twilight would mask the fear in his eyes.

Daleview Manor was laid out in a horseshoe. Reece and I flanked Mulray as he walked to the row of units on the opposite wing. Mulray stood on the mat in front of the peep hole. Reece stepped back to the left and I took the right, where I wouldn't have to cross Mulray to get to Lincoln. I nodded to both men.

Reece drew his sidearm. As Mulray knocked, I unsnapped the catch on my holster but left the gun on my hip. Reece would cover both of us.

"Mr. Wilson."

No answer. No noise at all from inside.

"Maybe he's in the bathroom," Mulray whispered.

"Knock louder," I said.

He pounded the door so hard Reece jumped.

"Mr. Wilson. It's Sid Mulray, the manager."

Still no sound.

"Wait a few minutes," I said.

We stood still. At least Reece and I did. Mulray's knees were shaking.

"Okay, try it again, but easier on the knock."

"Mr. Wilson." He pounded the door three times. Nothing.

I stepped closer to Mulray. "Do we have your permission to enter?"

He held out the passkey. "Be my guest."

I took the key from his trembling orange fingers and turned the lock. The door opened without the hindrance of a security chain. Shadows masked the details of the interior. I saw the outline of a coffee table, the shape of a sofa, and an indistinguishable lump sprawled across its cushions.

"Mr. Wilson." I stepped into the room and flipped on the lights.

An overhead bulb illuminated the room. Artie Lincoln was lying face up on the sofa, his head turned toward its back. An empty Seagram's bottle sat on the coffee table. There were no drinking glasses.

Reece laughed. "So much for me screwing up your arrest. He's dead drunk."

I walked forward a few steps and saw Lincoln's open eyes staring into the floral upholstery.

"No. He's just dead."

Chapter Thirteen

I went through the ritual of checking for a pulse. Nothing. Lincoln's skin felt warm, but the June night was warmer. Although I'm not a medical examiner, I estimated Lincoln had died within the hour. My cell phone rang. I glanced at the incoming number. The funeral home. Uncle Wayne probably had a question about Mildred Cosgrove's visitation. I let it go to voicemail. One body at a time was my limit.

"Reece, get Wakefield. And see if Asheville can spare their mobile lab."

Reece frowned. "That'll cost money."

"Damn it, we'll use the merchants' donation to cover it."

Asheville had a state of the art mobile crime lab and I didn't want to miss any evidence.

Reece still hesitated. "What about Clark?"

"Have the dispatcher page him, but I want that mobile here PDQ."

Ezra Clark was Laurel County's aging coroner. He'd held the elected position for nearly thirty years because the voters didn't have the heart to turn him out. Tommy Lee had an unwritten policy to have a more competent medical examiner review any death that occurred under suspicious circumstances. I'd have Lincoln's body sent to Asheville.

Reece holstered his gun. "That all?"

I knew Reece itched to be in charge and I didn't want him sulking underfoot. "Do what you think is best for controlling any media or gawkers. And if you could interview the neighbors that would move things along."

Reece nodded. "Yeah. Maybe Wakefield and I should split up to get to them faster. Before they start talking to each other and creating a story."

"Good point."

Reece smirked. "I have a good idea every once in a while. Let me know if you need anything else."

As Reece left, I turned to Sid Mulray. He was staring at Lincoln's body like it might jump up and bite him.

"Mr. Mulray, are you all right?"

He turned to me, his eyes enormous in his pale face. "You're saying he was murdered?"

"I don't know. Maybe he had a heart attack, maybe he mixed pills and booze." I looked around. The door to the bedroom stood open and the bed hadn't been touched. On the opposite wall, a small kitchenette had been customized where the single motel room's original bathroom had been. Two glasses were on the counter by the sink. "Do you see anything out of place?"

Mulray kept a safe distance from the sofa as he looked through his rental unit. I followed him into the bedroom. He reached for the bathroom door.

"Don't touch anything. I'll open it." The two glasses on the sink meant Lincoln might have had a drinking buddy. Someone could be hiding in the bathroom. I lightly grasped the doorknob with the tips of my fingernails, trying not to damage any latent prints. The hinges squeaked as I pushed the door inward.

The bathroom was empty. The fresh towels were undisturbed. No personal articles lay around the sink.

A search of the bedroom closet revealed neither hanging clothes nor a suitcase. To all appearances, Artie Lincoln had checked into Daleview Manor with just a bottle of whiskey.

I returned to the kitchenette. "Are there only two glasses in each unit?"

"Yes. Some of our long-term renters bring in cookware, but with only a small refrigerator and no dishwasher, most people eat out."

I bent eye-level with the counter. The glasses appeared clean. I opened the cabinet door under the sink and discovered a wastebasket. Two wads of paper lay on the bottom. "Do you use sanitary seals on your drinking glasses?"

Mulray peered over my shoulder at the crumpled pieces. "Of course. But why would he unseal the glasses and then drink from the bottle?"

"Good question, Mr. Mulray. And if he washed these, what did he dry them with?" There were no paper towels in the kitchenette. "Do you remember seeing any cars in the parking lot that didn't belong to a tenant since Lincoln checked in?"

"No. Someone could have come during our supper. Cars go in and out a lot around supper time." Mulray glanced back at the body. "Maybe someone else rode with him."

"Maybe."

I was anxious for the crime lab to arrive. The cleaned glasses suggested an effort had been made to destroy evidence. Maybe fingerprints, maybe traces of poison. Either way, the case I'd hoped to close by finding Lincoln had now taken a very strange turn.

Sid Mulray went back to his apartment. Ezra Clark arrived half an hour later. He waddled in toting his black medical satchel and wheezing from the short walk from his car. The portly coroner looked like he was minutes away from pronouncing his own demise.

"What've we got?"

I led him to the body. "I don't know yet. It could be a natural death or it could be a homicide. Possibly poisoning."

Clark's lips formed a small O. "Really?" He pushed his bifocals higher on his nose and leaned over Lincoln. "If he used poison, it must not have caused any pain. Some poisons contort the victim's face into all sorts of hideous expressions. This guy looks like his lights just switched off."

I pointed to the empty Seagram's bottle. "Poison could have been in the whiskey."

Clark nodded his head. "Could be. Enough alcohol could have acted as a depressant. You think suicide?"

"There were two glasses. They look like they were wiped clean."

Clark straightened up and folded his hands over his stomach. "Really?" He stared at Lincoln. "I wonder."

"What about barbiturates? They wouldn't cause pain."

Clark didn't seem to hear me. He opened his worn bag and extracted a pair of latex gloves. He stretched them over his pudgy hands. "Help me roll him toward us."

I grabbed Lincoln's hips while Clark twisted the dead man's shoulders. We rotated the body until Lincoln lay flat on his back. Clark lifted Lincoln's left forearm and examined the hairless skin of the inner side of the wrist up to the hem of Lincoln's short sleeve golf shirt.

"Nothing," he muttered to himself and laid the arm across Lincoln's chest.

"What are you looking for?"

Clark didn't answer. He picked up the right arm and repeated his examination. He extended Lincoln's elbow and peered over the top of his bifocals at the crook of the joint. "Take a look."

I leaned over the old man's shoulder. He made a circle with his thumb and forefinger to highlight the area in question. A small smear of dried blood discolored the pale skin. A darker red dot lay over the vein.

I understood what caught his attention. "Someone injected him."

"Sure looks like it. Somebody could have knocked him out with a drugged drink and then killed him by injecting him with God only knows what. No way of knowing for sure until an autopsy is done, but at least now the medical examiner will have a better idea of what to look for." Clark gently laid the arm down. "Sheriff's got a real reason to send this body to Asheville."

I heard the hint of sarcasm. "What made you look for a needle mark?"

Clark stripped the gloves off his hands and dropped them in his bag. "Cause I've been there."

His answer left me speechless. Doc Clark was nearly as old as Uncle Wayne. It never crossed my mind he'd been a junkie.

He saw the expression on my face and laughed. "You're thinking I was a drug addict?"

I sputtered a few incoherent syllables that proved I wasn't thinking at all.

Clark pointed to the empty whiskey bottle. "I was a drunk. Nearly cost me my medical license, and it's the reason Sheriff Wadkins double checks all my reports." He looked back at Lincoln. "Also why I doubt this poor devil got shit-faced. Toward the end of a fifth, half the liquor wound up on my shirt or splattered on the table. No way he could have drunk himself into a stupor and not have a single splash of hooch on him."

I stepped closer to Lincoln. "I'll put a rush on the blood work. Any guesses?"

Clark pulled his glasses off and pinched the bridge of his nose. Then he looked at Lincoln and sighed. "A fifty-cc syringe can pack a lethal dose of just about anything. Insulin would do it and be hard to trace if you didn't look for it right away. Or an epinephrine overdose would lower the blood pressure and send the heart into an arrhythmic flutter."

"That's adrenaline, right?"

Clark nodded. "Comes in vials to protect against overdose. People who are extremely allergic to bees carry it. EMTs stock it to jumpstart a heart."

A knock came from the door behind us. Reece walked in. "Barry, I need to speak with you."

"Wait a second. Ezra's found evidence proving this is a homicide."

Doc Clark gave Reece a dismissive glance. "As I was saying, the injection could have been a lot of things, from some high tech synthetic drug to something as simple as a syringe of air." He waved his arm in a wide circle. "Air's free, plentiful, and deadly. Fifty ccs will stop the heart like a well pump losing its prime."

Reece came right up beside me. "Barry, it's important."

I made no attempt to hide my exasperation. "Whatever it is, can't you handle it?"

Reece moistened his lips. "No, I can't. Your father's been rushed to the hospital. He fell down the stairs. We just got the call on the two-way."

My chest tightened and I couldn't breathe. The air Clark proclaimed to be so plentiful suddenly left the room. The safety gate. I'd been so anxious to find Lincoln I'd run out of the funeral home without replacing the damn gate.

Doc Clark grabbed my arm. "You want to sit down?"

"No. I'd better go. Cover Reece on what the autopsy should look for."

Reece pulled a small notepad from his shirt pocket. "I'll take care of things here. You need a driver?"

"I'm fine." I walked on rubbery legs out of the murder scene knowing I hadn't fooled either one of them.

Only four nights earlier I'd been in the same emergency waiting room because of my friend Tommy Lee and Helen's daughter Cindy. Tonight I found my mother in the same corner where Patsy had sat, not knowing whether her husband would live or die.

Mom looked up as I entered. Her lower lip quivered. "Oh, Barry. I tried to call you."

I sat down and put my arm around her shoulder. "I didn't know it was you. We were in the middle of something." My voice broke. "I forgot the gate. I'm so sorry."

Her face tightened. "Don't you even think that way. If anyone's to blame, it's me for not going up to check on him sooner. The gate's there to keep him from wandering through the house, not off the stairs. He'd never had trouble with them before."

"But the gate had been closed till I opened it."

"Not another word." Mom's reprimand left no room for argument.

I turned away and fought back tears. We were alone, but I didn't want to seem weak in front of her. Mom would start consoling me, and she needed her strength for Dad.

"How is he?" I asked.

"He's in X-ray. They think he broke a hip. Susan's been called in."

"Good. She's the best." I also knew Susan would level with me as to my father's prognosis. "Did you ride in the ambulance?"

"Yes. The EMTs were wonderful. They put me where your father could see me. He was in pain, but he wasn't scared."

"I'm sure they've given him something to sedate him. I'll ask Susan if one of us can be in recovery when he wakes up." My mind raced through the other details we needed to remember. "Did you call Uncle Wayne?"

"I tried a few times at the front desk. I got a busy signal. Maybe he knocked his phone off the hook."

"Maybe." I didn't tell Mom he'd more likely taken it off to avoid talking to one of his new girlfriends. "I'll call again after we know what's going on."

Mom and I sat for another fifteen minutes. A young Hispanic couple brought in a toddler. They were like so many new immigrants and illegal aliens who filled the area's demand for service jobs during the bustling tourist season. Their boy's face shone with perspiration. He whimpered and cupped his hand to his ear. The mother held him close and coaxed him to be quiet. I gave them a reassuring smile that their child wasn't bothering us.

A nurse escorted them to a treatment room and what I expected would be a shot of amoxicillin. They had just left when Susan entered. She was still wearing street clothes.

"Aren't you doing the surgery?" I asked.

Susan ignored my question and gave full attention to my mother. "Connie, I'm so sorry. But we've got Jack stabilized and he's resting as comfortably as he can."

Mom looked hopeful. "He didn't break his hip?"

"Yes, he did. But it's a clean break. I'll pin it and he should mend without need of a replacement."

I knew there was more to the story. "Why are you delaying the surgery?"

"Your father has pneumonia."

Mom grabbed Susan's arm. "Pneumonia? But it's summer."

"Pneumonia can be caused by a hundred different things. I suspect he might have aspirated some food. As we age, our swallowing muscles weaken. He might not always remember to chew properly, or thin liquids could have seeped down his windpipe."

"You think it's bacterial?" I knew viral was more difficult to treat and posed a greater risk.

"Yes. He's built up quite a bit of fluid in and around his lungs. We're tapping that to give him relief, and the fluid sample will enable us to get a more specific analysis of the infection. Right now we've got him on a heavy dose of general antibiotics, but when I know what we're dealing with, I can prescribe a more targeted treatment."

"Can I see him?" Mom asked.

Susan smiled. "I don't think that will be a problem. Let me see if he's been assigned a room yet."

I left Mom and followed Susan out into the hall. "When do you think you can operate?"

Susan glanced over my shoulder through the open door to the waiting room. I turned around. Mom sat with her head bowed and her lips moving in silent prayer.

Susan gently took my hand. "I didn't want to say this in there, but your father is very sick."

"But the antibiotics?"

"The antibiotics will work as fast as they'll work. I'm more concerned about your father's heart. The fluid build-up has placed a strain on it and revealed signs of congestive failure. Some of the fluid is from the pneumonia and some is from the heart's inefficiency. The combination is causing a downward spiral we need to break."

Even though I knew the answer, I had to ask. "What's the bottom line?"

Susan sighed. "I've called in a specialist in internal medicine because if the antibiotics don't reverse the infection soon, the broken hip will be the least of our worries." Susan's eyes met mine and I could read the pain in them. "Your dad might not make it through the night."

Chapter Fourteen

Time crept along, measured by the shallow breaths of my father. Mom and I sat by his bed helpless to do anything but watch the IVs of antibiotics and glucose slowly disappear into his veins.

I reached my uncle around eleven that night. "Wayne, it's me. I've been trying to call."

Wayne cut me off. "I just couldn't deal with those women tonight. I promise I'll talk to them tomorrow."

"I'm at the hospital. Dad fell and broke his hip. And he has pneumonia."

"Great day in the morning!"

I heard springs creak and I knew Wayne had sat down hard in his tattered recliner.

"How's my sister?"

"She's here." I looked over at Mom. She held Dad's hand.

"Tell him not to worry," Mom whispered.

Wayne jumped in before I could pass the message. "I'll be there soon as I can."

"We're fine. There's nothing you can do. You should get a good night's sleep before the Cosgroves' visitation."

Wayne didn't mince his words. "Are you guaranteeing your dad will be alive in the morning?"

I couldn't lie to my uncle. "He's in room 307."

Wayne arrived before midnight. For a few seconds, he stood in the doorway, his wrinkled face pale as he stared at my father.

Dad lay on his back, mouth open, cheeks bruised and swollen, and his forehead wrapped in a clean bandage.

I answered Uncle Wayne's unspoken question. "The cuts and bruises are superficial. Susan immobilized his hip and he's being kept sedated."

Wayne came to the foot of the bed, shook his head in disbelief, and walked behind Mom. He laid his hand on her shoulder.

She reached up and patted his hand. "They've done everything they can."

"How long they got to keep him doped up?"

Mom looked at me to respond.

"Depends on how soon the antibiotics begin to work. Susan can't operate on his hip till the pneumonia's under control."

"Is he in a coma?"

"No. Just sedated enough to ease the pain and keep him from pulling out the IVs." I thought about Crystal Hodges, who had to be put in a coma to control her cranial pressure—a coma she emerged from only long enough to die.

Wayne's lips disappeared in a grimace. He shrugged as in acceptance that he couldn't control the uncontrollable. "It's in the Lord's hands, no two ways about it." He turned to me. "You call Lester Pace?"

"Not yet. I'll get him first thing in the morning."

Wayne cocked his head and fixed me with a disapproving eye. "Your dad and Preacher Pace worked together nigh on fifty years."

Lester Pace was even older than Wayne and my father. Pace wasn't the minister at First Methodist in Gainesboro where Mom and Dad attended, but a theological dinosaur—a circuit-riding preacher who ministered to multiple congregations scattered in the hollows and coves of the mountains. Methodist preachers are normally reassigned every three to five years, but Pace had been so exceptional in his devotion to the mountain people that he had become an exception. And in the age of TV evangelists and mega-churches, a simple backwoods man of God wasn't the ecclesiastical model turned out by the modern seminaries.

Wayne stirred my feelings for the old gentleman, and if things were in the Lord's hands, Lester Pace was someone I wanted whispering in His divine ear. I stood up. "You sit down, Uncle Wayne. I'll get Reverend Pace's number from the hospital."

To my surprise, Pace didn't answer his phone. His simple "Leave a message" caught me off guard and I stammered the hospital room number and my father's precarious condition.

On my way back, one of the duty nurses stopped me in the hall. "Sheriff Wadkins knows you're here. He said if you take a break, come down and see him." She smiled. "He said everybody else in the damn hospital wakes him up, you might as well too."

"Thanks. I'll go down now. Please have someone get me if there's a change with my father."

Tommy Lee's room was dimly lit. I could see his eye was closed, and despite his instructions, I hesitated about waking him.

"Sorry to hear about your dad." He opened his eye. "How is he?"

"I thought you were sleeping. You must have been great on guard duty." I pulled a chair nearer the bed.

Tommy Lee reached out his arm, pulling the IV tube with it.

I clutched his hand and held it while I spoke. "We don't know. Touch and go until the pneumonia breaks. You hear how it happened?"

He nodded. "You gave me good advice not to blame myself for Mitch Kowalski's death." He gave my hand a firm squeeze and released it. I got his point.

"Did you hear about Lincoln?"

Tommy Lee pressed the control button on the bed until he sat upright. "Reece came by about eleven. That's why I can't sleep. Sounds like this time Doc Clark earned his election."

"I believe Lincoln got lured to his own execution. Unless the crime lab turns up something, I can think of only one lead."

"Me too." Tommy Lee wiped his hand across his grizzled chin. "But the dynamics don't seem right. Someone must have been running Lincoln. Daleview Manor was set as a meeting place."

I didn't understand where Tommy Lee was headed. "Are we talking about the same suspect?"

"Chip. Your Asheville junkie. Unless you've been holding back information."

"No. He's the guy I pegged. He knew I was looking for Lincoln and so he shut him up before I could get to him." I leaned forward. "And I let Chip get away."

"You were looking for Crystal. And your gut told you Chip was only a street doper." Tommy Lee held up a finger. "That's point number one that bugs me. You've got good instincts and I can't see Lincoln, a guy who can schmooze seniors like a Florida politician, let himself be controlled by Chip."

"You said Lincoln has to have a supplier. Those aren't the most savory characters."

"If we were talking about meth, you'd be right. But we agreed a connection to legal drugs means a more sophisticated source, someone that Lincoln is likely to cultivate directly."

Tommy Lee's objections to Chip as the murderer made sense. "So, why's he your lead?"

"Point number two. The speed with which Lincoln was eliminated. You saw Chip yesterday afternoon, he makes a break for it, and then tells someone else of our interest. That someone doesn't want Lincoln interrogated."

"Except we sent Fletcher's composite of Lincoln throughout the area."

Tommy Lee laughed. "Yes. There's that little detail that undercuts Chip for both of us." He held up a third finger. "Point number three. Tracking the whereabouts of every person who saw Lincoln's composite is beyond our capabilities. So, we're back to Chip, not because I think he's the murderer but because he's the easiest to find, and to hell with points one and two."

I wasn't ready to lose Chip as a suspect. "Sid Mulray said a young man phoned to book the room."

Tommy Lee looked out the window at the night sky. He seemed to be pulling his thoughts from some faraway star. "Did Mulray say anything more than it sounded like a young man?"

"You mean like he spoke with an accent?"

"Accent. Gruff. Soft. Whether the caller was trying to disguise his voice?"

"No. I didn't have time to ask him. He mentioned it before we found Lincoln's body. After that I focused on the crime scene."

Tommy Lee turned back to me and his eye narrowed. "How much do you know about Fletcher Shaw?"

"Our intern?" The accusatory tone of Tommy Lee's question jarred me. "Fletcher's been terrific. He's pitched in way beyond expectations. And he's the one who discovered Chip." I paused as if Fletcher's innocence should be self-evident.

Tommy Lee nodded in agreement. "Yeah. He did that real fast. What else has he done?"

"He made the composite of Lincoln."

"Damn good one given the circumstances under which he saw Lincoln."

Tommy Lee was thinking like a police officer and I'd been thinking like a proud mentor. My mind shifted gears. "He was in the room when Crystal died. And he found Lincoln's car."

"Did you have the car impounded?"

"No. I forgot. I also forgot to tell Reece to have the crime lab go over it."

Tommy Lee waved his hand, dismissing the oversight. "You were doing everything by the book up until you got the news about your father. Reece should have taken care of the car."

"Did he mention getting the car processed when he was here?"

"No. And I forgot to ask." Tommy Lee shrugged. "None of us is perfect."

I stood up and walked to the computer. The screen saver glowed in the dim room. The animated logo of the Laurel County hospital reminded me of another point. "I didn't know Fletcher had his computer drawing skills. He volunteered. Why do that when he could have left us floundering? Why find Chip? Why call me about Lincoln's car?"

"All good questions," Tommy Lee said. "On the other hand, if he helps with the investigation, he's able to monitor how it's going. If he killed Lincoln, then he knows the body's going to be discovered, so he phones in his discovery of Lincoln's car."

"That doesn't answer the Chip question."

Tommy Lee fiddled with the bed control, easing himself back to a more comfortable position. "Look. I'm not accusing Fletcher of anything. It's the pattern I don't like."

"You don't accept coincidences."

"I don't like coincidences. But I accept they happen. I just refuse to chalk up an event as a coincidence until every other possibility has been exhausted."

I'd heard Tommy Lee lecture the point many times before. He was right. My fondness for Fletcher couldn't blind me to the unusual circumstances surrounding him. "I'll start an inquiry in the morning. Fletcher's school records—"

"You'll do what you need to do for your family," Tommy Lee interrupted.

An involuntary shudder ran up my spine as Tommy Lee snapped me back to the reality of my father's condition.

Tommy Lee's voice softened. "Fletcher's not going anywhere. Give me some contact information and let me handle him. That'll also keep you out of the awkward position of spying on your employee."

I took a hard look at Tommy Lee propped in the hospital bed with an IV stuck in his arm. Simply walking to the bathroom would be a challenge. "Do you feel up to it?"

"Up to what? Talking on the phone? Using the computer? The damn doctors want me to walk up and down the hall three times a day now, flashing my ugly butt at whoever happens to have the misfortune to catch sight of the back of this ridiculous gown. If they're going to put me through that, they can spare me a little time at the computer."

I had to laugh. "Your butt in a chair is a definite improvement over your butt in the air."

"Tell me about it."

I sat down at the terminal and logged on. "I'm going to pull up the website for Fletcher's college and write down the contact information. There's a department that handles placing summer interns."

Tommy Lee shifted on his side and fluffed the pillows. "Might as well get me the number for the Asheville Parole Board. That's where I'll start my search for Chip."

I spent about ten minutes at the keyboard, compiling the information for Tommy Lee, and even searching the web for any reference to Fletcher Shaw. His name drew 4,350,000 possibilities. I refined the search to include Detroit. The number dropped to only 287,000—still too many for any practical application. I organized what contact numbers would be helpful to Tommy Lee by hand printing them on a notepad where he wouldn't have to find them stored on the computer. I turned around to explain what I'd done.

Tommy Lee was sound asleep.

In my dream, I kept clicking links to Fletcher Shaw, but each time the composite of Artie Lincoln kept appearing on the computer screen. Then the image called my name.

"Barry. The doctors will be in shortly."

For a few groggy seconds, I was disoriented as to how Artie Lincoln had turned into Reverend Lester Pace. The family waiting room came into focus and I remembered I'd gone there to rest a few minutes. Uncle Wayne and Mom had been sleeping at Dad's bedside and I hadn't wanted to disturb them.

"What time is it?"

Pace glanced at his old stem-wind wristwatch. "A little after six-thirty."

"When did you get here?"

"Around four. Emma Lou Carter went into labor last night and when she had birthing problems, the midwife called me." Pace straightened up and I heard a bone or two creak in his back. The old preacher usually carried a gnarled cane made from a rhododendron branch, but I didn't see it with him. He claimed a crooked cane made him look straighter.

"So, you've taken on delivering babies?"

Pace didn't return my smile. "Emma Lou wanted me there for a baptism, in case the little one didn't make it."

"What happened?"

"What I hoped." He took a deep breath. "I told her I'd baptize the baby if she had it in a hospital. She and her husband are scared of hospitals, and I suspect there's a worry about the money." Now a smile broke across his weathered face. "Don't know how theologically sound it is to hold an infant's spiritual life hostage, but it did the trick."

"Everyone okay?"

"Emma Lou and her little boy are fine, though I suspect he'll have a tough row to hoc."

"What's wrong?"

"They named him Lester." Pace couldn't mask his pride. "Imagine a little tyke saddled with that old-timey name in this day and age."

I stood up from the sofa that had been my bed for a few hours instead of just a few minutes. "Thanks to you I suspect this county has more Lesters per capita than any other in the state."

He laughed. "Somehow I can't see Mayor Whitlock printing that in a brochure."

We walked down the hall to my father's room. I let Pace enter first. Mom and Uncle Wayne were still sleeping. My father was fidgeting in his bed, his eyes fluttering in semiconsciousness.

Pace hurried to the bedside and grabbed my dad's hand. A bit of wisdom I'd learned from him flashed through my mind. Pace had once shared with me the most important lesson that he'd learned from his predecessor, who'd served the mountaineers since the early 1900s and had long ago gone to his heavenly reward. "Barry, the cruelest thing you can ever do is not take the hand of someone who's dying. No matter how great our faith or how sure we may be of our salvation, we all want to cling to this world. And though we make that transition alone, the warmth of a human hand will comfort us into the eternal warmth of

God's loving hands." Pace's words echoed in my head as I saw him calm my father with his touch.

"Barry?" Mom stirred in the hospital recliner. "I'm glad you got some sleep."

"Reverend Pace woke me so I could be here when the doctors make rounds."

Uncle Wayne wiped his eyes. "Any change, Preacher?"

Pace laid his hand on Dad's forehead. "Feels a little cooler. But if the fever had broken, I'd expect he wouldn't be so restless."

A knock came from the open door and we turned to see an older man in a Madras sport coat. A stethoscope dangled from his neck. "Good morning."

Susan stepped from behind him. "This is Dr. Madison. He's a pulmonary specialist from Asheville and was kind enough to drive over before his office hours."

Mom and Uncle Wayne started to get up.

Madison waved them down. "Keep your seats. I'll just give a listen to Mr. Clayton's chest and then we can talk a few minutes."

Reverend Pace retreated to a corner of the room. Madison rubbed the round chestpiece of the stethoscope against his palm to warm it, and then slipped it under Dad's hospital gown. The silence was broken only by the steady whoosh of the air-conditioning vents.

After a few minutes, Madison tucked the stethoscope in the side pocket of his coat. "Well, there's some good news. Although the fluid's not gone, there's less of it. I've read his chart and suggested a different antibiotic targeted to his specific bacterial infection."

Uncle Wayne edged forward in his chair. "Then he'll get better?"

"At this point, getting better is best understood as not getting worse." Madison studied the monitor beside Dad's bed. "His fever's down, but his pulse is weak and irregular. He's not out of the woods, but I'm cautiously optimistic that he'll recover." Madison turned to Susan. "Then he'll have to undergo the hip surgery."

"I hope we can do that within the next few days," Susan said. "I don't like keeping him overly sedated."

I knew Susan worried about the effects the narcotics were having on Dad's afflicted mental capacity. We were in a dilemma, risking what was left of his mind in a desperate attempt to treat his body.

Dr. Madison eased toward the door. "I'll continue to stay in touch with Susan and the hospital staff. Today's Wednesday. I hope by Friday he'll have turned the corner and we can move to the next phase of his care."

Susan left with Madison. She promised to come back after submitting the antibiotic changes to the hospital pharmacy.

Wayne stood and ran his fingers through his thick white hair. "I'd best go on to the funeral home. Y'all stay here as long as you need to."

"I'm going to wait for Susan," I said. "Then I'll be in. Fletcher will probably be early as well." I thought about Fletcher going under Tommy Lee's investigative microscope, but I certainly didn't mention that to my uncle.

"Both of you need to get some rest," Mom said. "We've got the Cosgroves' visitation tonight."

I patted Wayne's shoulder. "We'll take care of it, Mom. Everyone will understand you should be here."

"Barry's right," Wayne said. "I'll come relieve you later so you can get a shower and a change of clothes."

Pace cleared his throat. "I'll be glad to stay with Jack so all of you can run home for a few hours."

I jumped at his offer. "Mom, now might be the best time. We've gotten the latest update. Why don't you and Wayne leave now? I'll bring you back at lunch."

Wayne walked over and offered Mom his hand. "Come on, Connie. Reverend Pace will call us if anything changes."

Mom acquiesced. "All right. Barry, are you coming?"

"As soon as I talk to Susan."

When Mom and Wayne left, I motioned for Reverend Pace to have a seat. "Thank you. Mom wouldn't have left Dad with just anybody."

"I wouldn't have wanted her to. Your father's very special to me."

"He thought a lot of you too."

Pace stared at my dad and his eyes glistened. "I like to think he still does."

His words cut me. I hadn't meant to speak of my father in the past tense, but I did. Whatever hope the reverend's faith held out for him, I'd watched my father's mind fade beyond the point where I believed he'd ever come back to me. That realization weighed like a stone on my heart.

Softly Pace said, "He's not lost to God and so he's not lost to me."

A knock at the door spared me from facing my doubts.

Pamela Whittier entered. "I came in early for a meeting and just heard about your father. I'm so sorry."

Pace and I stood and I took Pamela's hand. "Thank you. Everyone's been wonderful."

"I saw Susan and she said Dr. Madison's consulting. You couldn't be in better hands." Whittier smiled at Pace. "And with the good reverend here I know your family's being well supported. But if there's anything we can do, please let me know. If you need to work here, we can set up a computer just like Sheriff Wadkins has."

"Thank you. That won't be necessary. But if something comes up, I won't hesitate to take advantage of your offer."

"That's what we're here for."

When she was out the door, Pace asked, "Who was that?"

"Pamela Whittier. The president of the hospital. She must have heard of you."

He chuckled. "And I've heard of her. But the name 'Old Iron Balls' didn't seem to be the appropriate way to greet her."

Susan returned a few minutes later and assured me Dad's new antibiotic would be administered immediately. I decided to run by the funeral home, pick up Democrat, and take him back to the cabin. I could grab a quick shower and get the clothes I needed to carry me through the Cosgroves' visitation. As I pulled into the driveway of the funeral home, I heard Democrat barking furiously on the back porch.

I ran from the jeep to find Wayne standing with a box held over his head and Mom tugging at Democrat's collar.

"What's going on?"

"Fletcher," Wayne said. "He's done it now."

"What's in the box?"

"Fluffy!"

I heard a cat screech. Democrat broke free of Mom and jumped up on Wayne.

I wrestled the dog away and manhandled him into the kitchen. With Democrat barking behind the closed door, I took the box from Wayne and set it on the floor.

A note on top read, "Mr. Shaw. Like we discussed, I want Fluffy's ashes put in an urn and placed in my mother's casket. Thank you for taking care of this delicate matter. Respectfully, Julius Cosgrove."

I opened the lid. A disheveled white cat who looked like its tail had been stuck in an electric socket cowered in a corner. The animal hissed and spat at us.

Wayne backed away. "What the hell did Fletcher think we were going to do? Cremate Fluffy on the barbecue grill?"

Chapter Fifteen

Fletcher hopped around the parlor like the floor was molten lava. "I had no idea the cat was alive."

Uncle Wayne and I sat on the sofa with Fluffy boxed between us.

"Stand still," Uncle Wayne said. "You're moving so fast I can't hear you."

Fletcher stopped and I could tell from his expression he was trying to make sense of Wayne's request. I knew Uncle Wayne had grown hard of hearing over the last few years, although he wouldn't admit that fact to anybody. These days he did as much lip reading as hearing and Fletcher's agitated gyrations were making reading his lips impossible.

I pointed to a winged-back armchair. "Sit down and we'll figure out what to do. What did Julius Cosgrove ask you yesterday?"

Fletcher sat down and rubbed his hands back and forth on his knees. "He asked for you or Wayne. Since both of you were gone, I said that I worked for you and would be glad to help if I could."

Wayne and I had been at the shuffleboard courts. I remembered Mom said Fletcher had done a good job dealing with the Cosgroves. Maybe too good a job.

"Mr. Cosgrove said he had a question about rule 6513," Fletcher explained. "I told him I wasn't familiar with it."

Uncle Wayne shifted uneasily on the sofa. He suddenly realized that somehow his clever stunt had bitten us in the butt.

"I'm sorry," Fletcher said, "I should have just taken a message, but I knew you were so busy that I thought I could handle the situation. Mr. Cosgrove said the rule had to do with animals and he wondered if a pet's ashes could be placed in the casket if they were properly sealed in an urn. Since cremation ashes are dispersed in a multitude of ways, I assumed that wouldn't be a problem. Mr. Cosgrove thanked me and said he trusted us to take care of things. He said he'd be in touch before the visitation."

"Rule 6513," Wayne muttered. "My own dang fault."

"Don't blame yourself," Fletcher said. "I should know the embalming laws of the state where I'm working."

"There ain't no rule 6513. I made it up. Julius Cosgrove wanted us to kill the cat and put it in the casket with Mildred. I told him it was against the law."

Fletcher stared at the box. "We can't give them back Fluffy."

Fluffy's claws scratched the cardboard at the sound of her name.

"What else can we do?" I asked.

The room fell silent for a few seconds. Then Fletcher's face broke into a broad grin. "Have you got a barbecue grill?"

Uncle Wayne flung his arm across the top of the box. "Great day in the morning! Have you lost your mind, boy?"

Fletcher's jaw dropped to his chin. "Ashes. I thought we'd get some ashes."

Again, silence. Then I started laughing. Uncle Wayne chuckled, and as Fletcher looked at us in bewilderment, the two of us degenerated into howls.

A light went on behind Fletcher's eyes. "You thought I meant to put Fluffy on the grill?"

That question brought tears to my eyes. Wayne snorted and gasped for breath. Nothing is more contagious than laughter, and Fletcher started giggling.

All of the pent-up tension—Tommy Lee's shooting, Crystal's death, Lincoln's murder, my dad's broken hip and his struggle with pneumonia—the entire list of terrible things weighing me down were, for an instant, offset by the absurd idea that Clayton and Clayton Funeral Directors would toss a cat on the Weber.

At last I caught my breath. "You're saying we should fake Fluffy's cremation?"

"It would serve Julius and Dot right," Wayne said.

The thought of tricking the Cosgroves was enticing, but I knew the scheme could blow up in our faces. "They'd be getting what they want, but if we're caught, we'd be accused of fraud."

Fletcher shook his head. "Not if we don't charge them anything. What's the worst that could happen? A headline reading 'Clayton Funeral Home Saves Cat'? And how long do you think Fluffy will last if we give her back?"

"They'll drown her sure as I'm sitting here," Wayne said.

Fluffy scrambled from one side of the box to the other as if she was following the conversation.

Uncle Wayne and Fletcher waited for my answer. "Well, I can't take her. Democrat would chase her and she'd probably kill my guinea pig George."

Wayne took his arm off the box. "I'm too old to be tied down by a cat."

My uncle never went anywhere and his little farmhouse and apple orchard would be perfect for Fluffy, but he was set in his ways and those ways didn't include a pet.

"I'll talk to Mr. Mulray at Daleview Manor," Fletcher said. "If I get Fluffy a kitty crate, he might allow me to keep her in the apartment. We won't have to worry about the Cosgroves seeing her."

Now that Fluffy's new home seemed secure, Uncle Wayne regained his enthusiasm. "We've got some sample urns in the storage room. We'll put the charcoal ashes in one of them."

"I cleaned the grill after our Memorial Day cookout," I said.

Uncle Wayne stood up. "Who wants barbecued hotdogs for lunch? I'm buying."

"I'll be back at the hospital," I said. "Just show the Cosgroves the urn and ashes at the private viewing. No sense getting the whole town involved."

While Uncle Wayne and Fletcher began the more serious aspects of preparing for Mildred Cosgrove's visitation, I went to my office. The small room had been used to conduct the business part of the funeral business since my great-grandfather opened it in 1930. Although I'd entered the office thousands of times before, this time I was struck by the history captured within the four paneled walls.

The large oak desk had belonged to my great-grandfather, a country lawyer who'd come to the mountains in the early 1900s because he believed the mill towns of the piedmont weren't a fit place to raise a family. He'd seen the need for a funeral home in the small community of Gainesboro and set his son up in the business. Photographs along the walls traced the story—from my great-grandfather and grandfather cutting the ribbon on the front porch of the Clayton Funeral Home in 1930, through my grandfather and Dad leaning against the new *Clayton & Clayton Funeral Directors* sign erected in 1952, to Uncle Wayne and Dad posing by our last ambulance in 1960 a few months before Laurel County took over emergency medical response.

I appeared in only one picture: my graduation from the Charlotte police academy. The color photograph hung in an eight by ten gold frame. That graduation was supposed to have stopped the timeline for Clayton and Clayton Funeral Directors, and my father had made peace with my decision. But his Alzheimer's had changed everything.

I sat down behind the desk, swiveled away from the wall of memories and picked up the manila envelope containing Mildred Cosgrove's release forms from the hospital. The packet felt thicker than usual. I thumbed through the contents and discovered either Cooper Ludden or the woman he had hounded for the paperwork had included more than the death certificates and release transfer. The printout of all Mildred Cosgrove's medical expenses was enclosed. I flipped through the sheets making sure I had what I needed for our files before passing the bulk of the information to Mildred's son Julius.

Most of the line item charges were coded with inventory numbers and brief descriptions: saline bags, IV kits, lab work, and dispensations from the pharmacy. One word jumped off the page. Oxycodone. The generic name for OxyContin. I held the fine print closer to the desk lamp. There was a twenty count number and eighty-milligram dosage. The same strength pill I had found in Lucy Kowalski's kitchen cabinet.

But I'd learned from Julius that his mother had spent her last few days in a coma. Any painkillers should have been administered intravenously. I laid Mildred Cosgrove's death certificate alongside the hospital's billing data. My assumptions proved correct. The oxycodone hadn't been given to Mildred Cosgrove while she was in a coma. She had been pronounced dead two hours earlier.

Had I stumbled across Artie Lincoln's supplier? If so, how could I investigate without alerting the culprit? The beauty of the scam lay in its simplicity. In the volumes of patient records generated each day in a hospital, even a small facility like Laurel County Memorial, who could double check that every prescription had been given to every patient?

I thought about Roy Spring in Delray Beach and the conspiracy the DEA had just broken. How many people could be involved here? Was the racket limited just to the hospital? Were we dealing with doctors, nurses, or pharmacists, or some combination of the three? I knew only one place I could safely start. I called Susan's clinic and told the receptionist it was an emergency.

"Did something happen to your father?" Susan's question came in a breathy gasp. She must have run to the phone.

"No. I'm sorry to have scared you. But something is wrong at the hospital." I shared my discovery and concern with how to proceed.

"You need to notify Hospital Security. They'll get answers faster than anyone."

"I don't want to stir the pot till I know what's in the stew."

Susan laughed. "You've been hanging around your uncle too long. I've no idea what you mean."

"Hospital Security will feel forced to do something immediately. I want to rule out other possibilities before making accusations." I turned in my chair and glanced at the photograph of me in my police uniform. "And we might need to bait a trap to catch not only those guilty in the hospital but a wider network as well."

"So how can I help?"

Since I'd been thinking out loud, I hadn't gotten that far. I stared at the papers on the desk. "Would you be able to tell who requested the OxyContin from the information on Mildred Cosgrove's printout?"

Susan hesitated. "Depends. I'm not familiar with those forms. They probably go to billing."

"I can fax them."

"Do it now," she said. "I've got afternoon rounds. Maybe I can get an explanation at the hospital for codes I don't understand."

"Be careful." The image of Lincoln's body on the sofa flashed through my mind. "We're dealing with people who kill anyone who threatens to expose them. We don't know who to trust."

I took Mom back to the hospital with me. We found Reverend Pace asleep in a chair with his broad hand resting on my father's.

"There'll never be another like Lester Pace," my mother whispered.

"The shepherd of the hills." I gently shook Reverend Pace's shoulder, mimicking the action he'd used to wake me earlier. "Hey, old timer, don't you have a home?"

Pace took a deep breath and looked up at me. "Yep. A home over yonder. I'm surprised the Good Lord hasn't called for me yet."

"You're still too ornery. Why don't you get some real sleep?"

Pace pushed up from the chair and steadied himself on the armrests. "Your dad's slept peacefully this morning. Nurse told me they're going to cut back on the sedation."

"Any word on when he might have surgery?"

Pace clapped a hand on my shoulder. "One step at a time." As if to illustrate his words, the old preacher walked carefully to the corner behind Dad's monitor and retrieved his rhododendron stick. I'd not noticed it before.

He pointed the worn end at me. "You fetch me if there's anything I can do." Then he went to Mom and leaned close over the walking stick. "I'll be praying, Connie, but whatever happens, God's with him."

Mom could only blink back tears. Pace turned, straightened his back, and strode out the door.

I left Mom with Dad and went up to see Tommy Lee. He sat at the computer, the IV pole beside him, and his pants belt cinched around his hospital gown.

"You look like Spartacus in that getup."

"I don't give a damn what I look like as long as it shuts off any unwanted summer breeze." He nodded to the computer screen. "Take a gander at this."

A head-on and profile mug shot were positioned side by side.

"That your boy?" Tommy Lee asked.

I recognized Chip's weasel face. The border beneath his picture read *Buncombe County Sheriff's Department.* "Great. They got him already."

"They got him too already. He was nabbed in a meth bust yesterday evening."

"Before Lincoln's murder?"

"Time stamp on the photos is 6:13 P.M."

"He still could have fingered Lincoln."

Tommy Lee clicked the mouse and a booking sheet appeared on the screen. "Possibly. But according to the arresting officer, Oswald Winters, aka Chip, has been living in his car the past two weeks. Not exactly the pedigree one would expect for someone in a well organized conspiracy."

"We have informants that aren't much above pond scum, why not the other side?"

Tommy Lee laughed. "This guy gives pond scum a bad name. I've been on the phone with Sheriff Wilkins, and his boys are going to lean on Chip about the murder." Tommy Lee shifted in his chair and his face got serious. "You don't have a photo of Fletcher Shaw, do you?"

"What for?"

"I thought I'd have them show it to Chip and say Fletcher had turned on him. See what shakes out."

"No. Clayton and Clayton doesn't use photo IDs yet. Maybe when we have more employees than I have fingers on one hand."

Tommy Lee held up his hand. "Don't get testy. We agreed Fletcher was a fair suspect."

"Did you try his college?"

"Yes. They want the request in writing and on official stationery. Fletcher had expressed a desire for privacy regarding any information beyond what the career placement office needed to arrange his internship."

That struck me as odd and I struggled for an explanation. "We're in the age of identity theft."

"Murder's the ultimate identity theft. I've instructed Reece to fax the request and have them email Fletcher's student photo."

My stomach turned at the thought of Reece's involvement. "To show Chip?"

"To make sure Fletcher's who he says he is."

I let the subject drop. "Mildred Cosgrove might have given us a lead."

Tommy Lee's eye opened wide with surprise. "Mildred? I heard she died."

"Yeah. And two hours later got twenty pills of OxyContin."

I gave him the background on my discovery and Susan's efforts to track down any leads.

Tommy Lee shook his IV pole. "Damn. I wish I wasn't stuck to this glorified water fountain. That's the best news we've had on this case."

"And what would you do?"

He thought for a moment, and laughed. "Come to the hospital. Ask Susan to do some quiet checking on who prescribed Mildred's medication."

"Good plan. I see why you're the sheriff. Now I realize you got yourself shot just as an excuse to go undercover. Brilliant."

Tommy Lee rose from the computer, turned around, and mooned me.

Chapter Sixteen

With Tommy Lee back in bed, I took over the computer and read Chip's file. He'd been caught selling meth on the street, and given his prior conviction, would be headed back to prison. Facing that prospect, Chip might want to deal if the Asheville D.A. would give us some leeway. Usually, competing jurisdictions yielded to the more serious crime and closing a murder case trumped a meth charge. But I had to agree with Tommy Lee that Chip seemed an unlikely prospect to be deeply involved in something as sophisticated as a prescription drug scam.

I moved on from Chip and checked email. A message had arrived from Lieutenant Roy Spring in Delray Beach. I turned to see if Tommy Lee was awake. He stared at the ceiling lost in thought.

"Roy Spring wants to know if we've found Lincoln. Guess I'd better bring him up to date."

At first I thought Tommy Lee hadn't heard me because he kept studying the tiles in the drop ceiling. Then my question must have registered. "Tell him about the murder and that we don't have any leads."

"But we do have some leads."

Tommy Lee shook his head. "Do you want the DEA stomping through our flowers? I guarantee you Spring has been told by his superiors to pass along any information."

I hit reply to compose my message. "Whatever you say."

"Wait." Tommy Lee raised the back of the bed so he could talk easier. "Ask him if the name Fletcher Shaw has surfaced in their case."

"Jesus, give the kid a break. And I don't want the DEA swarming over the funeral home."

"Leave it vague. Just his name. If Fletcher's innocent, then we need to clear him as soon as possible. The DEA's resources will do that in short order."

"And what about Mildred Cosgrove's prescription?"

"Let's wait a little on that and see what develops."

I'd finished my report to Spring and was reading it back to Tommy Lee when Susan opened the door.

"I can come back if you're in the middle of something."

Tommy Lee waved her in. "You're our leading lady and you're on stage. Everything else can wait."

Instead of the smile Tommy Lee and I expected, Susan nervously moistened her lips and closed the door behind her. She held the sheets I'd faxed.

I stood up. "You found something, didn't you?"

"Maybe nothing more than a coincidence."

The word "coincidence" pricked like a burr and I glanced at Tommy Lee. His face froze.

"Something about the pills?" I asked.

"The pills and the time." Susan stepped closer to both of us. "There were several prescriptions on that list I consider inappropriate for a patient in Mildred Cosgrove's condition."

"Were they all narcotics?" Tommy Lee asked.

"Yes."

He nodded. "Who was the doctor?"

"Nick Foster."

I turned to Tommy Lee. "I can't believe Nick Foster would be mixed up in this. He's practiced here for over thirty years."

Tommy Lee ignored me and focused all of his attention on Susan. "Nick Foster prescribing medicine for his patient is not a coincidence. What's the coincidence?"

Susan lowered her voice as if the walls had ears. "I checked all the medications on the printout that seemed irregular to me. There were five over a seven-day period. They were filled on different shifts, one even on a Sunday evening, but they all had one thing in common." Susan paused as if whispering had exhausted her breath. "The same pharmacist. Doug Larson."

"Doug?" I couldn't hide my surprise. "I'd sooner expect Nick Foster."

"That's why it must be a coincidence," Susan said. "His family's had that drugstore as long as your family's had the funeral home."

"Is there any cross-reference between the hospital pharmacy and the patient's actually taking the medicine?" Tommy Lee asked.

"You mean does the duty nurse report back to the pharmacy?"

"Or some way the medications are tracked from the pharmacy to the patient."

Susan laughed. "That's why we have a chart. The nurses mark everything down. It's my job to review the chart, see that my prescriptions are being administered, and note any effects they might be having."

Tommy Lee rubbed his fingers over his chin. I could tell her answer didn't satisfy him. "And if a pharmacist forged a prescription, how would the dispensation of the medication be traced? How would you know a phony prescription had been written in your name?"

Susan's eyes widened. "I depend on the pharmacists to call me if they get a suspicious prescription."

Tommy Lee grunted. "See the problem? We might have put a fox in charge of the henhouse."

I remembered my earlier conversation with Doug Larson. "He told me he took on shifts at the hospital to help make ends meet."

"If he's our man, he's meeting a lot of ends," Tommy Lee said. "Forty bucks a pill times twenty. Eight hundred dollars for a couple of minutes' work, and in Mildred's case the government picks up the tab."

Susan seemed to have tuned us out. "Pyxis," she murmured.

"What's that?" I asked.

"Pyxis. It's a system of hospital inventory management. They make med stations, controlled substance safes, barcode equipment. A prescription wouldn't be filled and billed until it had been coded and placed in a transport safe that the duty nurse would open. Most of the big hospitals have gone to it."

"But not Laurel Memorial?" I asked.

Susan shook her head. "When Pamela was hired, one of the first things she did was form a task force to look into the feasibility of going to the Pyxis system. Doug Larson was on the task force. He wasn't working at the hospital at the time, but as the only private pharmacist in town, it seemed natural for him to offer an outside, unbiased opinion."

"Don't tell me," Tommy Lee said. "The system was too expensive and couldn't be justified."

"Sounds like you read Doug's summary," Susan said.

I saw broader implications. "So Doug could not only be writing some forged prescriptions here at the hospital, but think of how many he could be moving through his drugstore."

Tommy Lee gave me a look like I'd announced the sky was blue. "What do you think? Doug pays wholesale and then sells at street value. A thousand percent markup. Plenty of margin for a sales force like Artie Lincoln." He thought for a second. "Damn. I guess the acorn doesn't fall far from the tree."

"What do you mean?" I asked.

"Doug's son Delbert's serving an eight-year sentence at Central Prison in Raleigh. He was ordering huge quantities of cough medicine through Larson's Discount Drugs and using it to manufacture crystal meth."

I remembered the story. I'd been in Charlotte and Mom told me how upset everyone was. One of those things the whole town talks about and then sweeps under the rug.

"Didn't Doug testify against Delbert?" I asked.

"Not exactly. He was subpoenaed to explain their recordkeeping. Evidence showed that Delbert had set up a separate checking account with a bank in Asheville. He paid through that account, had the order shipped to an Asheville warehouse, but used the pharmacy's authorization to obtain the cough medicine."

"What about prescription drugs?"

"As the licensed pharmacist, all those purchases came through Doug. There was no trace of impropriety. We considered Doug a victim of his son's greed."

"Maybe Doug Larson is smarter than anyone has given him credit for," Susan said. "Maybe he set up a protective shell and let his son take the fall."

Tommy Lee looked from Susan to me. "Maybe. He's still innocent till proven guilty."

My message to Roy Spring was displayed on the computer screen. "Should I add Doug Larson's name to my email?"

Tommy Lee nodded. "But don't go into any detail. Just ask if his name has ever come up in their investigation."

I didn't understand Tommy Lee's obsession with secrecy, but I did as he said. "How are we going to prove anything? How did Doug Larson find out we were onto Lincoln? He must have been the one who killed him."

"Find out where he was last night," Tommy Lee said. "And then there's Chip."

"Who's Chip?" Susan asked.

I saw the pieces Tommy Lee was putting together. "A meth head in Asheville. He has an alibi for the time of Lincoln's murder, but he could have booked the room at Daleview Manor and set Lincoln up."

"More than that," Tommy Lee said. "He did time. I wonder if it was in Central Prison. I'll place a call to the warden and see if Chip and Delbert knew each other."

"What can I do?" Susan asked.

"Any ideas?" Tommy Lee asked me.

"Maybe Susan can check on her own prescriptions in a way that wouldn't arouse suspicion."

Susan waved the papers in her hand. "I can't ask for these sheets. That would raise a flag." She eyed the chart at the foot of Tommy Lee's bed. "Unless I kept my questions within the pharmacy. Claim I saw an error on a chart and want to cross-reference a patient history."

"Sounds good to me," Tommy Lee said.

"I'll have to do it when Doug isn't there."

"But we'd want you to check more than one chart," I said.

"Once I'm logged onto my patient list, I'm free to view all my prescription files. I'll be prepared with those I think could have been likely targets."

"How soon can you do it?" Tommy Lee asked.

Susan studied a few notes she'd scribbled on the back of the billing pages. "Doug doesn't work in the pharmacy till after he closes his drugstore this evening. The current shift changes at three and I wouldn't want to return before then. If I'm down there twice, someone will remember."

Tommy Lee glanced at his bare wrist, expecting to see his watch. He swore under his breath. "Better be there between four and five. I don't want you crossing paths with Doug."

"And if Susan finds he's falsified her prescriptions?" I asked.

"Then we'll confront Doug with the evidence. By then, I hope to have word from Central Prison about any connection between Delbert and Chip. Be nice if everything comes back wrapped in a neat package."

I walked over to the monitor. "Better check his vitals. Tommy Lee's delusional."

He grinned. "I can always hope, can't I?"

"Neat package or not, promise me you won't interrogate Doug Larson till I'm here. It's my case too."

Tommy Lee gave me a mock salute. "And where are you going to be?"

"At my other job. Preparing a funeral service. For a dead cat."

My most difficult task of the day turned out to be convincing Mom she didn't need to be at the Cosgroves' visitation. In her heart, Mom knew she needed to stay with Dad, but in her mind, she didn't want to abandon Uncle Wayne, Fletcher, and me. In my heart, I also knew Mom needed to stay with Dad, and in my mind, I didn't want her anywhere near the Fluffy scam we were pulling. "Fluffygate" would be more than she could handle. I prevailed by convincing her I would be too worried about Dad to give the visitation the proper attention unless she stayed. When I added I'd ask Reverend Pace to come to Dad's room, even though the preacher had been up all night, Mom relented.

I found Uncle Wayne and Fletcher in the Slumber Room. Doris Grimsby from Grimsby's House of Beauty, a name more suited for a Stephen King novel, bent over the casket with her blow dryer zooming in and out like a pesky mosquito. While Doris made final touchups on her client, Wayne and Fletcher arranged the flowers that had arrived.

"Everything okay?" I asked.

Uncle Wayne winked and jerked his thumb toward Fletcher. "This kid's a genius."

Fletcher set down a vase of black-eyed Susans on one of the floral pedestals. "Not really. Wayne found a miniature urn sample that's perfect. We shaved down a cork fishing bobber to seal it."

"And you missed some delicious hotdogs at lunch," Wayne said. "The charcoal burnt to a fine ash."

I nodded toward Doris and put my finger to my lips.

"Oh, she can't hear nothing with that hairdryer going," Wayne said.

Doris wheeled around and held the blower level like a ray gun. "You're the one deaf as a stump. I can hear just fine." Doris turned to me. "Don't worry, Barry. Some people might be offended by talk of food in the presence of the deceased, but I know life has to go on—complete with hotdogs and fishing."

"Thank you, Doris."

She glared at Wayne. Wayne retreated with the mumbled excuse of needing something from the supply room and took Fletcher with him.

Doris stepped back from the casket. "Take a look."

Mildred Cosgrove wore a lavender print dress too heavy for June, but appropriate for the conservative tastes of those who'd be coming to pay respects to an elderly lady. Reading glasses hung from a chain draped around her neck and all she needed was a ruler in her right hand to fit the mental image that had been imprinted in the mind of each of her former students. I felt a sense of childhood loss and a twinge of guilt at the trick we were playing on her family. If God allowed paddling in heaven, I was going to be in for it.

Doris brushed against me. "Well, do you think it's too blue?"

Too blue for what? I wondered. The ocean? The painted face of a Duke fan? Suede shoes? Blue isn't a word that should be used in the same sentence with hair. "Nicely complements the lavender."

Doris bubbled. "I thought so too. Wayne showed me the dress while we were working in the back. I made the tint richer. Mildred was always worried I'd go overboard."

"Just right," I lied. Just right for Bozo the Clown.

Doris made one more pass with the blow dryer in case a strand had gone untortured.

"Are you coming to the visitation?" I asked.

Doris wrapped the cord around her dryer. "Oh, yes, an artist must always face her critics."

I helped Rembrandt carry her tools out to her station wagon and gave a wave as she drove back to the House of Beauty. Four-thirty. Julius and Dot would be here at six. Plenty of time to be finished. I wondered if Susan was doing as well in her race against Doug Larson's arrival.

Uncle Wayne met me at the front door. "Doris gone?"

"Yes."

"She suspect anything?"

"No. She was too anxious to show off Mildred's hair."

"Best thing for Mildred's hair right now would be a sombrero." Wayne shouted back into the house. "Coast is clear!" He put a bony hand on my shoulder. "Wait a second."

At least half a minute passed before Fletcher called, "Okay."

I followed my uncle to the Slumber Room. Fletcher stood at the foot of Mildred's casket. He had lowered the bottom half of the split lid. On the flattened crest sat a small urn and a gold-framed eight by ten photograph. Fluffy stared out from a ring of black-eyed Susans. I looked from the picture to the vase of flowers and realized Clayton and Clayton had become a feline portrait studio.

"How'd you get her to sit still?"

"Hotdogs," Wayne said. "I'd hold a chunk above Fletcher's camera and he'd snap the shutter."

"You guys are dangerous together."

Wayne pointed at the frame. "Mildred wanted to be buried with her Fluffy and now she will be. That was Fletcher's idea."

"Where's Fluffy?" I asked.

"Up in the bathroom," Wayne said. "She's got a saucer of milk and a whole pack of hotdogs. That's one lucky cat."

"What about Mulray at Daleview Manor?" I asked Fletcher.

"I haven't asked him yet. The answering machine says the rooms are all rented and Mulray won't be back till six."

"I don't want that cat in the house when Julius and Dot get here."

"I'll take care of it," Fletcher said. "Check out the urn."

I picked up the four-inch-high plastic replica some supplier had sent as a sample. A fresh coat of brass spray paint sealed the cork stopper in place. A few smudges of ash darkened the rim. I tilted the urn toward Fletcher. "For effect?"

He shrugged. "We want them to draw the right conclusion, don't we?"

Very clever. I would have enjoyed the ruse more if I didn't know Fletcher was under investigation for cleverness that might have led to murder. A light went off in my head. "Damn it."

"We can clean the ashes off," Uncle Wayne said.

I realized I'd spoken out loud. "No. This is great. I left something at the hospital. I need to call."

I walked to my office, closed the door, and collected my thoughts. Fletcher had been in Crystal Hodges' hospital room when she died. That fact was one of the reasons he was a suspect. Now Doug Larson was a prime suspect. We knew he had enough pharmaceutical knowledge to kill Lincoln with anything from air to insulin. But we'd neglected to think about his connection to Crystal. What if Crystal had been murdered? Doug Larson didn't even need to be in the room. He could have learned about Crystal's progress from any nurse at the hospital and when it looked like she might recover, tampered with the medication being sent to her room.

The intensive care nurse could have hooked up any poison to Crystal's IV, and unless a toxicology report was ordered, no one would ever know. Given her injuries, the prospect of dying had been a statistical reality—a tragic, but not unexpected outcome. I wanted to know if Doug Larson had been anywhere near Crystal's medications.

Susan didn't answer her cell phone. I left a message for her to call. Then I dialed the hospital switchboard and asked for the pharmacy. Maybe Susan had turned her cell phone off while in the bowels of the hospital complex or was shielded from a signal.

"Pharmacy. Larson speaking."

I slammed down the receiver and looked at the desk clock. Four-forty-five. Doug Larson had come to the hospital over an hour ahead of when we'd expected him.

Susan called ten minutes later. "I couldn't talk. Larson came in the pharmacy as my cell was ringing."

"I know. Did he believe your story?"

"I heard his voice and slipped out another door. I had to leave the computer logging out so unless he walked straight to that terminal, we should be home free. Why were you calling?"

"I wanted you to see if there was any way Doug could have laced the medications that went to Crystal Hodges."

Susan took a sharp breath. "You think he murdered Crystal?"

"If we think he murdered Lincoln, then why not Crystal? At that point he was trying to protect Lincoln's identity. When we found Lincoln anyway, Doug had to take him out."

"I can't go back to the pharmacy now," Susan said. "We'll have to check after he leaves tonight."

"Did you have any luck with your prescriptions?"

"Yes. Some of my surgical patients had been prescribed unauthorized painkillers. I didn't have time to plot them against Doug's work schedule, but I couldn't find any irregularities beyond six months ago."

"Why's that important?"

"Because six months ago Doug started working at the hospital."

"Good job, Nancy Drew. If you ever get tired of cutting people up, you'll make a hell of a detective. Tell Tommy Lee what you learned. I'll be there as soon as I can leave the Cosgroves."

At ten till six, Julius, his wife Nora, and daughter Dot arrived to preview Mildred. I guided them from the front door through the foyer to the Slumber Room. Fletcher had started a CD of soft piano hymns. Wayne had dimmed the lights except for the far end where the casket rested. Julius held his wife's hand and I gently took Dot's arm as her pace slowed. As we walked through the arched doorway, Julius gasped and Dot started crying. The photograph and urn gleamed in the spotlights.

Julius stopped, mesmerized by the sight. "It's, it's—"

"Silly," his wife muttered.

"—beautiful," Julius whispered. "It's perfect." He broke free of his wife and hurried to the casket with Dot right behind him.

Nora looked at me and shook her head. "How much did this nonsense cost?"

I gave her my best funeral director smile. "Nothing. Your mother-in-law was my teacher."

Nora seemed to calculate how much she thought the nonsense could have cost them, and then returned my smile.

Julius and Dot were so engrossed in examining the photograph and urn that Mildred Cosgrove could have been dressed in a burlap sack. Wayne and Fletcher stood at either end of the casket exchanging sly glances.

Nora came up beside me and peered into the casket. "Doris finally got her way. My mother-in-law looks like a grape popsicle."

By seven-thirty, the Slumber Room was filled with visitors and a line stretched out the front door. People reminisced over forty years of first grade adventures in Mrs. Cosgrove's class. The photo of Fluffy drew compliments while only Julius, Nora, and Dot knew about the urn discreetly tucked under the casket cushions, and only Wayne, Fletcher, and I knew Fluffy had used one of her nine lives.

The long day of sunlight and the logjam of mourners raised the temperature in the funeral home above the cooling capacity of our old central air conditioning system. A little after eight, I left Fletcher with the "Guests Who Called" signature book and Wayne in charge of moving folks through the receiving line as fast as possible. Rather than swim upstream, I ducked out the rear and down the hall to the work rooms. The evening air was now cooler and I wanted to open the back loading door to create cross-ventilation.

The sun had set behind the high ridges and thrown the valley into murky shadows. As I propped open the outside door, I saw a blur of motion in the parking area where we keep the hearses and our personal cars.

An ear-piercing shriek drowned the sound of crickets and katydids. Before I could move, a man yelled in pain and stumbled from the far side of Fletcher's Honda. His arms flailed around his face and he spun like a drunken ballerina. Then he hurled something toward me. A white streak flew through the floodlights, landed on the concrete driveway, and accelerated like a torpedo aiming to blow me out of the water.

Fluffy shot between my legs and into the funeral home. The bloody face of Reece Hutchins registered for a split-second by Fletcher's car before I whirled around and chased after the cremated cat. I burst into the Slumber Room as a blood-chilling scream hit me with the force of a sonic boom. Dot Cramer toppled backwards in a dead faint. Julius fell to his knees calling for "Sweet Jesus." I looked at the casket, fully expecting Mildred Cosgrove to sit up, blue hair and all. If Dot's scream didn't wake the dead, nothing would.

Beside her picture, back arched and claws red with Reece's blood, Fluffy reigned supreme.

Chapter Seventeen

"What right did you have to go through my car?" Fletcher's face burned crimson and the vein on his forehead threatened to explode.

"I'm a law officer. I heard something suspicious." Reece sat on the sofa parlor while Uncle Wayne dabbed Neosporin into the red streaks Fluffy had gouged into his cheeks and across the bridge of his nose.

Fletcher turned to me, his eyes flashing. "You went out there. Did you hear anything?"

I'd had time to piece together what had happened. Reece had cooked his own goose. I wasn't going to rescue him. "No. Just Fluffy's screech as Reece grabbed her out of the box."

Uncle Wayne backed away as Fletcher bent over Reece till their noses nearly touched. "That cat had food, water, and a towel to sleep on. I'd slipped out twice to check on her. You just broke into my car, didn't you?"

"It wasn't locked."

"It's a damn convertible. Lock it and somebody cuts in through the top." Fletcher wasn't backing down. For a college student, he showed no fear of Reece or the badge he wore. "If we get sued by the Cosgroves for what happened tonight, you're going to pay the price if I have to hire the lawyers myself."

The Cosgrove visitation had dispersed faster than a riot shot full of teargas. Nora had told Julius and a revived Dot to keep their mouths shut and let people believe the story Fletcher had concocted. Fluffy was his cat and happened to look like Mildred's beloved. But Reece didn't know that.

"Hire lawyers? Got a lot of money for a college student," Reece said. "I priced that car at over thirty grand."

Jesus. Hand Reece a can of gasoline and he'll throw it on a fire. A fire he's in the middle of. I placed my hand on Fletcher's shoulder and nudged him back. "It's not a crime to have an expensive car, Reece."

"Where'd he get all that money?"

Fletcher's muscles stiffened under my fingers. "That's my business. I'm going to talk to the sheriff about you minding your own business."

Reece paled. He knew Tommy Lee would probably come down to the funeral home, dragging his IV pole behind him, and beat him with it. "You are my business." He folded his arms across his chest as if that closed the matter.

Fletcher backed away from me. "What's he talking about?"

"Look," I said. "It wasn't my idea, but certain things had to be checked out."

"Certain things?"

I felt like I was on a high wire and Reece had just pulled the net out from under me. His bumbling had put me in an awkward position between Fletcher and the case I was trying to protect. "Certain information has leaked. Someone knew we were onto Artie Lincoln. That's the only motive we know for his murder."

Fletcher threw up his hands. "So I'm a suspect?"

"You're one of the people who knew Artie Lincoln's identity. We're checking everyone out."

"And Lincoln died at my apartment complex. And Crystal Hodges died while I was in her hospital room." Fletcher glared at Reece. "And the big clue—I drive a nice car." He spun around, turning his back on all of us, and stormed out the front door.

Uncle Wayne broke the silence. "Reece, you were born stupid and you've been losing ground ever since."

Tommy Lee clenched his teeth. I'd learned that when he was really mad, he didn't say anything. I sat by his hospital bed and hoped he was far enough away from his surgery that his blood pressure wouldn't blow out his stitches. He'd listened to my account of Reece's screw-up and with each sentence his jaws tightened. Now I waited for his anger to vent somehow. I just didn't want to be in its way.

Tommy Lee did something I never expected. He laughed, and then he cried because laughing still hurt. "Oh, God, why couldn't I have been there?"

"Believe me, you wouldn't have found it funny at the time."

"The hell I wouldn't have. I'd loved to have seen Reece sticking his face in that box like he'd discovered the crown jewels." He started laughing again. "Then the cat's on Reece like ugly on a hog."

My grandmother's favorite expression had never been used more appropriately.

"Tell me, could Reece even see where he was going?" Tommy Lee asked.

I replayed the scene in my mind but this time from Tommy Lee's perspective. "No. It was like he was dancing with a bag over his head. Yelping and hollering. The white cat made him look like Santa Claus break-dancing."

Tommy Lee took a deep breath and sighed with satisfaction. "Serves Reece right. And it gives me a way to keep him in line with one word."

"What's that?"

Tommy Lee grinned. "Meow."

"He put me in a hell of a mess with Fletcher."

"Don't worry. If the kid's got any sense, he'll understand. If he's guilty and makes a break for it, then we'll know. My bet's that he was more upset with the Fluffy debacle than Reece searching his car."

"And if he doesn't bolt, then you think he's innocent?"

"No. Fletcher could be guilty and damn smart. He'll stay put as long as we don't have any real evidence." Tommy Lee looked at the wall clock. Nearly ten. "I'd hoped you'd be here sooner, but I understand the delay." He picked up a folder on the table beside him. "Here's what Susan brought me. She highlighted the prescriptions in question."

I flipped through the pages. None of the patient dates were any earlier than December of the previous year. "Did Susan tell you she didn't find any discrepancies before six months ago?"

"Yes. And that Doug didn't start working at the hospital till then."

"Yeah." I closed the folder. "Pretty damning, I'd say."

"Oh, he's tied to forged prescriptions all right. Now we need to know why."

The answer to that question seemed obvious. "How about a thousand percent profit."

"There's that, but then there's your statement that you'd sooner suspect Nick Foster of fleecing his patients."

"That's before I saw these printouts."

"Yeah. The evidence. But not necessarily the evidence of the motive." Tommy Lee kicked the bed sheet free from his legs. "I'm hot. Let's take a walk down the hall. I need some air and I'm supposed to get some exercise." He glanced at the folder in my hand. "Bring that with you."

The halls were quiet at this time of night. Tommy Lee clutched his IV pole with one hand and took slow, deliberate steps.

When we'd gone a few yards outside his door, he asked, "Is there a waiting room on this floor?"

"Down near the intensive care wing."

"Good. I might want to rest a few minutes before we head back." Tommy Lee gave a light cough.

"Don't overdo it."

"I'm all right. I heard back from the warden at Central Prison this afternoon."

"Did Chip and Delbert Larson know each other?"

"No. Turns out Chip did his time in Tennessee."

I wasn't surprised. Linking Chip, Delbert, and Doug was too much to hope for. "I'm still going to confront Doug about these prescriptions."

"It's your case, but maybe it would be better if I talked to Doug."

"Why?"

"Two reasons. One, I've known Doug all his life. Two, I want to talk to him about Delbert as well as the prescriptions."

"Delbert? You think Delbert's running this from his jail cell?"

"Not unless he could do it from the hospital infirmary." Tommy Lee stopped walking and caught his breath. "About six months ago, Delbert was beaten to within an inch of his life in the yard. The warden said Delbert had been a model prisoner, kept his nose clean, and stayed clear of the gangs. Somebody wanted him hurt real bad and knew what they were doing. Delbert won't identify his attackers."

"Six months ago?"

"I thought you'd like that." Tommy Lee started walking. "I'm thinking somebody sent Doug Larson a message, and now I've got to be a hard-assed son of a bitch and squeeze that message out of him."

"Maybe we've got things backwards. Maybe Lincoln was running Doug."

"Lincoln had to have long arms to reach inside Central Prison. Doug took quite a gamble if he killed Lincoln."

"What do you think?"

"I think our little town is playing in the big leagues, and you and I might be in over our heads."

I couldn't believe my ears. "You want to turn the case over to the feds?"

Tommy Lee stopped again. "You ever been in whitewater?"

"I've gone rafting on the Nantahala and Chattooga."

"The guides pointed out the hydraulics, right?"

"Yeah." Hydraulics are pools at the base of falls where the tumbling current creates a trap, the most dangerous spot on a river. The water churns in on itself like a giant washing machine and can catch someone in the powerful turbulence, keeping them submerged for days.

"So when you're in over your head in a hydraulic, there's only one way to break free," Tommy Lee said. "You have to dive deeper where the force of the water is weakest and hope to God it spits you out. We're in over our heads and we're going to have to dive deeper. I think Doug Larson's been in a hydraulic for six months and he's going to drown if he doesn't dive with us."

Six months ago, Delbert Larson was nearly beaten to death and Doug Larson began writing forged prescriptions. A bell went off in my head. Six months ago I got a call from the Cincinnati College of Mortuary Science that a student had requested placement in Gainesboro. I kept that thought to myself.

Tommy Lee pushed open the door to the intensive care waiting room. "Good. It's empty. I want to talk to Doug in here where I don't look so feeble."

"What if we're interrupted?"

"See if you can find a cleaning crew and borrow one of those signs they put outside the restrooms."

I turned to go.

"Wait. I want you to call Doug first. It'll take him a while to get up here. Tell him you'd like to talk in person about your father's condition. About what's being prescribed. I want to catch him off-guard."

I used the phone in the waiting room and got Doug's assurance he'd be up in about fifteen minutes. He sounded grateful to help.

With the "Closed for Cleaning" sign positioned by the door, I waited in the hall. Within five minutes, the elevator doors at the far end opened and Doug emerged. He wore a white lab coat with his hospital ID on the lapel. As he came closer, I could see the weariness behind his smile.

"Sorry to hear about your father." Doug noticed the cleaning sign. "Do you want to talk in his room?"

"No. My mom's with him. The cleaning crew's gone." I opened the door for him. "I asked them to leave the sign so we wouldn't be disturbed."

Doug took two steps into the waiting room and froze. Tommy Lee sat in one of the small upholstered chairs he had dragged to the center of the room. His IV pole towered over him like a royal scepter. In his lap lay the folder with Susan's prescription records. Directly in front of him was a second chair.

Tommy Lee pointed to the vacant chair. "Take a seat, Doug."

Doug glanced back at me. His weariness had been replaced with panic. "What's going on?"

"That's what we aim to find out," Tommy Lee said. "No one knows you're here. I hope to keep it that way."

Doug walked like a zombie to the chair and sat down. "There must be some mistake," he murmured.

Tommy Lee nodded for me to stay by the door. I wished I could see Doug's face but I realized Tommy Lee had created extra psychological pressure by keeping me out of Doug's line of vision.

"You're right, Doug. I think there's been a big mistake. Going back six months and ending with a murder."

"Murder?" Doug sounded genuinely shocked.

Tommy Lee calmly answered the question with one of his own. "Have you heard from Delbert lately?"

Doug's shoulders shook and he gripped the arms of his chair. "Has something happened to my son?"

"Yes. I asked the warden at Central Prison to place Delbert in protective custody away from the other inmates. I was sorry to learn about his—" Tommy Lee feigned a difficult word choice "—his unfortunate incident. But I don't know how long the warden can extend that little favor for me."

"What do you want?" Doug's voice had gone dry as withered grass.

"I want to know who threatened you."

Doug forced a laugh. "I don't know what you're talking about."

Tommy Lee leaned forward. "We've known each other a long time. Your dad used to slip us free cokes from the soda fountain when we were kids. The Doug Larson I grew up with isn't a criminal. Somebody changed that." Tommy Lee picked up the folder. "Since Delbert was attacked, you've been falsifying prescriptions through the hospital pharmacy. I suspect you've been doing the same thing through your drugstore. One call to the licensing board will have them going through your records. That will be the least of your worries. I'll press for a murder charge. Someone's got to be held accountable."

Doug twisted in his seat to look at me. The sheen of perspiration glowed on his forehead. "I never harmed that girl. I swear."

The back of my neck tingled. Tommy Lee hadn't mentioned Crystal Hodges. He'd been referring to Artie Lincoln's death.

"I'm offering you a way out," Tommy Lee said. "Take it."

"I can't." Doug buried his face in his hands.

"Look at me," Tommy Lee said. "I know what you're up against. Are they from Florida? Raleigh? Detroit? New York? You've got to help me before I can help you."

Doug lifted his head. "I don't want your help. I know what I'm doing."

Tommy Lee struggled out of the chair. "Bullshit!" He leaned on the IV pole for support. "You're lying. You know it. I know it. Barry knows it."

Doug stood up and held out his hands. "Then arrest me."

Tommy Lee gave him an icy smile. "No. I've got a better idea." He motioned me to step away from the door. "I'm going to let you walk out of here. But not back to the hospital pharmacy. You've worked your last shift there. Tell them you're not feeling well and have to go home."

Doug stared at Tommy Lee with a defiant expression.

"I'm giving you till eight o'clock tomorrow morning to come to your senses and tell us the whole story. If you don't, then I'm going to arrest you and charge you with drug trafficking."

The faintest outline of a smile appeared on Doug's face.

"And as soon as I do," Tommy Lee continued, "I'm filing a report naming you not only as a co-conspirator but as a cooperating witness in our investigation. I'm sending the report to the police at Delray Beach where we first tracked Artie Lincoln. They'll pass it along to the DEA where your name will be added to their witness list. Next, I'm calling Central Prison and instructing them to return Delbert to the general inmate population."

"You don't know what you're doing." Doug's voice was almost a wail.

Tommy Lee's one eye stared at Doug without blinking. "We both know exactly what I'm doing. Now get out of here."

Doug seemed to shrivel under Tommy Lee's gaze. He turned and walked past me, his breath coming in slow sobs.

I closed the door behind him. Tommy Lee collapsed in his chair.

"I need to get you back to bed."

He didn't argue. "All right. Give me a moment." He raised his hand to his forehead. His fingers trembled.

"You heard the reference to Crystal," I said.

"Yeah. He thinks she was murdered. He wouldn't break even though he's terrified."

"Are you going to do what you said?"

Tommy Lee shook his head. "How heartless do you think I am? But I want Reece to organize a tail on him and I'll get Judge Wood to issue a search warrant for his house and business."

"Is that why you didn't want much about Doug in my report to Roy Spring? You were afraid it would leak?"

"I don't like losing control of a case."

Maybe, I thought. And maybe Tommy Lee had already made the connection I was making. We were looking at everyone who could have marked Artie Lincoln for execution because they knew we were closing in on him. Lieutenant Roy Spring of the Delray Police had that information, and I had only his word that he'd never heard of Lincoln. Had he really not known about the pending bust by the DEA? Could Spring be dirty? Could that be why Artie Lincoln came north with a stolen credit card?

We were tumbling in turbulent waters all right. But how could we dive deeper when we didn't know which way was up and which way was down?

Chapter Eighteen

Mom yanked the lever on the side of the recliner and brought the chair upright. Light blue yarn and someone's half-knitted Christmas present bounced in her lap. "How'd the visitation go?"

I nudged foam from the nozzle of the antiseptic can mounted just inside Dad's hospital room and pretended to concentrate on cleansing my hands. I didn't want to lie to Mom's face. "Fine. A lot of people asked about Dad and send you their love."

"That's kind. It's almost eleven. They must have hung around."

I walked to the far side of the bed where I could be closer to Dad. "We had a little excitement. I left the back door open and a cat got in."

"A cat?"

"Yeah. It startled Dot since it looked like one Mildred used to have. You know how people read omens into the slightest things. Fletcher shooed it out."

"I hope it doesn't start hanging around the funeral home."

"How's Dad?" I laid my palm on his forehead. His skin felt warm.

"Fever's back up a little. The doctor said that's not necessarily bad if his body's helping to fight the infection."

Or the fever's back up because the antibiotics aren't working. I knew Mom was well aware of that possibility. "You've had a long day. I'm going to run you home, and then I'll spend the night here."

"I'm fine. You've got your pets to look after and the Cosgrove funeral in the morning."

"Freddy and Uncle Wayne can handle the service. Everything's up at Crab Apple Valley Baptist." I stepped back from the bed and leaned against the wall. "Democrat and George have plenty of water and food, and I've got some things to do with Tommy Lee." I saved my strongest argument for last. "I'm sure Freddy and Wayne would appreciate a hot breakfast."

I saw Mom waver as her pride in her culinary skills took over. "Okay. But call me after the doctors have been through." She thought for a second. "You didn't mention Fletcher. Is he off?"

Is he off? I hadn't faced the question of Fletcher yet. Maybe he was off for good. "Fletcher worked through last weekend. I thought he deserved a break."

Mom grabbed her knitting basket from the floor beside her and packed away a skein of yarn and her needles. "Then he'll probably be up here with Cindy. Helen said he's usually in once a day. I think he's sweet on her." Mom got to her feet. "We'd better go so you can get back."

It was a little before midnight when I walked Mom into the funeral home to make sure everything was all right. Uncle Wayne and Freddy would be in around seven so I hoped she'd get a good six hours of sleep. I decided I could use a change of clothes for the morning and raided the closet in the guest room, where I keep a couple of spare outfits.

I was on my way to the car when my cell phone rang. I flipped it open and recognized Fletcher's number. "Hi. You okay?"

"No. I'm embarrassed." Fletcher also sounded nervous. He cleared his throat. "Sorry to call so late but I couldn't go to sleep without apologizing."

I kept walking to my car, trying to hold my shirt and pants hangers high with one hand. "No apology needed."

"I shouldn't have lost my temper and I shouldn't have walked out. I'll understand if you want to end the internship."

"You know what Tommy Lee did when I told him?"

"I guess he got mad."

I looked for a relatively clean spot on the jeep's hood and laid my clothes across it. "He laughed. Laughed till he cried. So this is not a big deal."

"You're saying this happens all the time?"

I opened the jeep door and watched the vibration slide the hangers off the fender and onto the dusty driveway. I gave up and sat down in the back seat. "No. You witnessed a first for Clayton and Clayton, but you've now been initiated into membership in the funeral directors' disaster club. You got off easy. I once had the deceased's relative slug me."

The nervousness left Fletcher's voice. "I also understand why I'm under a cloud of suspicion. I just can't believe the murder happened at Daleview Manor."

"Whoever killed Lincoln knows a lot about us. Tommy Lee and I are working on that." The connection to Fletcher's apartment complex triggered a question. "Have you mentioned the investigation to anyone? Friends or family back in Detroit? Classmates?"

"No. The only one I've talked to about it was Cindy. She's got a vested interest in the case."

I wondered who Cindy had talked to. Most likely her mom, Helen, and if Helen knew our progress, she would make it the topic of conversation at her diner. Other than the barbershop, the Cardinal Café was Grand Central Station for Gainesboro gossip. "Given the circumstances, you'd better keep Cindy in the dark."

The phone went silent for a second. Then Fletcher blurted out, "Oh God, I hope I haven't put Cindy in danger."

"No. But be careful what you say and who you say it to."

"I will. And I'll be in tomorrow."

"Be here by seven, and you'll get Mom's breakfast. I guarantee it's worth getting up for."

I slept fitfully. Dad started moaning around two and the duty nurse had to increase the flow of his morphine drip. Someone seemed to come in every half hour, which made me feel good about the care, but made sleep impossible. Sometime around four-thirty, I dozed off and didn't wake up till Susan and Dr. Madison came in at seven-fifteen.

"How's our patient?" Dr. Madison asked.

I rubbed my eyes and got out of the recliner. "He was in pain last night."

"I'm afraid that's to be expected." The pulmonary specialist ran his stethoscope over Dad's chest and frowned. "Fluid's coming back."

"The pneumonia?" I asked.

"Not necessarily. The IV keeps him hydrated. Could be just too much liquid in his system since he's getting no exercise and his kidney function has slowed." Dr. Madison turned to Susan. "I suggest we increase his furosemide." He smiled at me. "That's a diuretic that helps form urine and lowers the fluid level in his body. Let's give him another full day on the antibiotic before we start to worry. I'd hoped for more improvement, but at least his vital signs are stable."

Madison left and Susan wrote some notes on Dad's chart. "I'll get him on the heavier dose of furosemide right away. How did things go with Doug Larson?"

I told Susan about the previous night's confrontation, including Doug's unsolicited denial that he had anything to do with the death of Crystal Hodges.

"I guess that takes us back to square one," Susan said.

"We might have to have Crystal's body exhumed. I hate raising that issue with the family."

Susan clicked her ballpoint pen open and closed while she thought. "There's a chance you won't have to. Let me call the lab."

Susan asked for the supervisor and gave Crystal's name and approximate time of death. She cupped her hand over the mouthpiece. "I should have thought of this earlier. Patient lab samples aren't automatically discarded in case there's a technical problem with the readings or we need a new benchmark." She brought the phone back to her lips. "Yes. That's great. I'll bring you the screening instructions."

"They have something?" I asked.

"Oh yeah. The lab has a blood draw from Crystal. The nurse took it about fifteen minutes before Crystal died. In the confusion, the sample went to the lab without instructions."

"Is the sample still good?"

"Better than exhuming a body that had embalming fluid pumped through it. The results will depend upon what agent might have been used to kill her. But, yes, isolated from decay, the sample should reveal traces of a number of substances."

I remembered Doc Clark's opinion of Lincoln. "What if Crystal had been injected with air?"

"Then I'm afraid nothing short of an exhumation could prove anything. But that would have been much more dangerous to pull off. Contaminate the IV bag and you could be miles away rather than plunging an empty syringe while standing by her bedside where anyone could walk in and see you."

"How fast can the lab turn the tests around?"

"I'm going down there now. This is their busiest time since most surgeries occur in the morning. I hope we'll have a preliminary reading by this evening. If we can't find anything, Tommy Lee should send the sample to the state toxicology lab, but then you're looking at thirty days before you'll hear anything."

"More people could be dead by then."

Susan headed out the door. "Keep your fingers crossed we find something."

I called Mom and relayed Madison's report. She said the boys were eating breakfast and Fletcher had even come in on his day off. I changed clothes and told the duty nurse I was heading down to Tommy Lee's room. I found him chasing some rubbery scrambled eggs around his plate with a fork.

"Are you the worse for wear after last night's interrogation?" I asked.

"Me? You look like you slept in your clothes."

"I did. But these aren't them."

"I'm the worse for wear from starving to death. Patsy's bringing me some Krispy Kreme doughnuts to counteract this so-called health food."

"Maybe I've got some news to cheer you up." I pulled the chair away from the computer station and sat down. "Susan found a blood sample from Crystal taken shortly before she died. We should have results this evening."

"If Doug prepped her last IV infusion, we'll really have some leverage on him. Then I'll have Reece pick him up and we'll charge him."

"Any word from Doug?"

"No. Reece called at seven to say Doug didn't go anywhere last night and got to the drugstore before six this morning. Wakefield's on surveillance."

"What if Doug's in there shredding his records?"

Tommy Lee gave up on breakfast and set the plate to the side. "So what? We've got the hospital's pharmacy records and he'll still have to account for the distribution of controlled substances. That's why he needed the falsified prescriptions in the first place."

I felt my face burn. I must be tired. That was an obvious point and I should have thought of it.

"Of course, if you mean other records, then you could be right. Doug could have incriminating correspondence or emails he's planning to purge. That's why we've got the search warrant." Tommy Lee looked at the hospital wall clock. "It's ten till eight. Hand me my phone. I've got it charging."

"You want this one?" I grabbed the room phone with the long extension.

"No. I've got Wakefield's cell programmed. I'm telling him to go ahead and pick Doug up."

"I want to give it one more try. See what Doug's doing and tell him I've convinced you to hold off announcing he's a cooperating witness until this afternoon. Maybe he'll have second thoughts."

"You mean play good cop, bad cop?"

"Who said play? We're just being ourselves."

Tommy Lee tossed me his phone. "Okay. It's your case. Glad one of us is thinking. But if there's any sign Doug's destroying evidence, or bolting, bring him in. I can hold him on probable cause until we get Crystal's lab tests. Then we'll see how brave he is."

When I got to Main Street, I spoke to Wakefield as he sat in an unmarked car at the corner. Tommy Lee had had Reece roust Judge Wood out of bed at one in the morning to issue a search warrant. Wakefield gave me the warrant and I told him to watch the front. If Doug came out alone, Wakefield had orders to pick him up.

I parked the jeep in the alley between Larson's Discount Drugs and a trendy new coffee and antique emporium. Nobody opened a plain store anymore. I went to Larson's back loading dock and pounded on the door.

After a few minutes of continuous thumping, Doug yelled from the other side. "We're closed. Come back at ten."

"It's Barry Clayton. We need to talk and we need to talk now."

"I've done all the talking I'm going to."

"I've got a search warrant, Doug, and if you make me serve it, you'll have thrown away your last chance. I've convinced Tommy Lee not to brand you as a cooperating witness, at least for now. I think we can work this out, but you've got to open the door immediately."

I could hear him breathing on the other side. If he left, I'd call Wakefield to break in the front.

Metal scraped against metal as an inside bolt withdrew. With a jerk, the double-wide sliding door opened. Doug wore the clothes he'd had on at the hospital. His eyes were red and puffy. He made me look like I'd stepped out of *GQ*.

"All right, Barry. Five minutes."

I pushed past him without agreeing to his timeframe.

"Barry. Wait."

I ran straight to the back of the pharmacy where Doug kept the safe. The door was open, but instead of pills, the floor was covered with bank envelopes. An open attaché case lay beside the safe. I couldn't tell whether the envelopes had gone in or were coming out.

"Stop it!" Doug tried to push me away, but I tore open the unsealed flap of one of the envelopes and pulled out a handful of checks. The account name read D & D Wholesalers.

"What's D & D? Delbert and Doug? Is this where you stash your loot?"

Doug's entire body shook. His voice constricted into a harsh whisper. "I never took one penny."

"I believe you. I think this is the account they use to funnel money to you so you can buy the drugs and then they turn them out on the street. They threatened to kill Delbert, didn't they? We can stop them."

"You think this is all about drugs? You've got no idea who or what you're dealing with. No one can stop them. They know everything the police are doing. Hell, they could own the police for all I know."

"They don't own Tommy Lee or me and they don't know what we're doing or who we're talking to."

Tears streaked down Doug's cheeks. "They do and you don't even know it. They already knew you suspected me." His eyes went wide. "No one can stop them from killing my son but me." He ran to the cash register at the pharmacy counter.

Too late I understood what a man who feared being robbed would keep there. Doug yanked open a drawer and spun around. He held a pistol level with my chest. My thirty-eight rested on my hip. It might as well have been on the other side of the moon.

"Take it easy, Doug. I know you haven't killed anyone." I let the bank checks flutter to the floor. "Don't make a terrible mistake. Deputy Wakefield's right outside."

The tremor in his hand ceased and the gun went rock solid. I shifted my gaze to Doug's face and saw the hard edge of his resolve.

"I couldn't kill you, Barry. And now they'll have no reason to kill Delbert."

"No!"

The deafening shot smothered my cry.

Chapter Nineteen

My ears rang as the room wavered in and out of focus. I don't know how long I must have stood there, probably only a few seconds, but time stopped. Doug had disappeared. In his place, a haze hung in the air. The acrid smell of gunpowder snapped me back to my senses.

I heard pounding and the shattering of glass.

"Barry!" Wakefield crashed through the front door, gun drawn. He moved quickly to the protection of the shelves, uncertain what he was facing.

Then I saw Doug lying at my feet, blood oozing from his head.

"Wakefield! Call an ambulance." I dropped beside Doug, frantically feeling the side of his neck for a pulse. I swore at him. "Damn it, you can't die on me!" My fingers dipped into his warm blood as I kept probing for any sign of life.

I felt a hand on my shoulder. I looked up and saw Wakefield. He seemed oblivious to Doug. He stared at me.

"Are you all right?" he asked.

Was I? A chill rose from the pit of my stomach. How can I be all right when I'd just driven a man to shoot himself?

Wakefield grabbed my upper arm and lifted. I got to my feet.

"Maybe you can find a pulse," I told him.

Wakefield holstered his pistol and radioed for an ambulance. Then he checked Doug again. "He's gone, Barry."

I took a couple of deep breaths, trying to clear my head. I'd seen suicides before when I'd worked as a patrolman in Charlotte, but never someone I knew. Never someone who killed himself right in front of me.

"I should have seen it coming. I should have stopped him."

Wakefield shook his head. "Doug had a gun. He could have just as easily shot you."

But Doug had told me he couldn't kill me. As Doug pulled the gun back, I should have wrestled it from his hand. I could have saved his life.

Wakefield walked to the front and peered out the window. "There was no one on the street but me. I think the shot went unnoticed." He turned and waited.

I realized he expected me to take charge of the scene. What happened here had been horrible, but I was a police officer and the situation demanded action. I felt a surge of energy as my adrenaline kicked in. "Call Reece and tell him to bring officers through the alley. Keep the closed sign in the front window and a deputy at the door. Release no information unless Tommy Lee or I authorize it." I pulled my phone from my belt. "I'm going to tell him."

I doubted Tommy Lee could reach his phone before I was routed to his voicemail, but he'd call back immediately.

Patsy picked up after the second ring.

"It's Barry," I said. "I need Tommy Lee."

She caught the urgency in my voice and handed her husband the phone.

"I'm eating my second doughnut."

"I botched it. Doug's dead. He shot himself."

The chewing in my ear abruptly stopped. "Damn. I pushed him too hard. I should have taken him into custody yesterday." Tommy Lee sighed. "Damn."

"I was the officer on the scene and I just watched him grab his gun and blow his brains out."

Neither of us spoke for a moment. What can you say when your best efforts have gone terribly wrong?

A bitter thought came to my mind. "I guess I wasn't the good cop after all."

"Somebody's going to pay. Somebody put Doug Larson in such a bind that he saw no other way out. Is Wakefield there?"

"Right beside me."

"Emphasize to Wakefield to clamp down on what happened. I'll call Reece and read him the riot act on how we want this handled. First report will be that Wakefield discovered a suicide and we're investigating. That's all. I don't want your name mentioned."

"Why?"

"I've got my reasons. Just get back here as soon as you can."

"But there's evidence."

"What evidence?"

"Checks. I think Doug was taking them somewhere. I saw one account and there are probably more. I accused Doug of using the accounts to funnel money. He didn't deny it."

"What else did he say?"

"That we didn't know what we were dealing with. That they owned the police. That they owned us and we didn't know it."

Tommy Lee took a few seconds to digest my words. "Tag anything else that seems suspicious. Bring one example of each bank account that you find. Have Wakefield take charge of the rest, but under no circumstances is he to say anything other than he discovered a suicide."

"What are you thinking?"

"I don't want Crystal Hodges or Doug Larson to have died in vain. Doug might have given us a way to flush out our enemies, but we'll only get one shot and we've got to be careful."

I felt a twinge of excitement cut through my despair. Maybe something good could come out of this tragedy. "I've got your back."

Tommy Lee chuckled in spite of the situation. "Fine. But I got shot in the front."

Reece arrived within fifteen minutes and took charge of securing the scene. He only nodded at me and told his deputies that I was following up a possible lead on the street dance shooting and as far as they were concerned, I wasn't there. Reece got a couple of curious stares from his colleagues because his face looked like a patchwork quilt of scratches. No one said anything, not even a meow.

I identified ten bank accounts from three different banks. I pulled a range of statements from the previous six months and noted the number of cancelled checks was small in comparison to wire deposits and withdrawals. None of the transactions were over $8,000.

I asked Wakefield to search Doug's body in case he'd hidden something on himself when he heard me pounding on the door. Wakefield pulled two wads of cash out of the pockets of Doug's pants.

"Explains why there was nothing but change in the register," Wakefield said.

"And no money in the safe. Doug was making a break for it, and somehow these bank statements were an insurance policy. Tag all the statements as evidence and I'll take them with me to show Tommy Lee."

"And the rest of the safe's contents?" Wakefield had found a few boxes of OxyContin in the rear I hadn't noticed at first.

"Take everything," I said. "Note the lot number on the pills. Maybe we can match them to an invoice or purchase order."

Wakefield pulled a pad and pen from his shirt pocket. "You know, it's really sad." He glanced down at Doug lying in a pool of blood. "The Larson family has been part of this community as long as I can remember, as long as my daddy can remember. To end up this way. Dead in your own store and by your own hand. Who could have seen this coming?"

I knew who should have seen it coming, but I kept that thought to myself.

Tommy Lee was chasing rubbery chicken around his plate with a fork.

"Your egg from this morning must have hatched." I walked across the room and set the pile of bank envelopes by the computer.

"This hospital must have an inexhaustible supply," Tommy Lee said.

Patsy raised her head from a magazine and gave me a sympathetic smile. "Tough morning, huh?"

"I've had better."

An unspoken cue ran between Tommy Lee and his wife. Patsy stood up and curled the magazine in her hand. "I'll leave you two to talk business. How's your Dad?"

"About the same. The doctor hopes the antibiotics will start making more headway today. I stopped in before coming here. Mom's sitting with him."

Mom had just sat down and begun knitting when I'd arrived. She'd given me the report that Mildred Cosgrove's funeral had gone without a hitch.

"I'll say hello to her if that's okay," Patsy said.

"She'd love the company."

Patsy closed the door, leaving Tommy Lee and me to talk in private.

I sat in a chair next to his bed. "I really screwed up big time."

Tommy Lee gave up on his chicken and pushed the plate aside. "What else could you have done?"

"A thousand things. For starters, I could have taken Wakefield in with me to watch Doug. I could have paid more attention to what Doug was doing. But no, I had to go in there like the cock of the walk, expecting Doug to fall at my feet and confess everything because I'm such a wonderful detective."

"And I should have invested in Microsoft when Bill Gates was just another geek. Hindsight's perfect, but it doesn't mean a damn thing to whatever's over and done. Especially in police work."

Tommy Lee's one eye fixed me with a hard stare. "You have to make too many split-second decisions based on too little information to try and predict human behavior. Yes, if you'd arrested Doug the second you walked in the store, he'd be alive. If I'd arrested him yesterday here at the hospital, he'd be alive.

We both made decisions based on information we had and did what we thought was best at the time. That's what a policeman does. Sometimes the decisions turn out to be wrong."

"In this case, dead wrong."

"That's right. And no amount of wishing or second-guessing is going to change that. We'll both have to live with it. But in the final analysis, Doug is dead because he got into a situation he couldn't see any way out of. We can sit here and feel sorry for him and ourselves till the cows come home, or we can concentrate on catching the scumbags who really killed him. Now let me see those checks."

I handed him the statements from May postmarked only a few days earlier.

Tommy Lee flipped through the pages slowly, and then examined the five checks that had been enclosed with the statement. "The checks are made out to pharmaceutical companies and signed by Doug."

"That's the story with all the envelopes. And deposits are either recorded as cash or wired in."

"Some transactions are wired out. Some of the numbers repeat."

I opened one of the envelopes and ran my finger down the lines. "I spotted funds going back and forth between the accounts."

"Always different banks I bet." Tommy Lee folded the sheets and replaced them.

"Why?"

"I think your first guess was accurate. Doug was buying drugs that could be laundered on the street. Cash is coming in and out in small enough amounts that those transactions stay beneath the radar."

"And the funds wired out?"

"They probably wind up in the accounts of individuals who don't want their names on a check. Then the bigger profits from the street sales go straight to the muscle behind the operation."

Tommy Lee's theory sounded right on the money. "And you've got a plan to uncover the muscle?" I asked.

"I already know who the muscle is, and you do too if you think about it. Organized crime."

"Here in Gainesboro?"

Tommy Lee sailed the bank envelope back to me like a Frisbee. "I told you we were in over our heads."

Hydraulic pools were one thing. Being thrown in a hydraulic while wearing concrete shoes was another. "Maybe we should give this case to the feds."

"We will. But Doug Larson was one of us. And Crystal Hodges lost her life trying to find justice for her brother. They were our people. Mountain people. And I want someone to learn a hard lesson. You don't come into these hills and screw us over without paying a price."

The old warrior may have been shot and hooked to an IV, but if it was Tommy Lee versus the Mob, I knew where to place my bet.

His mention of Doug reminded me. "Doug said something else right before he shot himself. 'They already knew you suspected me.' Nobody but us knew about Doug except for Susan and she wouldn't have told anyone."

Tommy Lee took a deep breath. "Nobody but us and the state of Florida."

"What?"

"We added Doug's name to the email you sent Roy Spring. We wanted to know if his name had come up in their investigation." Tommy Lee chewed on his lower lip. "Damn. Even if Spring's clean, he has to share his information with everybody from his supervisors to the DEA."

An idea flashed through my head. "If you ask me, two can play at this game." I moved to the computer. "If somebody in Florida is so interested in what we're doing up here, I say we tell them."

Tommy Lee laughed. "I'm reading your mind."

Together we composed an update of our case. I wrote that Doug Larson had been uncovered as the source for the pills that Artie Lincoln had been selling. He'd been forging prescriptions through the hospital, his own drugstore, and possibly area nursing homes. Also, Doug had probably killed Lincoln and Crystal Hodges. We expected a lab report to confirm the girl's murder. Doug may have been acting out of fear for the safety of his son who is incarcerated in Central Prison. When confronted with the charges this morning, Doug had committed suicide. As an officer had attempted to serve the arrest warrant, Doug had refused to open the door and was seen running to the rear of his store where he locked the safe and then grabbed a pistol from his cash register. He suffered a single self-inflicted shot to the head. We suspect more incriminating evidence might be in his safe and are bringing in an expert to open it tomorrow.

"The safe's the bait," I said.

"Yeah. We'll have the store staked out."

"I don't think Roy Spring's dirty."

Tommy Lee shook his head. "I don't know. Somebody's been staying a step ahead of us. Send the message and then don't contact him by any other computer. We know this one's been heavily fire-walled, but we don't know who has access to the one in Delray Beach. If you need to talk to him again, use this phone so I can hear the conversation."

"In case something happens to me?"

"I've got your back, remember?"

I hit send and then phoned the Delray Beach Police Department. Roy Spring was out on a case, but the dispatcher radioed him that the email message would be waiting.

"Now what?" I asked.

Tommy Lee got up and rolled his IV back to the bed. "Log out." He sat on the edge of the mattress and glanced at the wall clock. "Nearly one. No need to stake out the drugstore till closer to dark. Nobody's going to break into a store in town until the other stores have closed. I'll have Reece board up the front door and release the deputy. You take these bank statements to Special Agent Lindsay Boyce at the FBI in Asheville. She's expecting both you and the statements."

I was surprised at the speed of the appointment, but part of me was glad for the extra help, especially the resources of the FBI. "When did you make that appointment?"

"I didn't. I told Patsy to call from her car while you and I were talking." He ignored my confused expression and stared at the empty bedside table. "Damn. She took my last doughnut."

Chapter Twenty

Lindsay Boyce opened the door of a small conference room and motioned me inside. The round oak table and four matching chairs could have been found in any bank branch in Asheville. In fact, the entire décor of the FBI office wasn't much different from the Wachovia offices a few blocks away. We could have been closing a loan.

Special agent Boyce reminded me of Elaine Vincent, who had shown me the video of Crystal Hodges only a few days earlier. Both walked with a confidence born of training and achievement—Elaine from her years in the military and Lindsay from surviving the rigors of Quantico. Lindsay had the body of a runner and I estimated her age to be around thirty, a few years younger than me. I had no doubt she could break me in two.

She took the near chair, where she could be between me and the door. "I understand Sheriff Wadkins has some bank accounts he'd like us to run."

I slid the envelopes across the table. "What did he tell you? I'm surprised you set this meeting up so quickly."

Lindsay laid the bank statements to one side. "Aunt Patsy told me what you found in the safe."

"Aunt Patsy?"

Lindsay smiled. "She's my mom's sister. I try not to refer to Sheriff Wadkins as Uncle Tummy—that's the way I pronounced his name as a kid."

"Tommy Lee didn't tell me he had a relative in the Bureau."

"I'm out in San Francisco. Mother died five years ago. We'd lost touch, but I heard about the shooting."

I remembered Patsy's family had lived in California, and five years ago I'd still been with the Charlotte Police Department.

Lindsay leaned over the table and lowered her voice. "Two days ago Tommy Lee called asking for any information I had on a DEA operation in Florida. When he told me why, I got permission to travel on the government's nickel."

Now I understood why I was sitting in an FBI office. If Tommy Lee and I were in over our heads, he'd want to deal with someone he could trust. Lindsay Boyce wouldn't betray Uncle Tommy.

She patted the stack of envelopes. "You think Mr. Larson was financing drug purchases through these accounts?"

I shrugged. "If we're talking about organized crime, Doug might have been using the accounts to balance his books while moving extra pills through his store. But you probably know more about organized crime's financing schemes."

"That's what got me my ticket here." Lindsay pushed back from the table and relaxed. "I find it interesting that Larson was a small-town pharmacist."

"Why?"

"Are you familiar with the term blowback?"

As a policeman, the first thing that popped in my mind was the small blood spatters often found on the hand and gun of a suicide victim with a head wound. I'd seen blowback only hours earlier on the hand of Doug Larson as he lay dead in his own store.

When I hesitated to answer, Lindsay continued. "Blowback is when some action has bad consequences that no one anticipated. In this case, I'm going back over forty years to when the President and Congress did something nice for senior citizens."

"Are you talking about Medicare? My father's medical bills would have bankrupted us without it. As a matter of fact, I enrolled both him and my mother in Part D last year. What's the blowback?"

"In a word—fraud. Fraud to the tune of thirty billion dollars a year."

The enormity of the number staggered me. "Thirty billion?"

Lindsay smiled at my obvious shock. "And rising. We estimate ten percent of all claims are now fraudulent. Last year the government spent over three hundred billion on Medicare. You do the math."

"That's incredible," I said.

"Not really. Fraud used to be by individuals, but in the past decade organized groups have become more sophisticated and vicious. We've seen rings take over the healthcare system for an entire area. They usually start with fraudulent drug claims because that's the easiest and quickest money to make. When Tommy Lee told me a man who'd been an honest pharmacist all his life started forging prescriptions, I got interested."

"You've seen this before?"

Lindsay nodded. "You mentioned Medicare Part D. That's triggered its own blowback by squeezing down drug prices, which might be fine for the big chains like Wal-Mart and CVS, but puts the small, locally owned pharmacy in a terrible bind. Prescriptions for which Medicare might have paid four dollars to dispense have been cut to a dollar and a half. And Medicare Part D is administered by private insurance companies, some of whom delay the reimbursement checks to the pharmacists for months. So we're now seeing fraud occurring to a disproportionate degree in small towns and rural areas."

"I know Doug was having a tough time."

"But when Tommy Lee said Doug began forging prescriptions at the same time his son was assaulted in prison—well, that's quite a coincidence."

I laughed. "Don't tell me. You don't like coincidences."

"Runs in the family."

"If drugs aren't the point, then what are these rings after?"

Lindsay held up her empty palms. "It's simple. They want the whole damn thing. Once they get their foot in the door through the drugs, they expand to other healthcare providers who get reimbursed by Medicare. False claims are like printing money. They gain control of area nursing homes, home healthcare services, medical laboratories, and equipment companies, anybody who can feed from the Medicare trough. Violence like Larson's case is rare. There are plenty of people either hurting for money or greedy for a fast buck. But once they cross the line and these rings get their hooks in them, they can't get out."

Laurel County Memorial's efforts to combat fraud and theft took on new significance. I thought of Artie Lincoln and Crystal Hodges. Maybe he'd been recruiting her to do more than skim a few OxyContin pills. A smart girl like Crystal could work her way up into the facility's administrative staff and open up lucrative doors. Multiply Crystal across the many nursing homes, hospitals, and clinics in our area and the scale of the operation became huge. Millions of dollars of fraudulent claims pouring into Medicare—everything from lab tests that were never run to wheelchairs that were never delivered.

And I saw another possibility. "A ring like that could be run from anywhere. From Detroit to Delray Beach."

Lindsay smiled at my not-so-subtle locations. "Anything's possible. That's why I'm hoping these bank accounts will get us one level higher up the food chain."

"So Tommy Lee did ask you to check out Lieutenant Spring and Fletcher Shaw."

"He mentioned several names." Lindsay got up from the table. "Perhaps it would be better if you asked him yourself."

When I returned to Laurel County Memorial, I found Dr. Madison and Susan in my father's room.

"Where's my mother?"

"She went to the cafeteria for coffee." Susan spoke in an emotionless monotone. "We wanted to do a more thorough examination and she preferred to be out of the way."

"You don't like the way things are going, do you?"

Susan turned to Madison. He set my father's chart in the holder at the foot of the bed. "The antibiotics are having an effect. But they're extremely powerful and place an added strain on the body."

"You mean his heart," I said.

"The cardiologist was in earlier. He's determined your father's left side's pumping at only fifty percent efficiency. That creates pulmonary fluid. The furosemide helps, but increased urine formation has put a strain on his kidneys."

"Fixing one problem causes another," I said.

"Yes. So we're proceeding cautiously."

"What's the bottom line?"

Madison kept his eyes on mine. "We're in a pickle. That's the best non-medical way to describe the situation, and probably more accurate. Pneumonia, heart failure, kidneys. Any one could be fatal."

Susan stepped closer. "But he has a chance. We're not giving up on him. He's tough."

I hugged her, and whispered, "But does he have the will to live—to live as the shadow of himself?"

Susan had no answer. I kissed her cheek and backed away. "Mom and I appreciate what you're doing. My power of attorney for his healthcare decisions is on file. If it comes to it, there's to be no resuscitation."

Susan and Madison nodded in agreement.

"I'd better bring Mom up to date." I left the room startled that tears blinded my vision. How could things have gotten so bad so fast? Alzheimer's progressed relentlessly but slowly. We'd gotten used to the corrosive way that disease destroyed Dad's personality. But to be in critical condition in only a few days. I wasn't prepared.

Mom sat alone in a corner of the cafeteria. A few late afternoon patrons consumed coffee and soft drinks. Dinner wouldn't be served for another hour.

She looked up from the depths of her cup. "Did you see Susan?"

"Yes. She and Dr. Madison say Dad's in a tight spot. But they've got hope."

Mom reached across the table and gripped my hand. "I'm fine, Barry. I'm praying for the best, so I know that will be what happens."

"Do you want me to run you home for a while?"

"No. My place is here." She released my hand. "Have you seen Fletcher? He was looking for you earlier."

"No. What did he want?"

Mom rose from the table. "He didn't say. He told me he'd be in Tommy Lee's room if I saw you."

When I got to Tommy Lee's room, the door was open. Patsy sat beside his empty bed.

"Where is he?" I asked.

"They took him to physical therapy. He told me not to leave the room."

"Uncle Tommy's on his guard."

Patsy smiled. "You met Lindsay. She's something, isn't she? Always idolized Tommy Lee."

"I bet she's a good agent. I'm looking for my intern Fletcher Shaw."

"He was here about forty-five minutes ago. Tommy Lee had just gone."

"Did Fletcher follow him to physical therapy?"

"No. He sat down at the computer and spent about ten minutes going through different screens."

"Is that all Fletcher did?" I asked.

"Yes. He seemed excited and told me he'd return in a few minutes." She glanced at her watch. "Almost an hour now. I expect Tommy Lee to be back soon."

What would Fletcher have been doing on the computer? His skills far outstripped mine. I logged in and everything appeared normal. One email had arrived from Roy Spring saying he had no records of Doug Larson or Fletcher Shaw, but to let him know what we found in the safe and he'd cross-reference the information. His answer could be truthful or it could be what he'd need to say if he was shielding someone. We'd know tonight if the drugstore stakeout was successful.

I logged off, my heart racing from the possibility that Fletcher had hacked into our files. Why? If the leak was coming from Delray Beach, why would Fletcher need the information? Unless he was covering the tracks of someone else who had somehow left a signature.

"What's wrong?" Patsy asked.

"I'm going to look for Fletcher. He might be with Tommy Lee."

The hospital's rehabilitation center included a large room with a variety of activity stations. Some patients climbed steps, some walked between parallel bars, and others did exercises on a floor mat with a physical therapist. Tommy Lee stood next to the wall with his right arm raised against a measuring strip. A therapist wrote data on a clipboard.

"You come to watch me suffer?" he asked.

"I came to watch her suffer." I smiled at the woman with the clipboard. "I've got some police business for the sheriff whenever he can take a break."

"He's earned a rest." She grabbed Tommy Lee's IV pole. "There's a table over here not being used."

I followed them to a table on which were scattered pieces of a wooden puzzle.

The therapist helped Tommy Lee into a wheelchair. "I don't want you trying to walk to your room. I'll wheel you back when you're ready."

"I'll do it, if that's all right," I said.

"Fine." She patted Tommy Lee on the head. "Not bad for an old guy."

"See if I ever fix a ticket for you," he said.

She laughed and walked away.

"That woman knows her stuff." He inched the wheelchair closer to me. "What's up?"

"Fletcher was on the computer in your room."

"You saw him?"

"No. Patsy said he spent about ten minutes going through different screen pages. She thought it was all right since he works for me. He didn't try to hide anything. She said he seemed excited and said he'd be right back. That was almost an hour ago."

Tommy Lee grabbed one of the puzzle pieces and turned it over and over. "So we have to figure he knows about the safe."

"Yes. But why'd he take such a risk? If the leaks are coming out of Delray Beach, why would he need to access our computer here?"

Tommy Lee shook his head. "I don't know. Unless they think we've got more information in the case files. Fletcher was searching through that computer only a few hours after you sent Spring the email. Maybe they're desperate to know what Doug told you before he shot himself."

"Do you want me to find Fletcher?"

"Yes. He was on a computer that's technically the property of the Sheriff's Department. If we didn't ask him what he was doing, that would be unusual. I like the idea that somebody might be getting desperate."

"Makes the stakeout all the more important. Who do you want with me?"

Tommy Lee tossed the puzzle piece back on the pile. "You don't have to do this, Barry. I know your dad's not doing well. We can cover the drugstore without you."

"Right now I'm a police officer. I understand the demands of the job have to override personal concerns. The hospital can get me if the worst happens." I said that, and believed that. But the stakeout was also personal. If Fletcher were involved, I wanted to be there and confront him face-to-face.

"All right," Tommy Lee said. "We're stretched pretty thin with two deputies on vacation. I think Wakefield's off tonight and Reece isn't in rotation. I'll ask Reece if he and Wakefield will work it."

I got up and grabbed Tommy Lee's IV and wheelchair. "Let's get back to your room. We'd better be in position at the drugstore by eight, and I want to find Fletcher before then."

I started to pull him back from the table, but he grabbed my hand. "Barry. I want you to promise me you'll bail out if your mother needs you. Reece and Wakefield can handle the drugstore. Otherwise I'm telling Reece you're not to be on the premises."

"You've got my word."

Fletcher had disappeared. His convertible was parked in the hospital lot, but I couldn't find him anywhere. Cindy and Helen Todd said he'd stopped in before going up to Tommy Lee's room, but they hadn't seen him since. Uncle Wayne said he hadn't been by the funeral home. Sid Mulray let me into Fletcher's apartment, but all I found were Fluffy sleeping in her crate and a half-eaten pepperoni pizza on the counter.

At seven-thirty, I met Reece and Wakefield at the Sheriff's Department. We stocked up on thermoses of hot coffee. Wakefield and Reece each drove an unmarked police car and I drove my jeep. We parked all three vehicles in a used car lot several blocks away where they wouldn't be noticed. Reece brought a walkie-talkie and earpiece so he could be in touch with the dispatcher. The night shift was thin and additional backup would be unlikely with only two other deputies on duty.

The drugstore hadn't been decorated with crime scene tape. The closed sign was in the window and three-quarter-inch plywood now covered the door Wakefield had smashed through when he'd heard Doug's fatal shot only twelve hours earlier.

We entered through the alley, spacing our arrivals by five minutes. Wakefield went first, taking up an inside position near the front where he would be shielded by the free-standing magazine rack. Reece settled in a corner behind some boxes in the storage room next to the back loading dock. I wanted to be closer to the safe and hid in a nook behind the pharmacy counter. We'd closed the safe but hadn't spun the tumblers since we didn't know the combination. To the casual observer, the safe appeared locked.

Our locations were far enough from each other that we couldn't risk talking. I sat on a stool, sipping coffee and watching the shadows intensify from gray to deep purple and then black. One low-watt bulb above the front door came on when triggered by its photocell.

In the darkness, my mind wandered. Why would Fletcher use the computer right in front of Tommy Lee's wife? Where had he gone afterwards? Would FBI agent Lindsay Boyce link Doug's bank accounts to any outside criminal network? The words "Mob" and "organized crime" were such catchall phrases as to be almost meaningless. Who had devised such a sophisticated scheme and was willing to kill to protect it? Who had gotten their hooks into Doug Larson, one of our own, as Tommy Lee had said? Who else had they targeted?

Fragments of a conversation came back to me. Cooper Ludden on the loading dock at the hospital, accepting some shipments, refusing others. Setting aside a split carton for later. "My job's to at least get the stuff in the door. Then it's Hospital Security's problem." What if Cooper was ripping off shipments before they went into inventory? And pulling out drugs and supplies that had been ordered but never delivered within the hospital? "When you've been here as long as I have, you can shortcut the system," Cooper had said. Only I hadn't been listening.

I had no proof, just pieces of a puzzle and no picture to guide their assembly. Fletcher Shaw was still the most baffling piece of all.

Thursday night crossed into Friday morning. By two o'clock, I began to doubt whether we would have any intruders. By two-thirty my legs were cramping and I risked exposure by slowly walking in a tight circle to get the blood flowing again. Then I heard a sound from behind me.

"Barry." Reece crept close to me. "Dispatcher says they've had a bomb threat at the hospital."

"Jesus." That's a law officer's worst nightmare. The public place where people are most vulnerable. "What's happening?"

"They're doing a sweep floor by floor. Buncombe County's lending their unit, but they need more manpower. I'm releasing Wakefield to assist."

"Sure. It doesn't look like anything's going to happen here anyway."

Reece slowly maneuvered toward Wakefield.

Was this a coordinated ruse to divert our attention? I had to admire the brain behind the plan. With the Sheriff's Department tied up at the hospital, even if someone witnessed a break-in at the drugstore, the response time would be seriously delayed.

Twenty minutes passed. Again, Reece whispered from the dark. "Barry. Dispatcher reports a fire."

My heart jumped. "At the hospital?"

"No. The Econo Lodge by the interstate. One of the fire trucks is being pulled from the hospital. We'd better abort."

"We can't. That's what they want us to do. They've got to be behind the bomb threat and the fire."

"Maybe. But the fire's real. I've got to have an officer on the scene."

"Then go."

Reece didn't move. All I could hear was his breathing.

"Reece?"

"I don't like leaving you alone. Two officers should be minimum."

"We don't have a choice. I'm in charge of this case and I'm not leaving. Go. You're needed at the fire."

He hesitated. I was touched by his concern for my safety.

"I'll be all right, Reece. We know their game so I'll be ready. If this is a stunt to pull us off, they must have seen us come in the back. Maybe they can't watch both doors. If you go out the front, they might think we're both still here."

"Okay. Take the walkie."

"No. You might need it for emergency services at the fire. I've got my cell."

"I'll be back as soon as I can."

But Reece didn't leave.

I realized he was holding out his hand in the darkness. I shook it. "I'm proud to serve with you."

He didn't say anything, just gave my hand an extra squeeze. I saw him leave through the dim glow of the front door night light. Reece and I would never be close, but at that moment the bond of the badge was stronger than our differences. That's what I missed most about being a police officer.

Since both doors were uncovered, I returned to my position by the safe. The entry point didn't matter because any intruder would have to come to me. I stepped closer to the wall where I could reach the light switch. Then I unholstered my revolver and waited.

No more than fifteen minutes had elapsed when I heard the back door slide open. There was no sound of the lock breaking or a crowbar prying out the latch. Whoever was coming had a key.

I drew back the hammer and cocked my pistol, but I kept my finger on the trigger guard. My left hand poised over the light switch. Footsteps came closer. Then they stopped.

A voice spoke out of the darkness. Not in a whisper, but as strong as if we were chatting about the weather at three in the afternoon instead of three in the morning.

"You may as well turn on the light. No sense bumbling around in the dark."

I flipped the switch. A man stood at the other end of the counter, his back to me with his hands raised over his head. At first I thought he held a gun, but as my eyes adjusted, I saw only an open cell phone.

"Turn around slowly," I ordered.

"Certainly." The man kept his hands high and obeyed. "Sorry to keep you waiting, Deputy Clayton."

Chapter Twenty-one

Joel Greene was smiling, but the glint from his eyes was as cold as steel. For a few seconds, I could only stare at him. Then my mind shifted into overdrive and the pieces of the puzzle I'd assembled into one picture created an entirely new one.

"You're under arrest," I said. "Keep your hands up."

"On what charge? Opening a drugstore with a key the owner gave me? Holding an open cell phone?" He laughed. "Using minutes beyond my calling plan?"

"Medicare fraud for starters. Extortion. Illegal sale of prescription drugs. Trafficking in stolen goods. Murder."

"Murder? Of that man the papers identified as Artie Lincoln?"

"That's one count. Crystal Hodges is the other."

"The girl? She died of brain trauma." Greene gave a quick glance up at his phone. "Or if it was murder, the only person near her was your intern."

"That's right. But the drugs used on her had to come from somewhere. You should have checked Crystal's chart more carefully. The lab still had a blood draw taken from her a few minutes before her death. We've run the tests."

For a second, the smug expression on Greene's face wavered. "Fascinating speculation, but I'm afraid I don't have time for games. I believe poor Doug Larson left something for me."

"I said you're under arrest."

Greene slowly lowered his hands. "I don't need to convince you how people can die since you've already figured out what happened to that Hodges girl." He put the phone to his ear. "You've got five seconds to hand over your gun, or my partner at the hospital gives your father a dose of the same drug that killed the girl. And Sheriff Wadkins, I believe, is still on an IV."

The tingle in my neck exploded into a cold shiver down my spine. The words I'd spoken to Doug Larson on this very spot echoed in my head. "They don't own Tommy Lee or me." Doug had answered with the truth. "They do and you don't even know it."

A police officer is trained never to give up his gun to an offender under any circumstances. If Tommy Lee's life was in danger, he knew the risks, and I knew he would want me to take Greene out right then and there. But my father wasn't a police officer. And as sick as he was, he wouldn't become a murder victim through my actions. Greene had barely counted to three before I handed him my gun.

Greene spoke calmly into his phone. "Everything's under control here. I'll call back in a few minutes." He flipped the phone closed. "Very sensible, Deputy Clayton." He crouched down at the safe, reached to turn the dial, and then noticed the number. "It's not locked." He yanked down the handle and pulled open the door.

The empty space looked as big as a double garage. Greene stared into the safe as if expecting something to materialize.

I played the one card I had left. "You don't think we'd be stupid enough to leave evidence here? We found nothing. We have nothing. It was a bluff."

Greene jumped to his feet. "You don't think I'm stupid enough to believe you? Why do you think I know the combination and have a key to the drugstore? Doug Larson was in a panic after you and the sheriff grilled him. He was emptying the safe when you confronted him, wasn't he?" He jabbed the gun at me. "You're wasting time. Give me the contents or your father dies."

"I can't. They're not here."

"Where are they?"

If I told Greene the FBI already had the bank statements, I'd lose my bargaining power. Would he just shoot me? If I answered "locked in the Sheriff's Department," would he force me to take him there? What then? We were only a few minutes away. I needed time to think. Time to allow Greene to make a mistake. I still had my own cell phone. Maybe I'd get the chance to call for help.

"At my cabin," I said.

"Not in an evidence room?"

"No. I'm the officer in charge. I signed out for everything in the safe so I could catalogue the evidence at home. Frankly, we didn't know who to trust. There was a leak and we were afraid it was in our department."

Greene smiled. "There was a leak in your department and you were it. Nice of you to keep those emails going to Florida. How do you think I knew you hadn't gotten in the safe yet? I don't know what that fool Larson left in there, but I can't take a chance that it leads back to me or the people I work for."

Of course. The leak wasn't in Florida like we thought. Neither Spring nor anyone else down there was involved. Greene or his accomplice had simply installed another password when they set up the computer in Tommy Lee's room, a computer I'd asked for. Was that what Fletcher had been doing? Erasing any trace of another way into our files?

"How far's your cabin?" he asked.

"Twenty-five or thirty minutes. It's on the back side of Bear Ridge."

Greene frowned. "I don't know where that is, but you'd better not be leading me on a wild goose chase."

"Ask your friend on the other end of the phone. He'll tell you it's the truth."

"Keep your hands where I can see them." Greene flipped open his phone and punched re-dial. "Clayton says the papers are at his cabin on Bear Ridge twenty-five to thirty minutes away. Does that sound right?" Greene listened a few moments. "Then we're headed there. I'll keep calling every five minutes." He stared at me and barked his orders into the phone. "Stay close to them. If Clayton is stupid enough to try anything and you don't hear from me, tie up the loose ends and get out."

I didn't need a glossary to understand what he meant.

We left by the back door. Greene held the gun inside his suit coat and walked a few yards behind me. "My car's around the corner from the alley. A black Cadillac STS. Get in the passenger side. But first toss your cell phone in that dumpster. You weren't planning on calling anybody, were you?"

Greene was smart. He wasn't making any mistakes. I threw my phone in the dumpster.

When we were about twenty feet away from his vehicle, he pushed his remote key. Headlights flashed twice and the locks popped up.

"Back seat?" I asked.

"So you can strangle me with your shoe lace? I don't think so. Sit in the front and buckle up. Then tuck your arms under the shoulder strap."

Greene waited until I'd secured my seatbelt before he slid behind the wheel. He closed his door, transferred the pistol to his left hand, and rested it in his lap with the barrel pointed at my stomach. "Which way?"

I gave him directions out of town. The route wasn't the most direct one, but he didn't know that. I had to stop him before we reached my cabin and he discovered I'd been lying. My only chance lay in overpowering him when he was most vulnerable, navigating the twisting road that scaled Bear Ridge. I played the path of the old two-lane blacktop in my mind, searching for the best place to make my move. We'd need an impact hard enough to deploy the airbags, but not so violent that I was pinned in the car or knocked unconscious. Some of the hairpins bordered drops nearly five hundred feet deep. The road crossed several streams that wound down the mountain. Those drops weren't as severe and the plunge into a shallow stream not as dangerous as tumbling end over end into the trunk of an ancient pine.

As we left the town limits, the black starry sky swallowed us. Memory and the halogen throw of the Cadillac's headlights were all I had to guide me.

"Are you the brains behind this operation?" I asked.

"Curiosity killed the cat. Remember?"

I'd had one too many cats this week already. "Just wondering. The setup seems well thought out till you get to a two-bit hustler like Artie Lincoln."

In the soft glow of the illumined dash, I could see Greene's face tighten.

"Artie Lincoln was a damn fool. None of that was my idea. We were making good money off the Medicare scams, but the OxyContin was too tempting. Too much profit for too many greedy people."

Greene stopped talking and hit his phone's re-dial button as the road began the sharp ascent toward my cabin. "We're still on the road. What's happening there?" Again he was silent as he listened. "You mean to tell me those country bumpkins haven't figured out the bomb threat is a hoax? That just makes it easier for you to do what you have to do if Clayton decides to become a hero." He hung up.

"It's not too late to work out a deal," I said. "I can hook you up with an FBI agent who will probably give you immunity if there's no evidence you killed anyone."

"And wind up with a new name in Arizona?" He laughed derisively. "I may as well take a lesson from Larson and shoot myself. No, I'm out of here. Out of the country. But somebody else screwed up, so Joel cleans up. Cuts the losses, contains the investigation."

The bitterness in Greene's voice meant he was telling the truth. I had no doubt I was part of that containment. Whether he found what he wanted at my cabin or not, he meant to kill me. I thought about the five minutes between calls to his accomplice. Maybe Greene had made a mistake after all. He should have stayed on the phone the entire time to insure I wouldn't do anything. Maybe he was worried about the call being tracked or his cell battery dying. Maybe the other person couldn't stay tied to the phone without raising suspicions. Whatever, I had five minutes to overpower Greene, call the hospital, and get someone to my father's room. Five seconds had meant no chance for my father, but five minutes was a chance I was willing to take. More importantly, a chance my father would want me to take. Dad would want me fighting to the end. He had been fighting his own battle for survival for years, and now he was lying in a hospital fighting for every breath. He would want me to do the same.

A few minutes later, the road took a dip to a narrow bridge over the first stream. I tensed as Greene opened his phone again. My timing would need to be perfect. Would he fire the gun or use both hands to fight me for the steering wheel? As much as I feared the pistol, my first concern was the phone. I had to get it away from him.

Greene slowed to forty-five as the slope bottomed out at the narrow two-lane bridge. "Clayton's been a good boy. Everything's going to work out." He hung up without waiting for a reply.

I saw the gap between the trees and the bridge widen. The headlights disappeared in the blackness. I snapped my arms from under the shoulder belt and clamped both hands on top of the steering wheel. I yanked hard to the right. The car lurched, lifting the right tires off the road.

Greene fought to regain control and for a second I thought we would slam into the facing of the bridge guardrail. Then we were airborne over the bank. Greene screamed as rocks and churning whitewater rushed toward us. I grabbed his phone and pulled so hard the plastic belt clip broke.

The dashboard exploded as the airbags were deployed. I had turned in the seat and the impact hit my shoulder like a two-by-four swung by Babe Ruth. The car rolled onto its left side, cracking the windows. Greene fell against his door, stunned by the blow from the airbag.

I twisted my legs from under the dash and pulled the seatbelt release. My body dropped on Greene and I stomped his arm with both feet, hoping to dislodge the gun if he'd managed to hold on to it. Cold water soaked through my shoes. The stream surged through the broken glass.

Greene was screaming, reaching with both hands to pull himself out of the rising water.

I pushed up my door and stood up like a sailor emerging from a submarine. The interior lights were still working and I looked down to see Greene trapped behind the wheel and tangled in the deflated airbag. His face paled with panic.

"Help me." He reached a hand toward me.

The car lay on its side across the stream and had become a dam. Water flowing in had no way out. The pressure of the current forced the level higher. Greene could drown in water that only came up to my knees. At that moment I didn't care if he did. I called Tommy Lee's number, praying that the bomb scare at the hospital hadn't separated him from his cell phone. Patsy answered after the first ring.

"Put Tommy Lee on quick," I said.

"He's right here."

Immediately Tommy Lee's gravelly voice came on the line. "Are you all right? I just tried to call you. This bomb threat and fire have got to be a setup. They're coming for the safe."

"They already have. It's Joel Greene. I've got him but he has an accomplice at the hospital who's going to kill my father. I don't know who it is, but Greene's going to tell me. Get to my father's room now!"

Tommy Lee's breath came in gasps. "I'm on my way."

I looked down at Greene. "Who did you talk to? Who's after my father?"

"Help me and I'll tell you."

I pushed Greene's head beneath the water with the heel of my shoe. After a few seconds, he came up sputtering for air.

"Who's going to kill my father?" I screamed.

Above the rush of the water, a bang sounded from the trunk. I hopped out of the car, worried it was toppling over. I sloshed through the stream and found the left rear wedged on a rock. The bang came again. Someone was inside.

I pounded on the trunk and what sounded like a kick came in response.

"I have to get the key," I shouted.

"Clayton! Clayton!" Greene's shrill cries echoed through the hollow.

I wriggled back inside the passenger door, dodged Greene's frantic grasps, and wrenched the keys free of the ignition.

"Get me out. I'll tell you. I swear!" The water swirled around the back of Greene's head.

"No deal. You tell me first."

I stumbled over the slippery rocks and located the lock by the red glow of the taillights. The trunk lid swung to the left until it hit a boulder. The open space was no more than nine inches wide. A head fell through. Fletcher Shaw turned his face to me. His eyes shone bright with fear. Gray duct tape covered his mouth. I reached in and grabbed his shoulders. As carefully as I could, I twisted him through the gap and pulled him free.

Duct tape bound his hands and feet. Dried blood caked the back of his head. I dragged him to the bank where the light from the car was barely strong enough to see him. He whimpered as I peeled the tape from his mouth.

"I'll get your hands," I said.

"Clayton! What do you want? What do you want to know?"

I ignored Greene's cries and felt for the edge of the tape. Greene had looped Fletcher's wrists at least ten times, but once I got it started, the tape quickly came off.

Fletcher flexed his fingers.

"Can you do your feet?" I asked.

"Yes." His voice sounded thick and husky.

I left him picking at the tape around his ankles and waded to the Cadillac. Greene strained against the belt, trying to keep his head above water.

"The game's changed, Greene. I don't care whether you live or die." I pulled his phone from my pocket. "I'm betting Tommy Lee got to my father in time. All I want to know is who's helping you at the hospital?"

As if on cue, Greene's phone rang. I was afraid to answer. I'd talked big just a few seconds before, but what if this was the accomplice calling to say the job had been done. Had I miscalculated the time?

Greene stared at the phone like it was a life raft. "You still need me, Clayton. Go ahead, answer it."

After the fifth ring, I flipped it open. "Yeah," I said, trying to do my best impersonation of Greene.

"This is OnStar," a woman said. "We've received notification of an airbag deployment on a vehicle belonging to this cell phone owner. Has there been an accident?"

"Has there ever."

"Does anyone require medical attention?" Her voice grew even more concerned.

"Yes. Do you have our location?"

"We have a GPS fix."

"Then send an ambulance and the police as soon as possible." I waited till she clicked off and kept my eyes on Greene. "And better send a hearse." I flipped the phone closed.

Chapter Twenty-two

"Whittier," Greene screamed. "Pamela Whittier."

I dialed Tommy Lee without giving Greene a second look.

"Your father's all right," Tommy Lee said before I could speak. "Susan's been with him for almost an hour, and no one else has been here."

Relief swept over me. I leaned against the car, the whitewater swirling around my knees. "Thank God."

"Is Greene talking yet?"

I struggled to keep from crying.

"Can you hear me, Barry? Who's the accomplice?"

Finally I forced the words out. "He says Pamela Whittier."

"Whittier? Are you sure he's not jerking us around?"

"Greene's not in a position to jerk us around."

"Pamela was here," I heard Susan tell Tommy Lee. "A little after the bomb threat came in. She said she was checking to see if everything was all right."

Tommy Lee came back on the phone. "Susan says—"

"I heard. Any idea where she is now?"

Before Tommy Lee could answer, I heard metal scrape over rocks as the Cadillac tilted farther on its side.

"Clayton. Help me!" Greene's words ended with a strangled cough.

"I'm at the bridge over Little Buck Creek on Bear Ridge. Find Whittier." I jammed Greene's phone in my pocket.

The weight of the trapped water began to wedge the car deeper. I pulled myself up to the passenger window. Greene pushed against the steering wheel trying to keep his head out of the cold stream. He struggled to free himself, but kept falling back into the water.

"My leg's pinned against the door," he cried.

I reached down and locked my hand around his wrists. He dug his fingers so deep into my skin that pain shot up my arm. I braced myself against the door jamb and tugged as hard as I could. Greene's leg bent against the bottom of the steering wheel and he screamed.

I released his wrist and jerked my arm free. "Fletcher. Can you help me?"

"Yes." He splashed through the water, kicking spray that glistened like red drops of blood in the glow of the taillights.

The pit of my stomach churned. Joel Greene might drown right in front of me. I turned to Fletcher. "The stream's flowing in through holes in the side windows. The hydraulic pressure's raising the level higher." Hydraulic. The wrecked car was creating an artificial hydraulic. The trapped water couldn't flow back against the stronger current, but Greene couldn't escape by diving deeper.

"Come on." I stumbled over the slippery rocks, using my hands to steady myself until I reached the front windshield. Through the glass, I could see the water tumbling like a giant washing machine. "Find a rock. We've got to smash through as low as we can so the water has a way out."

We felt along the bottom of the stream. A small rock wouldn't have enough mass and a large boulder would be too heavy to lift.

I gripped my hands around a stone the size of a cinderblock and pried it free. "This should work."

Fletcher helped me lug the rock closer to the car.

"We should throw it together," he said. "Safety glass is tough."

"Aim for the lower corner right above the stream. On the count of three."

We stood side by side, the heavy rock swinging between us. With a groan I put all my strength into hurling it against the glass. The windshield shattered, spitting the stone back out as the trapped water rushed for an exit. I saw a flash of metal and snagged my pistol as the torrent flushed it free. I waded to the side of the car and climbed up to the passenger door. As I bent down to drag Greene out, he waved me back.

"Thanks, Clayton. I can wriggle up out of this mess now. I owe you one."

The tone in his voice spooked me. I jerked back as Greene snapped a small caliber pistol clear of the frothy water. A bullet whizzed past my ear, buzzing like an angry hornet. Sheer reflex took over and I fired two rounds as I fell backwards into the current.

"Barry!" I heard Fletcher scrambling after me.

"Stay down!"

I bumped over rocks a few yards before hitting a fallen log. Without taking my eyes off the upturned passenger door, I crawled back toward the front of the Cadillac, careful to stay out of the spill light. A pink tinge colored the water flowing out of the smashed window. Greene's bloody head bobbed against the windshield. He no longer needed rescuing.

I crawled over to Fletcher.

He was shaking. "He was going to kill you. After we saved his life, he was going to kill you."

I gave Greene's body one last look. "That's the way people like Greene repay kindness."

We found a mossy patch on the bank and collapsed on the ground. Fletcher couldn't stop shivering and I was afraid he was going into shock. No telling what he'd been through before I found him. I needed to get his mind off what had just happened until the ambulance arrived.

"How'd you wind up in Greene's trunk?"

"I got an attack of the stupids," Fletcher said in a shaky voice. "I knew you were right that someone was leaking information and I knew it wasn't me. I thought about how you and Tommy Lee always discussed the case in his hospital room and that the computer was the link for all the emails. I didn't know the password, but I know enough about computers to see if the data was being accessed by someone else. Even though you were on the hospital network, the shielded files shouldn't allow another terminal to read them. I saw multiple interactions from a different IP address occurring with your protected zone."

"IP address?" I'd heard the term but wasn't sure what it meant.

"Internet Protocol address. Every computer connected to the internet has one. I thought it was probably a computer in Florida since that seemed to be the link to Artie Lincoln."

"Nothing sounds stupid so far," I said. "I wish you'd told me your suspicions."

"I was hurt that I was a suspect, and I wanted the satisfaction of proving my innocence to you and the sheriff." Fletcher laughed. "So I went down to see Joel Greene. I learned he'd set the password up for you. I gave him the IP address and asked if he had a way to trace it. He wanted to know if I'd mentioned this to you or the sheriff, and like a dummy, I said no. He reached in his desk drawer and pulled out a pistol. He forced me out to his car. He said he just wanted to have a little chat. As I started to get in the passenger seat, he knocked me unconscious with what must have been the butt of the gun. I woke up in the trunk of the car a few minutes before the wreck."

Fletcher had been out cold for almost ten hours. Greene must have injected him with something.

Fletcher shuddered. "I wonder why he didn't kill me."

"Too risky to fire a shot at the hospital. He'd wait till he'd devised a way to dispose of our bodies. Who knows? He might have planned to make it look like you and I killed each other at my cabin." The thought had come spontaneously, but as I said it, I also shuddered.

The wail of a siren echoed off the ridge. A second, higher pitch joined in. Wakefield and an EMT crew were only minutes away.

"What now?" Fletcher asked.

"Tommy Lee's tracking down Pamela Whittier. I want the medics to check you out, and you should be taken to the hospital. No telling what Greene put in your system."

"Okay. Man, none of my friends' internships can top this. I almost got to be the body."

I sat up and couldn't help but laugh. I liked Fletcher. Sitting beside him, I couldn't believe I'd thought he'd been on the other end of Greene's cell phone. "I'm sorry you wound up being a suspect. We just couldn't get enough information to rule you out. Your college wouldn't release anything."

Fletcher stretched his arms and legs, still trying to work out the stiffness. "That was my doing. I was afraid I'd be treated differently."

"Treated differently?"

"My mother's maiden name was Sealey."

"Sealey? Like in the Sealey Corporation?"

"Yes."

The Sealey Corporation was the largest owner of funeral homes and related supplies in North America. They'd started in Canada and through smart acquisitions and product development had become the major player in the industry. What Sam Walton did for retail, Neville Sealey did for the funeral business. I'd flirted with an offer from the Hoffman chain the year before, but they were small change compared with the Sealey Corporation.

"Was Neville Sealey your uncle?" I asked.

"My grandfather. You know your uncle Wayne reminds me a lot of him. Plain spoken and down to earth. Grandpa died while I was in high school, but he'd always told me the funeral business was the ultimate people business. Only go into it if you understand that."

"Is that why you're here in Gainesboro?"

"Yes. My uncles and my mother don't understand why I'd come to such a small town, but Grandpa would have approved. Now his company's all lawyers, bankers, and accountants. I don't think he'd be happy with his creation. He was a funeral director first and a businessman second. I wanted to get a feel for what Grandpa understood."

Blue lights strobed through the treetops as a patrol car and ambulance crested the ridge behind us. "Keep an eye on the car." I got to my feet and walked up to the bridge.

The ambulance trailed the patrol car. Wakefield pulled onto the bridge so that the EMTs could be closer. For the first time, I saw the skid marks where the Cadillac had left the road and plunged into the stream. Wakefield ran toward me, his eyes wide as he took in the scene. I stood in the ambulance's headlights, sopping wet and shaking from the cold water.

"Good God, Barry. Sheriff told me what he knew. Are you and the kid okay?"

"Yeah."

"We've got to stop meeting like this," a voice said from behind me.

I turned around and recognized one of the EMTs from the shooting at the square dance. Hard to believe that was only a week ago.

"Anybody hurt," the second EMT asked.

"Yes," I said. "Fletcher Shaw has a head injury and possible shock." I nodded to the Cadillac. "Greene's dead. I had to shoot him."

"Let's see what we've got," Wakefield said, and headed for the stream.

The EMTs started working on Fletcher just as Greene's phone rang in my pocket. The caller ID showed Tommy Lee's number.

"Did you get Whittier?" I asked.

"No. Hospital Security said she left an hour ago. Told the officer she'd come in because of the bomb threat. She took a call on her cell and left before the all-clear."

"She's running."

"That's the way I read it," Tommy Lee said. "I don't think she had the stomach for what Greene wanted her to do."

"Or she couldn't do it because Susan was there. Did you put out a BOLO?"

"I got nobody to do the looking out. State highway patrol and neighboring counties are lending assistance."

"What about her home?" I asked. "She may need to pack."

"Next on my list."

"Where is it?"

"Indian Moon Estates."

I knew the exclusive development. "That's only five miles from here."

"What's your status?"

"Wrapped up. Greene's dead."

For a few seconds all I heard was Tommy Lee's breathing as he thought about what must have happened.

"You can fill me in later," he said. "I'll send Wakefield to Whittier's."

"No. Pamela Whittier's mine."

Tommy Lee's voice rose in my ear. "Don't be an idiot. I just want Whittier tailed till I can free up reinforcements."

"My case. You gave it to me. I can tail her as well as Wakefield."

I waited for his answer, glad that Tommy Lee hadn't rejected my request out of hand.

He sighed. "Okay. But use your head. And for God's sake, report in."

"How's my dad?"

"He's hanging in there. They changed the antibiotic bag as a precaution. Susan's still monitoring his condition."

That's when it really hit me. For Susan to be personally checking on my dad at four-thirty in the morning meant his condition had to have deteriorated even further. Part of me wanted to go to the hospital right then, but another part urged me to finish the job. "I'll have to take Wakefield's car. He'll have to ride back with the ambulance."

I told Wakefield the plan and he gave me his keys. I pushed the patrol car as fast as I dared. Fortunately no one was on the road at that time of night. The dispatcher gave me directions to Pamela Whittier's home. She'd had enough of a head start that she could already have run.

As I sped along the two-lane blacktop, I thought about the unfolding events. Lindsay Boyce's scenario had been right on the mark. Doug Larson's forged prescriptions were only a small piece of the scheme. Greene and Whittier controlled so much more—an entire hospital. The potential take from Medicare fraud was astronomical. And that could still only be the tip of the iceberg. There was no way of telling how many other people in the area might be involved.

Doug Larson had been blackmailed into cooperating. What was Pamela Whittier's motive? From what Susan said, she was a highly intelligent and respected administrator. Was she also being blackmailed, or had the temptation for big money been too great? Were she and Greene equally involved?

I had no doubt that Greene had been responsible for the deaths of Crystal Hodges and Artie Lincoln. I had come too close to being his next victim to doubt Greene was a cold-blooded killer. But Pamela Whittier? Had she come to my father's room tonight as Greene's accomplice? Greene had never missed his five-minute phone calls until it was too late. I had no proof of what Whittier would have done otherwise. At this point, I didn't care.

Because of Whittier, good people like Crystal Hodges and Doug Larson were dead, and my own father could have easily been added to that list. Greene had paid a price for his crimes, the ultimate price. Pamela Whittier would have to go through me before she'd escape justice.

Ten minutes later, I turned onto her street. All of the houses were dark except hers. A side window glowed. A silver Lexus SUV sat in front of a two-car garage, blocking both doors. Pamela Whittier had parked ready to leave.

If I were going to tail her, I should have withdrawn to a spot where I couldn't be seen and picked up the Lexus as she left through the gate.

Thoughts about my father kept gnawing at me. Pamela Whittier stood between me and my dad's bedside. Did I really want to waste time following her to the Charlotte or Atlanta airport if she literally took flight?

I parked the patrol car three houses down in a dark spot between two street lamps. I pulled a set of handcuffs from the glove box and found a pair of bolt cutters in the trunk. Then I unsnapped the safety strap of my soggy holster.

The light still burned in Whittier's window. She could be packing clothes or destroying evidence. Probably both. I ran wide of her yard to avoid any spotlight wired to a motion detector. Clinging to the shadows, I hurried to the Lexus. There was enough moonlight that I could see the valve on the nearest tire. I wedged the bolt cutters under the expensive wheel cover and snipped the stem. Air whooshed out and the heavy vehicle sagged down on one corner. In less than two minutes, the Lexus sat level on four flats. My tailing job had just gotten a lot easier.

A short hedge of rhododendrons marked the boundary with Whittier's neighbor. I looped around the other side and sat down in the cool grass to wait. I should have reported in like Tommy Lee requested, but the radio was in the patrol car and I wanted to keep Greene's phone free in case Whittier tried to call him. Every connection between their two phones might prove to be evidence.

The light went out. I'd feel pretty damn stupid if she'd gone to bed. Maybe Greene had just thrown out a name to try and get me to help him. I began calculating how much four high-performance tires on a Lexus would cost me.

A back door slammed. No spotlights came on. Unusual unless someone didn't want to be seen leaving. I heard footsteps on the concrete drive. Then the headlights blinked as Whittier used her remote entry. The footsteps ceased a few yards from the driver's door. She must have seen the tires.

I stood up from behind the rhododendrons. I could barely make out her shape in front of the Lexus. She had what looked like a suitcase in her left hand and her keys in the right. A purse hung from her left shoulder. Beneath the hand with the keys, an attaché case sat on the driveway.

"Pamela Whittier, this is Deputy Barry Clayton."

Whittier jumped like she'd been shot. I felt a rush of adrenaline knowing that justice was about to prevail. I started walking around the rhododendrons, never taking my eyes off her hands.

"You're under arrest for conspiracy to commit fraud, extortion, and murder. You have the right to remain silent—"

"Barry, what are you talking about? You scared me half to death. Come out where I can see you."

"Anything you say may be—"

"Barry, you're making a terrible mistake. I'm leaving on vacation. I was supposed to have gone this evening, but I couldn't get away, and then we had a bomb scare at the hospital. I'm trying to make a six o'clock flight in Asheville."

I stopped on the driveway. Had Joel Greene duped me? Was Pamela Whittier innocent? But Greene thought he was going to drown. "Where are you going on vacation?"

"The Bahamas. I'm meeting friends. A reunion from nursing school. The ticket's in my purse."

The Bahamas. I tried to remember countries without extradition treaties. Surely the U.S. had such a treaty with the Bahamas. But there were other things in the Bahamas besides sun and surf. Banks.

"What's in the attaché case, Pamela?"

"Paperwork. I might be on vacation but the work for the hospital has to go on."

I slid along the side of the Lexus without turning my back to her. I yanked open the driver's door and the interior light spilled out in a pool reaching far enough to engulf us.

"Then open it."

Her face hardened. "Do you have a warrant?"

"I just placed you under arrest. We can go down to the Sheriff's Department and sort this out there. Of course, you'll miss your flight. Or you can open the case now, show me your ticket, and if everything's as you say, I'll personally take you to the airport."

Her lips tightened and her eyes seemed to cut into me. "Have you ever been abandoned, Barry?"

I had no idea what she was talking about.

"I have," she continued. "Alone, abandoned, and deceived. Did you know I put myself through nursing school?"

"I know people are dead because of you."

She kept talking as if she hadn't heard me. "Then I worked double shifts to put my husband through medical school. Guess what happened as soon as he got his degree and his residency behind him?"

I wasn't in the mood for hard luck stories. "He dumped you for a blond bimbo and a Mercedes."

She gave an icy laugh. "It was a Porsche, but the bimbo came with it." Her nostrils flared as her anger boiled over. "I vowed I would never be at the mercy of a man again. And I started over, this time preparing myself to run the game, not be a pawn."

I began to see the irony of her situation. "But you did become a pawn. You were seduced again, this time not by a man but by easy money. Why? Because life had once given you a raw deal? Because you felt you were owed something?"

The glint of tears trailed down her cheeks. She quickly wiped them away.

"Could you have killed my father?"

The anger in her eyes turned into despair. "No. That's why I left. After that first call from Joel, I wasn't even in the hospital. I wanted out." She looked at the attaché case and reached for her purse. "The key's in here." Her eyes focused somewhere in the night sky. "I just want a way out."

Unlike at the drugstore, this time I heard the anguish and knew what was happening. I lunged forward, grabbing both of her wrists, and wrestled the purse from her hand. A small black automatic pistol fell to the concrete.

She stared blankly at me.

"Enough people have died. I'm not going to let you. For what it's worth, I believe you."

Then Pamela Whittier began to sob.

Headlights swung across the front of her house as a car pulled in behind me. I glanced over my shoulder and saw Patsy Wadkins get out of her Taurus and cross in front of the headlights to the passenger side. A few seconds later Tommy Lee stepped into the beams, holding his wife's arm. He wore a hideous hospital gown and skid-proof socks. A bandage was wrapped around his wrist where he'd ripped out his IV. He looked like hell. The way a friend would look who'd gone through hell for a friend.

"Tommy Lee was going to drive himself," Patsy said. "Wouldn't even take time to borrow some clothes."

"Cuff her to the car," Tommy Lee whispered. "Take the patrol car and get to the hospital now."

My breath caught in my chest. Patsy could only nod in agreement.

"She was making a run," I said. "She said the Bahamas. That's probably true. She's carrying a concealed weapon and that case which she refused to open."

"Go. I don't think there's much time."

The light in Dad's room was dim. Through the window the first hints of dawn lightened the sky. Mom and Uncle Wayne sat on either side of the bed. Susan leaned against the wall. She looked exhausted.

I stood in the doorway listening to my father's rapid, shallow breathing mixed with the soft beep of the monitor.

Susan crossed to me. "The infection's stopped responding to the antibiotics. His kidneys have shut down and the fluid's building. I'm so sorry, there's nothing we can do."

I kissed her cheek. "You did what you could."

Uncle Wayne got up from his chair. "Sit down. You need to get off your feet."

I didn't argue. I wanted to be near my father.

His head lay on a single pillow. His pale lips were cracked, and spittle had dried in the corners of his mouth. I grabbed his hand and was shocked by how cold it felt.

"We have to let him go, Barry." Mom whispered the words without looking at me.

"I know. But we can walk with him as far as we can." I could think of nothing better than to step into the eternal surrounded by the love of those whose memories you shared. I prayed to God those memories still existed for him.

Mom began to hum "Don't Sit Under the Apple Tree With Anyone Else But Me," a favorite song from their youth, and I thought I saw a slight twitch in Dad's lips, the trace of a smile. The old memories would be the strongest, the last to be extinguished.

Mom stopped and the silence seemed wrong. I started talking, softly at first, and then in a normal voice, telling the story of our first camping trip. I'd been six years old and I'd caught our tent on fire. I heard Susan laugh, and a stranger chuckle. I turned around and saw a nurse in the doorway, but that was fine. Our stories are to be shared. Our stories make us human. Our stories are all we have and what we leave behind.

Uncle Wayne picked up with a tale I'd never heard. He was speaking to Dad about the time the two of them had locked the keys in the hearse at a funeral and the only passenger was in no condition to open the door. The procession was delayed for two hours.

And we kept talking, filling the room with memories, the joys and sorrows acquired over a lifetime.

At seven o'clock, Reverend Pace came in. He said a prayer, one he spoke as if Dad were listening. And then Pace sang a song, the old standard "I Love To Tell The Story." One of Dad's favorites. Fletcher and an orderly were by the door, and we were singing along together, a group of family and friends and strangers in a dying man's room.

The first rays of the sun broke over the eastern mountain ridges. The light fell upon my Dad and woke him like a gentle breeze nudging him out of his sleep. The last note of the hymn faded and we watched as he opened his eyes, sweeping the room with a single turn of his head. He paused to stare at my mother. "Connie," he whispered.

Then he looked at me and I saw my Daddy again. His face was transformed into the man who had been there for me from my earliest memory. His eyes cast off the watery clouds of confusion and burned bright and blue and filled with love. "Barry." No question in his voice this time, but a peaceful certainty. He squeezed my hand.

He was gone.

Chapter Twenty-three

Tommy Lee slept sitting up in his hospital bed, a fresh IV hooked to his arm. He didn't look nearly as bad as when I'd last seen him standing in Pamela Whittier's driveway six hours earlier.

He opened his eyes at the sound of my footsteps. "I heard about your dad. Patsy and I are very sorry. He was the best."

"Yes, he was." I took the chair nearest Tommy Lee's bed. "Thanks for being such a stubborn old coot and getting me back here in time."

He shrugged. "You'd have done the same for me. How's your mom?"

"I hope she's getting some sleep. Uncle Wayne took her home. I just spoke to Williams Funeral Directors in Asheville. They're sending some men over Sunday to help Freddy and Fletcher with the visitation and the Monday morning service at First Methodist. Lester Pace will officiate."

"Sounds appropriate. You let Williams do everything. This time you and your mom need to let others serve you."

"But Uncle Wayne and I are going to do the prep. I know it will be tough, but we don't want to turn that part over to strangers." A lump formed in my throat. "That's what Dad would have wanted for his final undertaking."

"I understand."

Tommy Lee and I sat quietly for a few minutes. He let me pace the conversation.

"Did Pamela Whittier have anything to say?" I asked.

"We took her down to the department. Reece came to her house as soon as he left the Econo Lodge fire."

I'd forgotten about that. "Was anybody hurt?"

"Fortunately, no. We think Greene rented a room and then set the blaze. Probably a candle burning down to a more flammable accelerator. The night clerk identified Greene's picture this morning."

"Add arson to his other crimes," I said.

"You think Pamela Whittier's going to clam up?"

"No. I think we'll turn her. I bucked Patsy's demand that I return to the hospital long enough to see the more than one hundred thousand dollars in Whittier's attaché case. Lindsay came over from Asheville. The feds would have taken the case anyway, so I'd rather bring in someone who'll let us know what's going on. Maybe we'll be credited with more than 'and other local law enforcement agencies' when the Bureau brags about its big bust."

I thought about Pamela Whittier's bitter comments to me. "I hope you'll have enough leverage to get Whittier to talk. She's the one I think got in over her head."

"Susan didn't tell you?" Tommy Lee asked.

"Tell me what."

"The lab report on Crystal Hodges' blood sample came back with lethal levels of epinephrine. Susan says it's really synthetic adrenaline."

"Doc Clark thought that might have been what killed Lincoln."

Tommy Lee nodded. "An overdose can speed up the heart until it fails. Colorless, it could have been injected into Crystal's IV bag and gone unnoticed. That's premeditated murder and I've learned Joel Greene was seen in Crystal's room earlier the day she died. Link Greene and Whittier together with their cell phone records from last night and we have a very strong conspiracy case for murder as well as fraud. I bet Pamela Whittier's singing her lungs out to Lindsay before the week's over."

Fletcher Shaw rose to the occasion. Uncle Wayne and I asked him to help our part-timer Freddy Mott organize my father's visitation and service using the help offered by Williams Funeral Home. Fletcher had learned from Mom that my father had loved daisies, and a few phone calls to our local florists had insured that everyone ordering flowers was made aware of that preference.

There couldn't have been a single daisy left in Gainesboro or all of Laurel County. The simple flower was transformed into a sea of white blossoms, bordering our walk and lining the walls of the Slumber Room. The only things outnumbering the daisies were the people who came to offer their condolences.

Visitation started at seven, but cars began arriving at six-thirty. I'd thought on a Sunday night we'd have a respectable but not overwhelming crowd. Sunday night was church night for the Baptists, and as the predominant denomination, they'd be singing and praying in churches and chapels throughout the valley.

I realized I'd thought wrong when the first person to arrive was Preacher Stinnett from Crab Apple Valley Baptist Church.

"We cancelled prayer meeting tonight," Stinnett said. "This is where we wanted to be. Most of the congregation has had loved ones tended by your dad and I'd probably have been preaching to empty pews." He gave me a hug.

"You're welcome to preach on the lawn," I said.

"I thought about that, but we decided we'd bring lemonade and cookies instead, if that's all right. Sort of a variation on the feeding of the five thousand."

Other people had had the same idea, and by the time the visitation was scheduled to begin, several hundred people sat on lawn chairs enjoying the cool, clear evening. They watched the line streaming out our front door and kept the Slumber Room steadily filled.

Uncle Wayne stood near the entrance, but Mom and I withdrew closer to the casket to keep the room from jamming as people spoke with us. We'd dressed Dad in a light-weight blue suit, and although no one truly looks natural lying in a casket, Wayne and I had done Dad proud.

Mom and I tried to keep people moving along, but everyone had a story they needed to share.

Melissa Bigham, the top reporter for the *Gainesboro Vista*, had just returned earlier in the day from a week's vacation to Colorado. She offered her sympathies, and as she hugged me, whispered, "I'm never leaving town again. I won't bother you tomorrow, but Tuesday you're giving me every detail from Tommy Lee's shooting to Pamela Whittier's arrest."

I'd have been disappointed if Melissa had been any less pushy.

The visitation went an hour and a half beyond schedule. Finally, the last car left and Susan took Mom back to the kitchen for a cup of hot tea. I stood with Uncle Wayne and Fletcher by the casket. Dad looked at peace and I treasured the memory of the light in his eyes and the squeeze of his hand as he'd crossed into the ultimate mystery.

"Tonight was remarkable," Fletcher said.

"No," Uncle Wayne said. "Jack Clayton was remarkable. Tonight was simply people understanding that."

Someone cleared his throat. We turned and saw Tommy Lee standing at the door.

"Sorry to be so late. I stayed away because I knew everybody would want to see my scar."

"Thank God you're out of that hospital gown," I said.

Tommy Lee walked slowly across the room. I looked for a chair, but they'd been cleared out.

"You didn't have to come," I said. "We know how you felt about Dad."

"If you really did, you'd know I couldn't stay away."

Fletcher, Uncle Wayne, and I stepped aside and gave Tommy Lee space to pay his respects. He reached in and patted Dad's chest. "Good bye, old friend. Don't worry. I'll be in the lead car."

I knew what he meant. The Sheriff's Department provided the escort service for funeral processions and Tommy Lee was going to lead Dad's final one.

Tommy Lee took a deep breath and faced us. "And don't you worry. Reece will be driving."

"How'd you get here?" I asked.

"Patsy. She's in the kitchen with your mom and Susan. Susan's pissed that I left the hospital a day early, but what can she do, arrest me?"

"Why don't you and Tommy Lee sit in the parlor," Uncle Wayne said. "Fletcher and I'll finish up here."

I let Tommy Lee have the armchair with the firmest cushion. One that would be easiest to get out of. I sat on the sofa across from him.

"Anything new on the case?" I asked.

"Yes. Whittier fired her Philadelphia lawyer."

"What's that mean?"

"It means she's going to deal. Lindsay said the money, brains, and muscle is probably out of the Philadelphia families. The new generation is all MBAs and the Dugan branch has an affinity for white-collar scams."

"Dugan? That's not Italian."

Tommy Lee laughed. "You've been watching too many episodes of the Sopranos. Mergers and acquisitions aren't limited to corporate America."

"How'd Whittier get hooked up with them?"

"Little feelers go out. Through some crooked drug and equipment reps. Whittier took a few kickbacks on purchases, and before she knew it, she was swimming with the sharks. Greene was brought in as her executive assistant with the real purpose of squeezing as much out as possible. That's when things turned nasty for Doug Larson."

"Greene told me he didn't like crossing into the OxyContin world."

Tommy Lee waved his hand at me. "Yeah, and he loved his mother and gave money to orphans."

"What kind of deal is Lindsay likely to broker?"

"For starters, take the death penalty off the table and then see what Whittier's information's worth."

I thought about all the damage that had been done. "What kind of justice is likely to come for Crystal Hodges?"

"You tell me. Do you think Crystal would rather have Whittier executed or the whole operation that supplied her brother with pills brought down?"

I remembered Crystal's face at the ATM camera, trying to draw attention to the stolen card of Lucy Kowalski. "She did it, didn't she? Crystal set things in motion."

"Yes. And I want to make sure we get every piece of the cancer that's growing here."

I knew the way the feds worked. "Lindsay will be anxious to follow the leads to Philly. Unless Uncle Tummy's cut his own deal."

Tommy Lee winked at me. "Uncle Tummy's still in the game. But I need you to play my cards. Susan and Patsy have ganged up on me and I've been told I can't be back on active duty for six weeks. I hope through sheer orneriness to cut it to four."

"I've got a funeral home to run. What's left to investigate?"

"You've got Fletcher to help you here. I've seen enough of him to appreciate the kid's mettle. I want to find the rest of the Artie Lincolns out there. He was setting Crystal up in a nursing home. I doubt if Crystal was the first plant. Greene said he sent out the composite photos to all the healthcare providers. You can be damn sure he didn't fax them to any place where Lincoln's face would have been recognized."

I couldn't argue with Tommy Lee's reasoning, but I could argue that I wasn't the man for the job. "Get a commitment from Lindsay for help from the Bureau. Then you and Reece can follow up on their leads."

"I'm glad you're sitting down. Reece was the first one to ask me if you could stay on."

"What?"

"Reece's hardheaded, but he's not stupid. This is the biggest case the department has busted in a long time. Morale has never been higher. Whether you like it or not, Reece and the rest of the officers consider you part of the team."

I didn't know what to say. Tommy Lee's words touched me, but I realized my emotions were running raw. "I need to get through tomorrow. Then I'll talk with Mom, Uncle Wayne, and Fletcher."

"Fine," Tommy Lee said. "Take all the time you need."

Fletcher and Freddy must have worked during the night because when Freddy drove us in the family limousine to First Methodist Church, all of the daisies had been transported to provide a border along the sidewalk to the entrance of the sanctuary.

As Mom, Uncle Wayne, and I entered from beside the chancel, we found every pew occupied except the front one reserved for our family. The sound of so many people rising to their feet out of respect for us and my father took my breath away.

The service was short and simple. The passages of scripture and the hymns were my father's favorites, ones he had heard at thousands of funerals he'd conducted over the years. Reverend Pace delivered a eulogy that was structured as a conversation between him and my father, weaving in stories from half a century of serving the mountain people together. At the core, Pace held true to his creed that a funeral isn't for the adoration of the departed, but for the celebration of what God's love can do when it works through the hands and heart of His servant.

Tommy Lee and Reece led the long procession to the outskirts of town where the municipal cemetery lay on acres of rolling hills. My great grandfather had been the attorney who handled the legal matters for the cemetery's creation, and we'd always referred to our plots as "Clayton's Corner." The burial tent marked with *Clayton and Clayton Funeral Directors* stood over the freshly dug grave. The mourners surrounded us so that no matter where I looked, there was the face of a friend.

At the interment, Pace's remarks were brief and we closed with the Lord's Prayer. Few people came up to speak with us because most had said their piece the previous night. While Pace and Mom exchanged a few words, I slipped away to walk among the other graves in Clayton's Corner. Each had a vase of daisies on it. Fletcher Shaw had quite a bit of his grandfather in him.

I touched my hand to each of the simple headstones that were our family's custom to erect. Mom and I would choose Dad's in a few days. The marble felt cool in the warm June air. I stopped at the grave of my great-grandfather. Although he hadn't been a funeral director himself, he'd made it possible for our family to begin our business. He had seen the opportunity because he had seen the need. In that sense, he'd provided as much of a service as my father and grandfather.

To serve. That should be the calling for all of us. That was the message of Reverend Pace's eulogy. That summed up the life of my father and the reason so many people from town and from the backwoods, coves, and hollers had come to pay their respects. A funeral service was more than an event; it was an act of compassion and of being of service.

To serve. Those words were stitched upon the uniforms of the deputies of Laurel County, part of the motto borrowed from the LAPD. "To Protect and To Serve."

Maybe it was time I started doing both.

Chapter Twenty-four

"Thank y'all for coming out this evening. It's good to be back in Gainesboro." Roscoe Dickens hunched in front of the microphone, fiddle at his side, with the rest of the Dickens family poised for musical action.

In the three months since he'd uttered those same words at the June opening of the Friday Night Street Stomp, Roscoe and his clan probably hadn't ventured more than forty miles away from Gainesboro. But, technically, they were back, closing out the summer dances on the Friday night of Labor Day weekend.

"I don't think the banjo picker's grown an inch." Susan settled into her folding chair at the edge of the curb.

I studied the boy perched on a stool. The five-string still swallowed his lap. "No, but little Albert Dickens the Fourth picked up a nice tan since we saw him last."

Main Street bustled with people—from babies in strollers to seniors in wheelchairs. Along the sidewalk, vendors sold apples, the first of the fall harvest to come in.

Susan pointed across the street. "There's Mayor Whitlock. Of course, he'll have to make a speech."

Sammy Whitlock had his mouth wrapped around a caramel-dipped apple on a stick. The gooey coating appeared to be winning.

"We can always hope His Honor can't get his dentures free."

My words seemed prophetic as Tommy Lee walked up to the mayor and said something. Whitlock could only nod and point in my direction.

"Guess I'd better sit out this first number," I told Susan.

As the square dancers thronged onto the street for Roscoe's training lesson, Tommy Lee maneuvered through them. He'd been back on full duty only two weeks and still looked gaunt from his ordeal. His uniform hung a little too loose and the weight of his pistol and handcuffs dropped the belt lower on his hips.

Susan got up. "He looks like he needs to talk business. I'll get us two of those candied apples. They'll make your lips sweeter."

"Impossible."

She stepped up on the sidewalk and disappeared.

Tommy Lee stopped in front of her empty chair. "Did I run Susan off?"

"Yeah. That's her way of saying you need to sit down. She's still your doctor."

He grabbed the armrests and lowered himself, careful not to catch his police belt in the chair's nylon webbing. "I had a call from Lindsay late this afternoon. More indictments came down."

"Any of our people?"

"Yes. Two. The manager of the Shady Grove Nursing Home and the pharmacist for the Southern Senior Health Centers. Lindsay wants you to know you'll be called to testify."

"At this rate I'll be making more court appearances than Perry Mason."

In the two and a half months since the case broke, we'd uncovered a number of people involved in the Medicare fraud. Lincoln's composite had generated leads where he'd found jobs for nurse's aides who would short-count pills. Doug Larson had also been the pharmacist for several nursing homes where he delivered prescriptions and got the pills back from inside accomplices. The two most recent indictments were for fraudulent billings of wheelchairs, walkers, and even motorized scooters.

Tommy Lee tucked his legs under the chair as the square dancers swung closer to the curb. "But that wasn't the main reason Lindsay called. She was most delighted by one of the money trails Whittier provided. They got a link between our western North Carolina operation and the DEA bust in Delray Beach. That filters down to some nice brownie points for Lieutenant Spring because he was the first to cooperate with our initial investigation."

"Good." I'd felt guilty that I'd considered Spring a dirty cop, but at least Tommy Lee and I had never taken that theory public. "So the timing for my retirement seems perfect."

"When's Fletcher leave?" Tommy Lee asked.

"The same time he's always been leaving. Tomorrow. His classes start next Tuesday."

"And you're sure you can't do both—funeral serve and protect?"

"I gave Fletcher the last two days off to get ready for his trip. Believe me, working for the department and managing the funeral home are more than I can handle."

I expected some smart remark, but all Tommy Lee said was, "Damn. Somebody's gotta be ice skating in Hell."

I followed his gaze to the promenading couples on the street. There, with his arm wrapped around the woman I only remembered as "Liver Spots," Uncle Wayne high-stepped to the beat of "Alabama Jubilee."

"You're right," Tommy Lee said. "Maybe holding down two jobs is too tough when your help starts a-courting for the first time in seventy-five years."

I stood up. "Susan's got to see this. Can you save our seats?"

"Don't I look armed and dangerous?"

I hurried along the crowded sidewalk. People stepped aside, letting me move freely. The candied apple stand was in front of Larson's Discount Drugs and a line of customers stretched to the curb. Susan wasn't among them.

"Barry." Fletcher called from the head of the line. He juggled four apples while the vendor stuffed change in his shirt pocket. "Are you looking for Susan?"

"Did you see her?"

"Yes. I was already in line when she got here. Two of these apples are for her. She and Cindy went to look at some summer clothes on sale at the shop across the street. They said they'd be right back."

I took two of the apples. "'Right back' in shopping language could mean before the next millennium."

"Guess we'd better stay here unless you want to look at dresses."

"What do you think?"

Fletcher laughed a little too loudly. He seemed nervous.

"Can we talk a few minutes?" he asked.

"Sure."

He walked away from the apple cart to the door of the drugstore. A "For Lease" sign hung in the window, and what little daylight penetrated inside showed the inventory had been removed.

We stood facing one another, a caramel-coated apple on a stick in each hand. To passing pedestrians, we must have looked like some vaudeville juggling act.

Fletcher shifted his weight from foot to foot. "I was going to write you a letter, but I never could get it started the way I wanted. Now I've let it go to the last minute."

"You can tell me anything. I hope the summer's been a good experience, once that little unpleasantness resolved itself."

"Oh, no, it's been terrific. I thought what I had to say should be more official, but then Cindy said I should just ask you."

"Cindy?" Fletcher was losing me.

"Cindy. And Susan. And Tommy Lee."

"You talked to all of them?" I tried to lighten what suddenly seemed a serious mood. "Why not Uncle Wayne?"

Fletcher missed the point. "I would have, but he was always playing shuffleboard."

I'd missed that change in Uncle Wayne's behavior. So much for my detecting abilities. "What is it that required a panel of advisors?"

"You know I'm graduating this December. My family expects me to take my place in the corporate business."

"Great opportunity."

Fletcher shook his head. "You'd hate it. Meeting after meeting until you're meeting simply to plan more meetings."

"It's your family business," I said.

"No. It's a conglomerate that happens to have family members working there. Not like your family's business. When your dad got sick, you came back because you were needed. You make a difference."

"Then what do you want to do?"

"I want to come back here. After I graduate." He broke eye contact, afraid to see my reaction. "I should have talked to you earlier, but if you said no, I didn't want to make things awkward between us while I was still here."

"Fletcher, I'd love to have you work for me, but we're such a small operation. I couldn't afford to pay you anything like what you should be earning."

He nodded and cleared his throat. "This is the part I need to put in a letter. I don't want to work for you. I want to work with you. As a partner."

"Partner?"

"I asked Susan and Tommy Lee whether you'd even consider such a thing. They told me about the Hoffman deal you turned down. But I thought this could be different. You'd still be an owner. People in Laurel County would see us working like we've been doing these past few months. You could continue to help Tommy Lee."

"But you have so many opportunities even if you don't go the corporate route."

Fletcher raised his hands. "Now where else could a deal be made where the participants couldn't shake on it because they held candied apples?"

"You've got a point there," I said.

"Here's my pitch. You get me for a partner, the Sealey Corporation to handle centralized accounting if you want, volume purchasing for better discounts and customer savings, your mother gets some cash for her share, and you get the chance to step out of the day-to-day operations and chase down bad guys."

To protect and to serve, I thought. "And what do you get?"

Fletcher swept his two apple-filled hands in a wide arc. "The best end of the bargain. This town. These mountains. These people. What my grandfather started and lost through success, not failure."

The last sliver of the sun was setting behind the western ridges. The rapid-fire banjo rolls of Albert Dickens the Fourth rose above the sound of laughter and dancing. Locals and tourists swung from arm to arm in an undulating circle. The moment brimmed with the joys of being alive. I was part of it all—life and death. I had seen my father deal with both, for the community he served and for himself. I had witnessed the grace with which he descended into shadows and the triumph in the hospital room as he woke in the light. And I had been changed in the process.

In Fletcher Shaw I recognized a part of myself. This community would become his community.

A wave came from the crowd at the curb. I spotted Susan. She stood with Cindy and Tommy Lee. I realized Fletcher Shaw had been part of a conspiracy after all.

Fletcher saw them too. He blushed.

"Well," I said. "You'll get all that—this town, these mountains, these people—for better and for worse, for life and for death. But you'll also get a seventy-five-year-old funeral business. Before you put anything on paper for me to consider, you'd better know what you're in for. I'll update the documents I prepared for Hoffman Enterprises and send them wherever you tell me."

Fletcher beamed and clicked his apples against mine like sticky champagne glasses. "That's great, Barry."

"Maybe. See what you think after the Sealey accountants have had their say." I nodded toward Susan and Cindy. "I see the shoppers have returned. Take these and give mine to Tommy Lee." I handed him the apples. "I'm actually on my final night of duty so I'd better make a pass around the street."

Fletcher hurried off.

I looked in the empty window of Larson's Discount Drugs. The fading light had turned the plate glass into a mirror. I checked the uniform I'd been wearing the past two months while continuing the investigation. I looked good. Maybe I'd just keep it in the closet till Fletcher's graduation.

I started down the sidewalk away from the band. A family hurried toward me, a girl about six pulling her mother forward. A toddler sat on his dad's shoulders and gazed in wonder at the new world around him.

"Good evening, Officer," the young father said.

"Yes. It certainly is."

To receive a free catalog of Poisoned Pen Press titles, please contact us in one of the following ways:

Phone: 1-800-421-3976
Facsimile: 1-480-949-1707
Email: info@poisonedpenpress.com
Website: www.poisonedpenpress.com

Poisoned Pen Press
6962 E. First Ave. Ste. 103
Scottsdale, AZ 85251